FEARS

EDITED BY
CHARLES L. GRANT

BERKLEY BOOKS, NEW YORK

FEARS

A Berkley Book / published by arrangement with
the author

PRINTING HISTORY
Berkley edition / May 1983

Contents

Introduction

What frightens you? *Spiders? Snakes? Dark streets? The economy? The kid next door? Nuclear war? God? Getting together with friends and discovering you're discussing the "old days" with alarming frequency?*

What frightens you? *Death? Infirmity? Age? Failure? The fact that the world still doesn't know you exist? Talking to yourself? Grey hair? Liver spots? Not being able to run as fast as your kid? Not being as strong as the kid who mows your lawn?*

What frightens you?

The field of horror, terror, and Dark Fantasy has long accepted the idea that what its stories do is allow us to face up to Death vicariously, to the notion of our own unpleasantly true mortality. I suspect, however, that most of us don't spend a lot of time worrying about dying. We know we will, but for the most part we've deluded ourselves into believing that the other guy is the one who'll be in the cortege, not us. After all, once we're done, we're done, and we can imagine a great many things—from space travel to hideous monsters to excruciating pain—but we can't really imagine nothingness. So we don't.

What we do, then, is fear other things, things far more immediate than something that'll happen to that other guy.

Like spiders, and snakes, and shadows, and dark streets, and all the tangible critters that seem to stalk us; like looking at ourselves and seeing things we really don't want to acknowledge, such as the possibility that *we* really might be able to murder someone, *that* revenge might be fun, *that* getting even with people we thought we liked might not be so terrible; *like the erosion of youthful liberalism and compassion into intolerance and bigotry.*

Frightening enough in reality, why should a writer bother using such things in stories? Because they are real and are frightening, and because they're fun. It's less a matter of liking to leap out at you and saying boo! *as it is sneaking up behind you and releasing a single drop of iced water onto the back of your neck. A* boo! *you can forget; that shock, that running down your spine, that* clawing *feeling over your skin . . . you won't soon forget that at all.*

A good horror story is one that implies that the horror isn't over when the story is.

A better story is one that lets you think *it's all over.*

The best is the kind that does both.

And if you should discover that some of the people in the tales collected here are disturbingly like you, or your neighbor . . . remember that it's only fiction. It isn't real. If you get a chill, just close the book. If you get scared or sickened, just turn on the TV or the radio or the stereo. It isn't real. It's only a story.

What frightens you?

It isn't real.

Sleep well.

CHARLES L. GRANT
Newton, New Jersey 1982

We spend an extraordinary amount of time putting our lives into some sort of order, creating a lifestyle that at least to us is comfortably predictable, a haven from the chaos that exists outside our doors. To do less, we believe, invites failure, madness, and worse.

But when that order is incapable of dealing with what we thought were all the possibilities. . . .

Janet Fox lives in Kansas, has had her stories published in most of the major science fiction and fantasy magazines/anthologies, and writes far too little for my taste. But when she does, there's no doubt that she will be, in the best sense, provocative.

1

Surrogate

by Janet Fox

STEVE WAS REPAINTING the walls of what had been the guest bedroom when he heard the doorbell. "Diane," he shouted, and certain that he'd done his duty, turned back to rolling a pale yellow swath onto the wall. The new crib, bureau and bassinet that Diane had bought lay under protecting sheets and there were several unopened boxes bearing a toystore logo. His own attitude was as chaotic and half-formed as this room. Earlier he'd given up all hope of being a father, and it took a certain effort of will to resurrect that hope. He was trying, mostly for Diane's sake, but turning this room into a nursery still seemed a kind of fantasy.

The bell resounded through the house again, an impatient sound, and he shouted again, this time with less confidence. He put down the roller and listened but heard no footsteps. "Damn, she must have gone out." He wiped his hands and hurried toward the door just as the bell sounded again. Through the screen he saw a young woman very visibly pregnant under a cheap dress whose pink-and-yellow print was very nearly phosphorescent. Her eyelids drooped under a layer of blue eyeshadow, and lipstick more nearly black than red glistened on her lips. Her jaw worked a wad of gum.

"Mr. Winston?"

"Yes, I'm Steven Winston."

He felt a hand on his shoulder and realized that Diane was behind him.

"I'm Kelsy Adams," she said, thrusting out a small hand as several plastic bracelets clacked together on her wrist. Confusedly he clasped hands with her.

"I'm sorry—" he began.

She patted her stomach. "I'm your surrogate mother." He heard Diane's indrawn breath, felt her hand clutch his arm. The moment with its tension lengthened until it threatened to pull reality apart, yet here she was on their doorstep in a splash of sunlight. He'd never seen her before, yet it was his child she carried. Thrown badly off balance, he could feel only anger.

"You had no right to come here," he said. "According to the terms of our agreement—"

"Invite her in," whispered Diane.

"No. No, you'll have to go. This isn't right."

"The neighbors . . . invite her in."

Reluctantly he opened the screen. "All right, we'll talk," he said. "But only for a few minutes." Diane moved newspapers off the divan with a nervous motion. She wore what Steve called her white look—shocked but still functioning. It turned her normal fragile prettiness harsh somehow, masklike, hollow.

"Maybe I should've called," said Kelsy, settling herself on the cushions with the air of a cat getting comfortable.

"How did you find us? The terms of our contract stated that we were to have no contact."

"I got the information from a . . . friend who works in the office."

"Well, I'm calling Doctor Joshua," Steve said. "I think something is very wrong here."

As he moved toward the phone, a dribble of mascara melted down Kelsy's cheek. "I had to go somewhere. I got kicked out of my apartment. Those old biddies said I had . . . bad . . . morals." Diane moved to stand beside her, looking down helplessly. "I didn't know people would think I—" began Kelsy, the rest lost in the tissue that Diane handed her.

Diane made a warning gesture as Steve reached for the

phone. "Calling the doctor isn't going to change the fact that she's here. She's not just on paper; she's real."

"But this isn't how it's supposed to be. It can cause terrible complications. It must nullify the agreement."

"I'm causing trouble. I'll go. I'll go and you'll never have to see me again." Kelsy wiped her face, smudging streaks of blackness across her cheek, a strangely vulnerable gesture.

"How can anything be nullified?" Diane said. "Look at her. It's your—our baby. What does it matter about your agreements and pieces of paper?"

"I didn't mean to bother you; I just didn't know where else to go, but I see I can't stay here." For all of her protests Kelsy wasn't making any moves to leave the comfort of the cushions.

"Don't go. Not just yet. I'll fix us some coffee, no, some juice, that'd be better." A tentative smile appeared amid the ruined makeup. A simpleminded girl, Steve thought. That was all she was. This agreement might be the only stable relationship in her life. But even as he lectured himself, trying to find some compassion, he was wondering how a simpleminded girl could so easily break the security of a doctor's private files.

After Kelsy had downed her second glass of juice, Diane directed her to the bathroom so she could, as she put it, put on a new face. "I wonder if we shouldn't call the doctor," Steve said. "He shouldn't be so careless with confidential information."

"But what if he cancels the agreement? Did we wait this long for it to be like the other time, when I—" Her voice fell to a murmur. "Lost the baby." Her skin seemed translucent, stretched taut over the fine bones of her face, and he was afraid to say anything as if the sound of his voice would shatter her.

"Here I am, back to normal." The greasy layers of makeup had been replaced, making strangely harsh the youthful contours of her face. "And I'm ready to go. You've been really nice. I'm glad I could meet you even if it was only for a few minutes."

Steve followed her toward the door, amazed that this whole soap-opera episode was to be so easily concluded. "I'm glad

I met you, too," said Diane. Kelsy was going out the door, smiling back toward Diane. Steve shouted a warning as he saw her foot in its flimsy high-heeled shoe miss the step. Too late to catch her; he caught Diane, who was screaming and bolting forward. Kelsy had fallen full length on the sidewalk and for the moment she hadn't moved. Diane knelt beside her to cradle her head. "Maybe we ought to get an ambulance," Steve said, but Kelsy was already stirring, trying to rise.

"No, she's all right, but we'd better get her inside." Steve helped her to stand but she didn't seem too steady on her feet, so he picked her up. She seemed small somehow, and lighter than she should have been. He put her on the couch.

Diane was carrying a cheap plastic suitcase. "This was left out by the curb. Her things must be in it."

"But she can't stay here."

"Only for the night. In the morning I'll see that she gets to the doctor's office for a checkup."

"This is crazy."

Diane came closer and put her arms around him. "It isn't crazy, is it, for me to want your baby—no matter how it comes about."

Still half-asleep, Steve lurched across the living room on his way to the kitchen to make coffee. On the couch, Kelsy, covered to the neck with a wrinkled sheet, looked like something in a cocoon. Her face devoid of the makeup was youthful. She could be hardly out of her teens, he supposed, and as he looked at her, he speculated on the kind of life that would make a woman agree to the surrogate arrangement. He supposed he should feel pity and responsibility, yet as he stood there he was feeling a kind of anxiety, the feeling that at any moment she would awaken and blink and stare at him with eyes gone ferally red in reflected light. Stupid. He turned away.

As he was drinking the coffee, Diane joined him, her slim elegance enveloped in one of his old blanket-cloth robes. "It's been over a week," he said in a tentative voice. "Don't you think it's time she left to get a place of her own?"

"I hate to think of her being alone."

"But this situation, it's impossible. I can just imagine what the Cartons—or the Pendletons—are thinking."

"I told Midge Pendleton that she's my baby sister," said Diane with a pleased, wicked grin that was uncharacteristic of her.

"But her clothes, her appearance—"

"I've been meaning to take her shopping—get her some nicer things. We can afford it."

"But what about the money, the fee she got for the baby?"

"I'm afraid she has no head for money, poor thing, and, well, who cares about that. It's not as if we ever thought we could buy a child."

He paused. He guessed he *had* thought so, when the agreement was made. It had all seemed so clear, so businesslike.

"Don't you feel the least bit responsible?"

"Of course I do," he said, "but there's something wrong about this. It's—" He couldn't explain. He could talk about the social and moral viewpoints, but that wouldn't begin to touch it. The wrongness was the kind that made hair bristle at the back of the neck and brought an undefined sound of warning up from the throat.

"What are you trying to pull?" he had burst into the living room, startling Kelsy, who was sitting on the floor putting together a jigsaw puzzle. "I happened to run into Doctor Joshua today," he said, feeling as if he were playing the part of an irate father in a play. Kelsy's condition wasn't nearly so noticeable in the simple cotton smocks that Diane had bought for her, and with the makeup toned down, she looked like a teenager. "He told me that our surrogate mother had missed her last two appointments and that he couldn't locate her at her old address."

"What are you shouting about?" Diane stood in the kitchen doorway.

"I thought the reason for her being here was to care for her health."

As jigsaw pieces scattered, Kelsy scrambled to her feet and hurried to stand beside Diane. He couldn't tell if he were imagining it but her stomach seemed smaller under the loose blouse. It *was* smaller. Or did it only seem so?

"He doesn't like me," said Kelsy.

"She's afraid of Doctor Joshua," explained Diane, putting an arm around Kelsy's shoulders. "We were going to find another doctor, one with more understanding, but we've been so busy shopping and—"

"We can't have her living here—sleeping on the couch, taking up all your time."

"The couch, I've been meaning to mention it to you. I think it'd be a good idea if we set the guest bed up again in the smaller bedroom."

"But that's the nursery. It's all fixed up."

"Of course it is—it will be. But it's important for Kelsy to be comfortable."

He felt that he stood at a crossroads of sorts, yet how could he be certain that the bulge under Kelsy's smock was really diminished? And if it was, how did one explain it without sprawling over into the kinds of ideas that only crazy people believed in? He only knew that under the murky surface of doing one's duty and living up to one's responsibility to one's fellow man, he hated her, with all the hatred of one species for another.

The nursery was a pale yellow with large decals of teddy bears in various costumes. Huddled in a shadowy corner was the baby furniture. A mobile of glittering plastic animals hung over the bed and Kelsy was reaching up to touch it with a languid motion. As it spun, a music box tinkled out a tinny melody. She sat against the pillow with knees up, the posture easy for her now that her stomach had flattened. The absorption had been a gradual process which Diane had never mentioned, but Steve had watched each change with fascination, feeling a vague sense of loss. The process had given Kelsy an additional layer of fat so that the drawn-up knees were dimpled and her breasts were scarcely noticeable under the pink shift with its print of clowns and balloons.

Her face had grown rounder, fuller, and there was never any makeup on it now. She was smiling an odd, secretive smile, thinking, he supposed, that she'd won. He stepped closer to the doorway; a board squeaked; she saw him.

"You scared me," she said with a little pout. He could almost be charmed by it; he could see how Diane might be.

"You scared *me*," he said with a smile that was only an ironic twist of the lips. "What are you, really?"

She looked at him out of large shining brown eyes and was silent. Maybe she didn't know herself. Maybe this usurpation was as natural to her as the cuckoo laying its eggs in another bird's nest.

It seemed equally instinctual when he reached for her, locking his hands around the chubby throat. There was a moment of self-loathing, of unreality before he began to squeeze.

He felt a blow from behind, at first unlocalized until a pain spread through his chest. He fell to the floor, his scrabbling hand confirming the double-looped shape of the handles of Diane's sewing shears. Warm liquid flooded into his nose and mouth and he felt that he was drowning in lukewarm water, but the substance that dribbled out over his hand was red. His fading consciousness supplied a kind of glowing haze to the figures seated on the bed. Diane's expression was both fierce and gentle at once as she looked down on Kelsy's tousled head cradled against her breast. Somewhere in the background the music box was endlessly droning its mechanical lullaby.

All things being equal, being helpless isn't quite so bad as being not quite helpless. If there's nothing you can do in a given situation, there's nothing you can do, period; but if there is a persistent and often overpowering feeling that you ought to be able to do something, the terror therein is magnified twofold. As, for example, in being lost. Maybe.

Chelsea Quinn Yarbro is one of the most admired writers in the field, and not only for her creation of le comte, St. Germain. Her eye for detail and sympathy for character are envied, as well they should be, as well they are displayed in the following story.

Coasting

by Chelsea Quinn Yarbro

THERE MAY HAVE been an inlet or lagoon off to port, Courant was not sure because of the fog. It had come up a little more than an hour ago, first nothing more than a kind of fuzz over the water, then gathering into an insubstantial barrier that rose up between the sleek day-sailer and the shore. It muffled sound as if the coast had been wrapped in cotton, and forced him to keep silent in the wraithlike cocoon it made around his sloop. The occasional roar of the waves against the beach was distant, like gigantic yawns, and he feared he might be drifting out to sea, for although the tide was near turning, the wind had died away to almost nothing. Overhead the sail luffed, pulling the *ShangriLa* on with occasional languid jerks. The jib flapped once in a while. In time he would have to start the auxiliary engine, but he was reluctant to use it until he could discover how far away he was from the rocks and the beach.

It was late in the afternoon; in another hour the tide would be noticeably higher, and if Courant could not find the coast by then, he might be in a great deal of danger. He did not like sailing blind, and he was well aware of the risks he ran. As the light faded, his situation would become more precarious. He listened to the quiet lappings of the waves against the hull of his thirty-two-foot sloop and gave a halfhearted tug on the shroud-line.

The ocean was eerie in its silence, and the mists seemed to merge with the water so that he felt he was floating in the greyness, apart from the world, isolated in a place he did not know.

Why hadn't he brought Sammy along? It would not be so lonely with Sammy here, and they would joke about their predicament, or set the running lights together. Maybe they could cook up a story the Coast Guard would accept if they came into port after dark. Sammy would enjoy that. And with no one on board but himself, he had to admit that he would welcome the sight of the Coast Guard. In a fog like this, they would have to stretch the rules a little for day-sailers that could not reach their berths before the sun was gone. Even the best of sailors got caught out once in a while, Courant reassured himself. Anyone else out in this fog would have the same feelings that plagued him now, and would take the same precautions, watching, listening to the water so that he would not run aground or have the bottom of the boat clawed out by the rocks along the shore. He imagined he heard the first scrape of the keel against submerged, jagged boulders: he braced himself for the shudder that heralded ruin.

In an hour, he reminded himself when several minutes had passed without the dreaded wreck, there would be the onrushing tide, and no matter how muted the sound on the beach, he would be able to hear the breakers where they gnawed at the coast. It would be safe then to begin his search for the entrance to the harbor at the mouth of Barranca River, or, barring that, to drop anchor.

He pictured in his mind the breakwater at El Pescador. It was little more than an extension of a sandpit on the south side of the inlet. Rocks had been piled up over the concrete, and there was a diaphone at the end of it with a revolving light on top that did not always work. Inside the breakwater there was a jetty and facilities for about thirty boats, with deeper moorings for the occasional large pleasurecraft that put in at El Pescador in the summer. Most of the boats out of El Pescador were commercial fishing craft and party-boats. On days like this, in the chill of autumn, they often did not put out to sea—there were no tourists to hire the party-boats and the fishermen set aside these days for painting and repair, anticipating the storms that would come at the back of the cold, taking a fearful toll on unprotected boats. Courant doubted that he would see any of the boats he knew, should there be a break in the fog.

El Pescador, San Jorge, Anderson, Port Talbot, Puerto Real, Bronley, Green River, Stella del Mar, Princeton Beach— he ticked off the little coastal towns in his mind as he held the tiller steady. He should be able to put in at one of them. He had an uncle in Port Talbot, a crusty old Welshman who had been in the first generation of settlers. The Bakers, in Green River, would let him sleep on their couch for the night if he fetched up there. He decided that he ought to stay away from San Jorge, since that was where the construction was going on at the harbor entrance. Tim, the bartender at *The Pelican*, was always willing to let him sleep in the back room, but he did not want to chance it, not since he had been heading into port there the month before and had been warned off by half a dozen men in a forty-foot cruiser that bristled with antennae and other devices. No, he would not make an effort to reach San Jorge. Better to try for Anderson.

He would not be able to call Sammy when he had said he would. Sammy was over with Kate today, with Kate and Barry. Courant was not used to his ex-wife's second marriage, and in his mind he stumbled over Barry's name. A nice fellow, he supposed, and if the circumstances were different, he might be able to like the man. He was pleasant enough, was generous with his beer and had pretty good sense about politics. But the way things had turned out, Courant was certain he would never like Barry. It was bad enough that the man had married Kate, but now he was starting to work on Sammy. The boy liked spending time with Kate in Santa Marisa, and Barry encouraged it. It was just that Santa Marisa was a good-sized place, with two high schools and four movie theatres, and much more to do than was offered in El Pescador. Sammy was eleven, and was eager for the excitement of a town and new friends.

Courant was distracted by a soft, scraping sound against the sloop. He looked over the side. Kelp floated around him,

brown and leafy, the long fronds stretching out into the fog.
For a moment it appeared that the seaweed was rising out of
the ocean and winding its way up the striations in the mists,
like ivy going up a wall. In the mild swell the branches
appeared to gesture to him, beckoning him and reaching for
him. He had seen kelp before, and knew it for the hazardous
nuisance it was. If the engine had been on, the propeller
might be badly damaged or perhaps even broken if entangled
with the plants. There were kelp beds all along the coast, of
course, but he had thought that the largest of them was off
Green River. By the look of this—what little he could make
out in the thickening fog—it was extensive. Had he drifted as
far as Green River? Or was he farther out from the coast than
he thought? Was the remote sound of the shore caused by
distance and not another illusion of the fog? He did not let
himself worry too much about that. There were more immediate problems, because if there was kelp looped around the
propeller now, he would have to get it free or damage the
engine when he started it at last. He had seen other boats,
some of them quite large, with big engines powering them,
come limping into port with their screws fouled by the long,
trailing weeds.

He tightened the sails and pointed toward what little wind
there was, in the hope that there would be enough power in
the halfhearted gusts to pull the *ShangriLa* free. It meant that
he had to aim his bow directly at where he thought the coast
was, but he preferred that risk to remaining in the clutch of
the seaweed. If only the fog would clear so that he could tell
how far he was from the shore, and how much kelp was
around him. Inadvertently he might put himself more deeply
into the patch of floating plants, ensnaring himself inextricably,
so that he would have to drift with the kelp as it moved.

The cold had begun to bother him, the clammy mist that
held him insinuated its frigid breath into him. He had a
peacoat down in the cabin, but he did not want to leave the
cockpit, not with the kelp around him and the sails trimmed
enough to give him some real speed once he was away. His
sweater, however inadequate against the fog, would have to
do for the time being. Once he was safely away from the kelp
and knew where he was bound, he would be able to take a

few minutes to get warm. He might even break out the bottle of rum he kept under the hard bread in the food-locker. The rum would warm him up, and lend a festivity to this dull, terrifying afternoon.

The swell had been increasing as the tide made its first lunge at the shore. The *ShangriLa* rocked, and Courant eased it off the wind a point or two. He would bring the compass up from the cabin, too. In theory, it should always be in place near the tiller, but the brass had become encrusted and he had taken it below a few days ago to clean it, thinking that it was a good time to do it. He hardly ever used it anyway, and for that reason had not made much of an effort to put it back into place. He had been sailing along the coast here for more than five years and he knew almost all of it by heart. It was simple to navigate by the frowning, steep front of Steeple Rock, or by the arch of Green Point. He had boasted the year before that he could find his way from Sanchez to Hollyville by landmarks alone. A compass was redundant unless he was going farther, down to Guddiston or beyond to San Dismas. He recalled guiltily that the brass was not entirely cleaned and shined yet, but it was the compass itself that he wanted, not its housing. Once set in its place, he was convinced, he would feel relieved, and this worry that was growing within him would not be as nagging as it had become. There was something about having the compass in place that would give him a sense of ease that did not come entirely from the instrument's function; since he was a boy, he had always believed that if he had a compass, he could not be lost.

The wind picked up, and for a little while it gave Courant the vain hope that the fog would dissipate. But it only became thicker, blurring the water around the *ShangriLa* and making the boat itself appear ghostly. No wonder the old sailors had believed in ghost ships, he told himself, attempting to persuade himself that the idea was absurd. If he saw his own sloop gliding silently out of a fog like this one, he might easily believe he had seen a vessel that was supernatural. It was silly, he insisted, but that was the way that legends got started.

Sammy would not have liked the sail much, he admitted as he made a deliberate effort to turn his thoughts away from the myths he had heard all his life. The boy enjoyed the ocean, but this grey, enveloping mist, the persistent kelp and the slow, aimless progress he was making would have driven the boy to a state of frustration and annoyance that would soon have led him to whine and complain. He was glad that with all the other difficulties he had to cope with, his son's ceaseless demands were not added to them. It was not that he did not love his son. Of course he did. Of course. But he often lacked patience with the kid when he became obstreperous. It might be just as well that Kate had him for the afternoon. If the fog had drifted inland as far as Santa Marisa, she would have to deal with the boy's moping and smart back talk, just as he had done for the last three years. Then she would understand what he had been objecting to in Sammy on those few occasions when they had discussed the boy. And, for a change, when Sammy returned, he would be glad to see him, to be home with his dad, and would tell him all the awful things that had happened while he visited mommy and her new husband. It would be a pleasant change, he thought, allowing himself a hint of gloating. Then it would be Courant who would make the phone call, asking what Kate had done that had upset the boy so much. In the past, it had been her privilege to call with unkind inferences and innuendos. This would provide a good turnabout. It was high time that Kate learned that their child was not the most reasonable and intelligent kid in the world. He was okay, but he had his bad days, like everyone else. Then Kate would understand a little why he resented her phone calls and the notes she sent him, saying that Sammy ought to be taken to the dentist, or needed another pair of new shoes, or was not studying hard enough and ought to be encouraged. God, how he hated those conversations!

There was more kelp around him, and the *ShangriLa* wallowed through it, tossing on the increasing swell. He studied the water around him, and was more dismayed than he let himself know to see how thick the seaweed had become, and how densely it stretched away into the fog. He held the sloop steady while he searched for something that would help him clear it away. There was not much he could do by himself, that was plain. If Sammy were here with him, he could have the job of pushing the kelp aside as the *ShangriLa* got through the worst of it. One man, holding the tiller and minding the sails, could not take the time to sweep the kelp out of the way.

A wave slapped at the side of the boat and a frond hooked over the splashboard, for all the world as if it intended to haul itself aboard. Courant cried out in surprise and disgust, and reached out for the brown, wet thing to throw it back into the darkening sea. It was worse than any creeper growing around his house, he thought, and gritted his teeth as he pointed the prow back closer to the wind. The *ShangriLa* would pitch, but it was better than having that stuff all over the deck, he decided, cringing inwardly as he heard the slither of kelp brush the length of the boat.

His hands were stiff from the cold and the tension that gripped him. The tiller felt enormous to him, and as heavily leaden as his infrequent dinners with Kate. He tugged at it, dragging it closer to him, his shoulder beginning to ache with the strain of it. He stared into the whiteness that engulfed him, giving no light, concealing everything. Slowly the sloop moved forward, the aft settling lower in the water as if the *ShangriLa* were dragging something. He turned to look behind him. Christ! What was back there? His uncle in Port Talbot had told him stories of creatures that lived under the sea and would often attack solitary boats, pulling them down to hideous depths where the monsters could consume their catch at their leisure. His uncle always laughed when he told such tales, and once or twice explained that it was typical of sailors to invent nonsense when on long hauls. Courant had always nodded his agreement, but now the fear came back to him without the welcome denial of chuckles. As if in confirmation of his anxiety, the *ShangriLa* lurched sideways, then righted herself and bobbed in the water. Whatever it was, it no longer held the boat. He swallowed four or five times in succession to keep from being sick.

The wind carried him farther, and he seemed to hear the rustle of waves on the beach. There was no break in the fog, and although he strained to listen, there was none of the determined, exuberant crash of breakers. He gathered up his courage and reached over the side of the boat, and to his relief, did not touch the brown leaves he dreaded. The water, in fact, was a bit warmer than he had expected. Perhaps he had inadvertently entered the long lagoon at Green River. If that were the case, he would find the first of two long docks not far ahead on the port side. He was pleasantly light-headed at the realization that his horrible afternoon was nearly at an end. Once he tied up, he would go into town for a drink and a hot meal with Sophie. He might even call Kate and tell her that she could keep Sammy another night. Cautiously he let down the jib, gathering it up as the *ShangriLa* drifted forward. A sudden gust of wind could send the sloop careening into one of the piers, and that would be the perfect end, after a day as bad as this one had been. He made his way back to the cockpit and took the tiller once more. He estimated that it would be ten minutes at the most before he found a place to berth his boat.

But the ten minutes went by, and nothing happened. He continued to move forward slowly, the wake behind the *ShangriLa* hardly more than a gentle ripple, the fog as thick as it was at the entrance to the harbor. What made him think he had got into the harbor? A hard, cold fist knotted his guts. If this were a harbor, any harbor, the reasonable thoughts went on, without remorse, then there would have been some sign of life. There would be a light, a diaphone, a signal of some sort that he had arrived. Other boats had to be protected, too, and there would have to be some evidence that they could use as a guide.

"Hello!" he shouted suddenly, very loudly. He heard his voice echo distantly, so faint and distorted that it might have been another speaker entirely. "*Hello!*" he bellowed again. "This is the *ShangriLa*! Where do I tie up?" He half-stood, listening intently, and heard only the sigh of the water as it passed under the prow of his sloop. "Hello!"

Something came toward the boat, thudded against the side, rolled once and then submerged.

He stared at it. "It was a log," he said aloud, thinking that someone would hear him. It had to have been a log, for he could not believe that the distorted, blackened thing that he had seen turning in the water was a body. They were twigs he had caught sight of, not fingers. He pulled on the tiller, as if to bring the *ShangriLa* about, so that he could pursue the thing he had seen, but the tiller did not respond, not even when he braced himself and pushed at it with the limit of his strength.

"It's the kelp," he said, still speaking loudly, hoping that someone would hear. "There's kelp down there. I can't steer because there's seaweed on the rudder." As if to prove this to himself, he gave one more push to the tiller and nodded grimly when the *ShangriLa* continued on her course without the slightest deviation. It would mean hauling her out of the water and having Pete at the boatworks give her a complete going-over. It was an expensive waste of time, he told himself, so that he would not have to say that he longed for the familiar boatworks and the genial rapacity of the owner.

If this was Green River, the harbor would be dead ahead, and he would ram a dock or a boat, anything. He thought of the damage with affection and hoped that the *ShangriLa* was enough damaged to justify his replacing her with another boat. He would not be able to take her out again without recalling this endless fog and dead tiller.

How would he explain that to Sammy? The boy loved sailing, and thought of the boat with more affection than he often showed his father. Courant did not let himself be distracted, but as minutes passed and there was no impact, no sight or sound to catch his attention and reassure him, he began to invent stories. There was a storm, he would say, or the sloop was wrecked in the fog. That was close enough to the truth that it would be acceptable to his son, should he ever learn the truth. The truth? But what was that? That somehow, while coasting, he had lost his way in the fog. It had happened to other sailors. His uncle had once been becalmed three days out from Tahiti and had almost lost his ship when one of his three crewmen had got crazy and said that they were damned for their sins, and that the ocean would punish them. He could not remember how that story ended, but he did not think his uncle had done much sailing since that voyage. Small wonder.

The water was growing warmer and more quiet. The *ShangriLa* drifted in the stillness and continued into the fog. There was a splash as something broke the surface off to starboard, then dropped out of sight before he could peer through the fog to make out what it was.

Sammy, he thought, would be running around the deck by now, demanding that his father do something about what was going on. Sammy, who would never understand why it was that Courant could not solve anything in a moment, who insisted that his mother and father vie with each other in giving him the things he wanted most. And Kate encouraged him. She did not have to live with him, and so it pleased her to set him at odds with his father, paving the way for her own generosity and bribes to convince the boy that his mother was the only one who loved him.

There were reeds off in the fog, taller and stiffer than cattails, standing at odd angles, disappearing into the water. The wake of the *ShangriLa* when it touched them made them rattle strangely, but nothing more. The mists wreathed around them, making them turn into shadows, like an army with spears.

He released the tiller and moved to the far side of the cockpit, and dangled one hand over the side so that it dragged in the water, which was quite warm now, almost to a temperature that would provide a pleasant swim. He did not look at the sail, holding taut without his aid. He watched the little wake his fingers made until something, perhaps a submerged reed, cut his knuckles and he brought his hand to his mouth to suck away the blood.

The fog grew less dense, and a touch of wind heeled the *ShangriLa* over on its side, and in that short moment, through a gap in the mist, Courant saw a dreadful thing, and he recalled those men in the cruiser with all the equipment. But this was nothing so comprehensible. This was a machine, or a beast so huge, so monstrous, that his mind had no space for it. Objects were being discarded or dismantled, at a rate that was stupefying.

"It's the sawmill at Anderson," he said in a stifled voice, as if he did not want to tempt the thing he had seen to respond to him. It had to be the sawmill. He had been in the fog too long, and his eyes were playing tricks on him. That was it. Nothing was out there, taking the coast to pieces as easily as a stagehand pulls down a set. It was the sawmill, and the disorientation was because of the wind and the sloop responding.

The wind had stopped and the fog returned, thick; Courant welcomed it now, and stared ahead into the stiff, closing reeds, with their spearlike stalks, and the narrow path of warm, oily water that stretched through them, winding away in the mist, swallowing him up.

The public has always had a fascination for the seamier side of the past, though always managing to hold it at a safe, and rather comfortable, distance. What is forgotten is the fact that the past, and its people, have a habit of returning with a vengeance—not necessarily literally, but, if you will, spiritually. This is not a ghost story, however. Though Jack, I suspect, might think otherwise.

Susan Casper lives in Philadelphia, decided one day to join her writer friends, and shoved Gardner Dozois away from his typewriter. This is her first published story; there are more where this came from.

Spring-Fingered Jack

by Susan Casper

HE KNEW WHERE he was going as soon as he walked into the arcade. He moved past the rows of busy children, blaring computer voices, flashing lights and ringing bells. He walked past the line of old-fashioned pinball machines, all of them empty, all flashing and calling like outdated mechanical hookers vainly trying to tempt the passing trade.

The machine he wanted was back in the dimly lit corner, and he breathed a sigh of relief to see it unused. Its mutely staring screen was housed in a yellow body, above a row of levers and buttons. On its side, below the coin slot, was a garish purple drawing of a woman dressed in Victorian high fashion. Her large and ornate hat sat slightly askew atop her head, and her neatly piled hair was falling artistically down at the sides. She was screaming, eyes wide, the back of her hand almost covering her lovely mouth. And behind her, sketched in faintest white, was just the suggestion of a lurking figure.

He put his briefcase down beside the machine. With unsteady fingers, he reached for a coin, and fumbled it into the coin slot. The screen flashed to life. A sinister man in a deerstalker waved a crimson-tipped knife and faded away behind a row of buildings. The graphics were excellent, and extremely realistic. The screen filled with rows of dark blue instructions against a light blue field, and he scanned them sketchily, impatient for the game to begin.

He pressed a button and the image changed again, becoming a maze of narrow squalid streets lined with decaying buildings. One lone figure, his, stood squarely center screen. A woman in Victorian dress, labeled Polly, walked toward him. He pushed the lever forward and his man began to move. He remembered to make the man doff his cap; if you didn't, she wouldn't go with you. They fell in step together, and he carefully steered her past the first intersection. Old Montague Street was a trap for beginners, and one he hadn't fallen into for quite some time. The first one had to be taken to Buck's Row.

Off to one side, a bobby was separating a pair of brawling, ragged women. He had to be careful here, for it cost points if he was spotted. He steered the pair down the appropriate alley, noting with satisfaction that it was deserted.

The heartbeat sound became louder as he maneuvered his figure behind that of the woman, and was joined by the sound of harsh, labored breathing. This part of the game was timed and he would be working against the clock. He lifted a knife from inside his coat. Clapping a hand over "Polly's" mouth, he slashed her throat viciously from ear to ear. Lines of bright red pulsed across the screen, but away from him. Good. He had not been marked by the blood. Now came the hard part. He laid her down and began the disembowling, carefully cutting her abdomen open almost to the diaphragm, keeping one eye on the clock. He finished with twenty seconds to spare and moved his man triumphantly away from the slowly approaching bobby. Once he had found the public sink to wash in, round one was complete.

Once again his figure was center screen. This time the approaching figure was "Dark Annie," and he took her to Hanbury Street. But this time he forgot to cover her mouth when he struck, and she screamed, a shrill and terrifying scream. Immediately the screen began to flash a brilliant, painful red, pulsing in time to the ear-splitting blasts of a police whistle. Two bobbies materialized on either side of his figure, and grabbed it firmly by the arms. A hangman's noose flashed on the screen as the funeral march roared from the speaker. The screen went dark.

He stared at the jeering screen, trembling, feeling shaken and sick, and cursed himself bitterly. A real beginner's mistake! He'd been too eager. Angrily, he fed another coin into the slot.

This time, he carefully worked himself all the way up to "Kate," piling up bonus points and making no fatal mistakes. He was sweating now, and his mouth was dry. His jaws ached with tension. It was really hard to beat the clock on this one, and took intense concentration. He remembered to nick the eyelids, that was essential, and pulling the intestines out and draping them over the right shoulder wasn't too hard, but cutting out the kidney correctly, *that* was a bitch. At last the clock ran out on him, and he had to leave without the kidney, costing himself a slew of points. He was rattled enough to almost run into a bobby as he threaded through the alleys leading out of Mitre Square. The obstacles became increasingly difficult with every successful round completed, and from here on in it became particularly hard, with the clock time shortening, swarms of sightseers, reporters and roving Vigilance Committees to avoid in addition to a redoubled number of police. He had never yet found the right street for "Black Mary. . . ."

A voice called "last game," and a little while later his man got caught again. He slapped the machine in frustration; then straightened his suit and tie and picked up his briefcase. He checked his Rollaflex. Ten-oh-five: it was early yet. The machines winked out in clustered groups as the last stragglers filed through the glass doors. He followed them into the street.

Once outside in the warm night air, he began to think again about the game, to plan his strategy for tomorrow, only peripherally aware of the winos mumbling in doorways, the scantily dressed hookers on the corner. Tawdry neon lights from porno movie houses, "adult" bookstores and flophouse hotels tracked across his eyes like video displays, and his fingers worked imaginary buttons and levers as he pushed through the sleazy, late-night crowds.

He turned into a narrow alley, followed it deep into the

shadows, and then stopped and leaned back against the cool, dank bricks. He spun the three dials of the combination lock, each to its proper number, and then opened the briefcase.

The machine: he had thought of it all day at work, thought of it nearly every second as he waited impatiently for five o'clock, and now another chance had come and gone, and he *still* had not beaten it. He fumbled among the papers in his briefcase, and pulled out a long, heavy knife.

He would practice tonight, and tomorrow he *would* beat the machine.

Most people, feeling reasonably safe in their homes, with their lives, are willing to endure a great deal before they'll get their backs up. Or, they're not willing to endure the slightest change in their routines at all. Whichever it may be, it isn't pleasant when, as the title here suggests, the end has been reached.

Gardner Dozois has been an editor, slush pile reader, lecturer, and teacher of writing, and continues to be one of the most insightful, and disturbing, writers in the country. One sometimes wishes he didn't hone the truth quite so close to the bone.

Flash Point

by Gardner Dozois

BEN JACOBS WAS on his way back to Skowhegan when he
found the abandoned car. It was parked on a lonely stretch of
secondary road between North Anson and Madison, skewed
diagonally over the shoulder.

Kids again, was Jacobs' first thought—more of the road
gypsies who plagued the state every summer until they were
driven south by the icy whip of the first nor'easter. Probably
from the big encampment down near Norridgewock, he decided, and he put his foot back on the accelerator. He'd
already had more than his fill of outer-staters this season, and
it wasn't even the end of August. Then he looked more
closely at the car, and eased up on the gas again. It was too
big, too new to belong to kids. He shifted down into second,
feeling the crotchety old pickup shudder. It was an expensive
car, right enough; he doubted that it came from within twenty
miles of here. You didn't use a big-city car on most of the
roads in this neck of the woods, and you couldn't stay on the
highways forever. He squinted to see more detail. What kind
of plates did it have? You're doing it again, he thought,
suddenly and sourly. He was a man as aflame with curiosity
as a magpie, and—having been brought up strictly to mind
his own business—he considered it a vice. Maybe the car was

33

stolen. It's possible, a'n't it? he insisted, arguing with himself. It could have been used in a robbery and then ditched, like that car from the bank job over to Farmington. It happened all the time.

You don't even fool yourself anymore, he thought, and then he grinned and gave in. He wrestled the old truck into the breakdown lane, jolted over a pothole, and coasted to a bumpy stop a few yards behind the car. He switched the engine off.

Silence swallowed him instantly.

Thick and dusty, the silence poured into the morning, filling the world as hot wax fills a mold. It drowned him completely, it possessed every inch and ounce of him. Almost, it spooked him.

Jacobs hesitated, shrugged, and then jumped down from the cab. Outside it was better—still quiet, but not preternaturally so. There was wind soughing through the spruce woods, a forlorn but welcome sound, one he had heard all his life. There was a wood thrush hammering at the morning, faint with distance but distinct. And a faraway buzzing drone overhead, like a giant sleepy bee or bluebottle, indicated that there was a Piper Cub up there somewhere, probably heading for the airport at Norridgewock. All this was familiar and reassuring. Getting nervy, is all, he told himself, long in the tooth and spooky.

Nevertheless, he walked very carefully toward the car, flat-footed and slow, the way he used to walk on patrol in 'Nam, more years ago than he cared to recall. His fingers itched for something, and after a few feet he realized that he was wishing he'd brought his old deer rifle along. He grimaced irritably at that, but the wish pattered through his mind again and again, until he was close enough to see inside the parked vehicle.

The car was empty.

"Old fool," he said sourly.

Snorting in derision at himself, he circled the car, peering in the windows. There were skid marks in the gravel of the breakdown lane, but they weren't deep—the car hadn't been going fast when it hit the shoulder; probably it had been already meandering out of control, with no foot on the accelerator. The hood and bumpers weren't damaged; the car had rolled to a stop against the low embankment, rather than crashing into it. None of the tires were flat. In the woods taking a leak, Jacobs thought. Damn fool didn't even leave his turn signals on. Or it could have been his battery, or a vapor lock or something, and he'd hiked on up the road looking for a gas station. "He still should have ma'ked it off someway," Jacobs muttered. Tourists never knew enough to find their ass in a snowstorm. This one probably wasn't even carrying any signal flags or flares.

The driver's door was wide open, and next to it was a child's plastic doll, lying facedown in the gravel. Jacobs could not explain the chill that hit him then, the horror that seized him and shook him until he was almost physically ill. Bristling, he stooped and thrust his head into the car. There was a burnt, bitter smell inside, like onions, like hot metal. A layer of gray ash covered the front seat and the floor, a couple of inches deep; a thin stream of it was trickling over the door-jamb to the ground and pooling around the plastic feet of the doll. Hesitantly he touched the ash—it was sticky and soapy to the touch. In spite of the sunlight that was slanting into the car and warming up the upholstery, the ash was cold, almost icy. The cloth ceiling directly over the front seat was lightly blackened with soot—he scraped some of it off with his thumbnail—but there was no other sign of fire. Scattered among the ashes on the front seat were piles of clothing. Jacobs could pick out a pair of men's trousers, a sports coat, a bra, slacks, a bright child's dress, all undamaged. More than one person. They're all in the woods taking a leak, he thought inanely. Sta'k naked.

Sitting on the dashboard were a 35-mm. Nikon SI with a telephoto lens and a new Leicaflex. In the hip pocket of the trousers was a wallet, containing more than fifty dollars in cash, and a bunch of credit cards. He put the wallet back. Not even a tourist was going to be fool enough to walk off and leave this stuff sitting here, in an open car.

He straightened up, and felt the chill again, the deathly noonday cold. This time he *was* spooked. Without knowing why, he nudged the doll out of the puddle of ash with his foot, and then he shuddered. "Hello!" he shouted, at the top of his voice, and got back only a dull, flat echo from the woods. Where in hell *had* they gone?

All at once, he was exhausted. He'd been out before dawn, on a trip up to Kingfield and Carrabassett, and it was catching up with him. Maybe that was why he was so jumpy over nothing. Getting old, c'n't take this kind of shit anymore. How long since you've had a vacation? He opened his mouth to shout again, but uneasily decided not to. He stood for a moment, thinking it out, and then walked back to his truck, hunch-shouldered and limping. The old load of shrapnel in his leg and hip was beginning to bother him again.

Jacobs drove a mile down the highway to a rest stop. He had been hoping he would find the people from the car here, waiting for a tow truck, but the rest area was deserted. He stuck his head into the wood-and-fieldstone latrine, and found that it was inhabited only by buzzing clouds of bluebottles and blackflies. He shrugged. So much for that. There was a pay phone on a pole next to the picnic tables, and he used it to call the sheriff's office in Skowhegan. Unfortunately, Abner Jackman answered the phone, and it took Jacobs ten exasperating minutes to argue him into showing any interest. "Well, if they did," Jacobs said grudgingly, "they did it without any clothes." *Gobblegobblebuzz*, said the phone. "With a *kid*?" Jacobs demanded. *Buzzgobblefttzbuzz*, the phone said, giving in. "Ayah," Jacobs said grudgingly, "I'll stay theah until you show up." And he hung up.

"Damned foolishness," he muttered. This was going to cost him the morning.

County Sheriff Joe Riddick arrived an hour later. He was a stocky, slab-sided man, apparently cut all of a piece out of a block of granite—his shoulders seemed to be the same width as his hips, his square-skulled, square-jawed head thrust belligerently up from his monolithic body without any hint of a neck. He looked like an old snapping turtle: ugly, mud colored, powerful. His hair was snow-white, and his eyes were bloodshot and ill-tempered. He glared at Jacobs dangerously out of red-rimmed eyes with tiny pupils. He looked ready to snap.

"Good morning," Jacobs said coldly.

"Morning," Riddick grunted. "You want to fill me in on this?"

Jacobs did. Riddick listened impassively. When Jacobs finished, Riddick snorted and brushed a hand back over his close-cropped snowy hair. "Some damn fool skylark more'n likely," he said, sourly, shaking his head a little. "O-kay, then," he said, suddenly becoming officious and brisk. "If this turns out to be anything serious, we may need you as a witness. Understand? All right." He looked at his watch. "All right. We're waiting for the state boys. I don't think you're needed anymore." Riddick's face was hard and cold and dull—as if it had been molded in lead. He stared point-edly at Jacobs. His eyes were opaque as marbles. "Good day."

Twenty minutes later Jacobs was passing a proud little sign, erected by the Skowhegan Chamber of Commerce, that said: HOME OF THE LARGEST SCULPTED WOODEN INDIAN IN THE WORLD! He grinned. Skowhegan had grown a great deal in the last decade, but somehow it was still a small town. It had resisted the modern tropism to skyscrape and had sprawled instead, spreading out along the banks of the Kennebec River in both directions. Jacobs parked in front of a dingy storefront on Water Street, in the heart of town. A sign in the window commanded: EAT; at night it glowed an imperative neon red. The sign belonged to an establishment that had started life as the Colonial Cafe, with a buffet and quaint rustic decor, and was finishing it, twenty years and three recessions later, as a greasy lunchroom with faded movie posters on the wall—owned and operated by Wilbur and Myna Phipps, a cheerful and indestructible couple in their late sixties. It was crowded and hot inside—the place had a large number of regulars, and most of them were in attendance for lunch. Jacobs spotted Will Sussmann at the counter, jammed in between an inverted glass bowl full of doughnuts and the protruding rear end of the coffee percolator.

Sussmann—chief staff writer for the Skowhegan *Inquirer*, stringer and columnist for a big Bangor weekly—had saved him a seat by piling the adjacent stool with his hat, coat, and briefcase. Not that it was likely he'd had to struggle too hard for room. Even Jacobs, whose father had moved to Skowhegan from Bangor when Jacobs was three, was regarded with faint suspicion by the real old-timers of the town. Sussmann, being originally an outer-stater and a "foreigner" to boot, was completely out of luck; he'd only lived here ten years, and that wasn't enough even to begin to tip the balance in his favor.

Sussmann retrieved his paraphernalia; Jacobs sat down and began telling him about the car. Sussmann said it was weird. "We'll never get anything out of Riddick," he said. He began to attack a stack of hotcakes. "He's hated my guts ever since I accused him of working over those gypsy kids last summer, putting one in the hospital. That would have cost him his job, except the higher echelons were being 'four-square behind their dedicated law enforcement officers' that season. Still, it didn't help his reputation with the town any."

"We don't tolerate that kind of thing in these pa'ts," Jacobs said grimly. "Hell, Will, those kids are a royal pain in the ass, but—" But not in these pa'ts, he told himself, not that. There are decent limits. He was surprised at the depth and ferocity of his reaction. "This a'n't Alabama," he said.

"Might as well be, with Riddick. His idea of law enforcement's to take everybody he doesn't like down in the basement and beat the crap out of them." Sussmann sighed. "Anyway, Riddick wouldn't stop to piss on me if my hat was on fire, that's for sure. Good thing I got other ways of finding stuff out."

Jed Everett came in while Jacobs was ordering coffee. He was a thin, cadaverous man with a long nose; his hair was going rapidly to gray; put him next to short, round Sussmann and they would look like Mutt and Jeff. At forty-eight—Everett was a couple of years older than Jacobs, just as Sussmann was a couple of years younger—he was considered to be scandalously young for a small-town doctor, especially a GP. But old Dr. Barlow had died of a stroke three years back, leaving his younger partner in residency, and they were stuck with him.

One of the regulars had moved away from the trough, leaving an empty seat next to Jacobs, and Everett was talking before his buttocks had hit the upholstery. He was a jittery man, with lots of nervous energy, and he loved to fret and rant and gripe, but softly and good-naturedly, with no real force behind it, as if he had a volume knob that had been turned down.

"What a morning!" Everett said. "Jesus H. Christ on a bicycle—'scuse me, Myna, I'll take some coffee, please, black—I swear it's psychosomatic. Honest to God, gentlemen, she's a case for the medical journals, dreams the whole damn shitbundle up out of her head just for the fun of it, I swear before all my hopes of heaven, swop me blue if she doesn't. *Definitely* psychosomatic."

"He's learned a new word," Sussmann said.

"If you'd wasted all the time I have on this nonsense," Everett said fiercely, "you'd be whistling a different tune out of the other side of your face, *I* can tell *you*, oh yes indeed. What kind of meat d'you have today, Myna? How about the chops—they good?—all right, and put some greens on the plate, please. Okay? Oh, and some home frieds, now I think about it, please. If you have them."

"What's got your back up?" Jacobs asked mildly.

"You know old Mrs. Crawford?" Everett demanded. "Hm? Lives over to the Island, widow, has plenty of money? Three times now I've diagnosed her as having cancer, serious but still operable, and *three* times now I've sent her down to Augusta for exploratory surgery, and each time they got her down on the table and opened her up and couldn't find a thing, not a goddamned thing, old bitch's hale and hearty as a prize hog. Spontaneous remission. All psychosomatic, clear as mud. Three *times*, though. It's shooting my reputation all to hell down there. Now she thinks she's got an ulcer. I hope her kidney falls out, right in the street. Thank you, Myna. Can I have another cup of coffee?" He sipped his coffee, when it arrived, and looked a little more meditative. "Course, I think I've seen a good number of cases like that, I *think*, I said, ha'd to prove it when they're terminal. Wouldn't surprise me if a good many of the people who die of cancer—or a lot of other diseases, for that matter—were like that. No real physical cause, they just get tired of living, something dries up inside them, their systems stop trying to defend them, and one thing or another knocks them off. They become easy to touch off, like tinder. Most of them don't change their minds in the middle, though, like that fat old sow."

Wilbur Phipps, who had been leaning on the counter listening, ventured the opinion that modern medical science had never produced anything even half as good as the old-fashioned mustard plaster. Everett flared up instantly.

"You ever bejesus try one?" Phipps demanded.

"No, and I don't bejesus intend to!" Everett said.

Jacobs turned toward Sussmann. "Wheah you been, this early in the day?" he asked. "A'n't like you to haul yourself out before noon."

"Up at the Factory. Over to West Mills."

"What was up? Another hearing?"

"Yup. Didn't stick—they aren't going to be injuncted."

"They never will be," Jacobs said. "They got too much money, too many friends in Augusta. The Board'll never touch them."

"I don't believe that," Sussmann said. Jacobs grunted and sipped his coffee.

"As Christ's my judge," Everett was saying, in a towering rage, "I'll never understand you people, not if I live to be two hundred, not if I get to be so old my ass falls off and I have to lug it around in a handcart. I swear to God. Some of you ain't got a pot to piss in, so goddamned poor you can't afford to buy a bottle of aspirins, let alone, *let alone* pay your doctor bills from the past half-million years, and yet you go out to some godforsaken hick town too small to turn a horse around in proper and see an unlicensed practitioner, a goddamn backwoods quack, an un*mit*igated phony, and *pay* through the nose so this witch doctor can assault you with yarb potions and poultices, and stick leeches on your ass, for all *I* know—" Jacobs lost track of the conversation. He studied a bee that was bumbling along the putty-and-plaster edge of the storefront window, swimming through the thick and dusty sunlight, looking for a way out. He felt numb, distanced from reality. The people around him looked increasingly strange. He found that it took an effort of will to recognize them at all, even Sussmann, even Everett. It scared him. These were people Jacobs saw every day of his life. Some of them he didn't actually *like*—not in the way that big-city folk thought of liking someone—but they were all his neighbors. They belonged here, they were a part of his existence, and that carried its own special intimacy. But today he was beginning to see them as an intolerant sophisticate from the city might see them: dull, provincial, sunk in an iron torpor that masqueraded as custom and routine. That was valid, in its way, but it was a grossly one-sided picture, ignoring a thousand virtues, compensations, and kindnesses. But that was the way he was seeing them. As aliens. As strangers.

Distractedly, Jacobs noticed that Everett and Sussmann were making ready to leave. "No rest for the weary," Everett was saying, and Jacobs found himself nodding unconsciously in agreement. Swamped by a sudden rush of loneliness, he invited both men home for dinner that night. They accepted, Everett with the qualification that he'd have to see what his wife had planned. Then they were gone, and Jacobs found himself alone at the counter.

He knew that he should have gone back to work also; he had some more jobs to pick up, and a delivery to make. But he felt very tired, too flaccid and heavy to move, as if some tiny burrowing animal had gnawed away his bones, as if he'd been hamstrung and hadn't realized it. He told himself that it was because he was hungry; he was running himself down, as Carol had always said he someday would. So he dutifully ordered a bowl of chili.

The chili was murky, amorphous stuff, bland and lukewarm. Listlessly, he spooned it up.

No rest for the weary.

"You know what I was nuts about when I was a kid?" Jacobs suddenly observed to Wilbur Phipps. "Rafts. I was a'ways making rafts out of old planks and sheet tin and whatevah other junk I could scounge up, begging old rope and nails to lash them together with. Then I'd break my ass dragging them down to the Kennebec. And you know what? They a'ways sunk. Every goddamned time."

"Ayah?" Wilbur Phipps said.

Jacobs pushed the bowl of viscid chili away, and got up. Restlessly, he wandered over to where Dave Lucas, the game warden, was drinking beer and talking to a circle of men ". . . dogs will be the end of deer in these pa'ts, I swear to

God. And I a'n't talking about wild dogs neither, I'm talking about your ordinary domestic pets. A'n't it so, every winter? Half-starved deer a'n't got a chance in hell 'gainst somebody's big pet hound, all fed-up and rested. The deer those dogs don't kill outright, why they chase 'em to death, and then they don't even eat 'em. Rum 'em out of the forest covah into the open and they get pneumonia. Run 'em into the river and through thin ice and they get drowned. Remember last yeah, the deer that big hound drove out onto the ice? Broke both its front legs and I had to go out and shoot the poor bastid. Between those goddamn dogs and all the nighthunters we got around here lately, we a'n't going to have any deer left in this county . . ." Jacobs moved away, past a table where Abner Jackman was pouring ketchup over a plateful of scrambled eggs, and arguing about Communism with Steve Girard, a volunteer fireman and Elk, and Allen Ewing, a postman, who had a son serving with the Marines in Bolivia. ". . . let 'em win theah," Jackman was saying in a nasal voice, "and they'll be swa'ming all over us eventu'ly, sure as shit. Ain' no way to stop 'em then. And you're better off blowing your brains out than living under the Reds, don't ever think otherwise." He screwed the ketchup top back onto the bottle, and glanced up in time to see Jacobs start to go by.

"Ben!" Jackman said, grabbing Jacobs by the elbow. "You can tell 'em." He grinned vacuously at Jacobs—a lanky, loose-jointed, slack-faced man. "He can tell you, boys, what it's like being in a country overrun with Communists, what they do to everybody. You were in 'Nam when you were a youngster, weren't you?"

"Yeah."

After a pause, Jackman said, "You ain' got no call to take offense, Ben." His voice became a whine. "I didn't mean no ha'm. I didn't mean nothing."

"Forget it," Jacobs said, and walked out.

Dave Lucas caught up with Jacobs just outside the door. He was a short, grizzled man with iron-gray hair, about seven years older than Jacobs. "You know, Ben," Lucas said, "the thing of it is, Abner really doesn't mean any ha'm." Lucas smiled bleakly; his grandson had been killed last year, in the

Retreat from La Paz. "It's just that he a'n't too bright, is all."

"They don't want him kicked ev'ry so often," Jacobs said, "then they shouldn't let him out of his kennel at all." He grinned. "Dinner tonight? About eight?"

"Sounds fine," Lucas said. "We're going to catch a nighthunter, out near Oaks Pond, so I'll probably be late."

"We'll keep it wa'm for you."

"Just the comp'ny'll be enough."

Jacobs started his truck and pulled out into the afternoon traffic. He kept his hands locked tightly around the steering wheel. He was amazed and dismayed by the surge of murderous anger he had felt toward Jackman; the reaction to it made him queasy, and left the muscles knotted all across his back and shoulders. Dave was right, Abner couldn't rightly be held responsible for the dumbass things he said—But if Jackman had said one more thing, if he'd done anything than to back down as quickly as he had, then Jacaobs would have split his head open. He had been instantly ready to do it, his hands had curled into fists, his legs had bent slightly at the knees. He *would* have done it. And he would have enjoyed it. That was a frightening realization.

Y' touchy today, he thought, inanely. His fingers were turning white on the wheel.

He drove home. Jacobs lived in a very old wood frame house above the north bank of the Kennebec, on the outskirts of town, with nothing but a clump of new apartment buildings for senior citizens to remind him of civilization. The house was empty—Carol was teaching fourth grade, and Chris had been farmed out to Mrs. Turner, the baby-sitter. Jacobs spent the next half hour wrestling a broken washing machine and a television set out of the pickup and into his basement workshop, and another fifteen minutes maneuvering a newly repaired stereo-radio console up out of the basement and into the truck. Jacobs was one of the last of the old-style Yankee tinkerers, although he called himself an appliance repairman, and also did some carpentry and general handiwork when things got slow. He had little formal training, but he "kept up." He wasn't sure he could fix one of the new hologram sets, but then they wouldn't be getting out here for another twenty years anyway. There were people within fifty miles who didn't have indoor plumbing. People within a hundred miles who didn't have electricity.

On the way to Norridgewock, two open jeeps packed dangerously full of gypsies came roaring up behind him. They started to pass, one on each side of his truck, their horns blaring insanely. The two jeeps ran abreast of Jacobs' old pickup for a while, making no attempt to go by—the three vehicles together filled the road. The jeeps drifted in until they were almost touching the truck, and the gypsies began pounding the truck roof with their fists, shouting and laughing. Jacobs kept both hands on the wheel and grimly continued to drive at his original speed. Jeeps tipped easily when sideswiped by a heavier vehicle, if it came to that. And he had a tire-iron under the seat. But the gypsies tired of the game—they accelerated and passed Jacobs, most of them giving him the finger as they went by, and one throwing a poorly aimed bottle that bounced onto the shoulder. They were big, tough-looking kids with skin haircuts, dressed—incongruously—in flowered pastel luau shirts and expensive white bell-bottoms.

The jeeps roared on up the road, still taking up both lanes. Jacobs watched them unblinkingly until they disappeared from sight. He was awash with rage, the same bitter, vicious hatred he had felt for Jackman. Riddick was right after all—the goddamned kids were a menace to everything that lived, they ought to be locked up. He wished suddenly that he *had* sideswiped them. He could imagine it all vividly: the sickening crunch of impact, the jeep overturning, bodies cartwheeling through the air, the jeep skidding upside down across the road and crashing into the embankment, maybe the gas tank exploding, a gout of flame, smoke, stink, screams—He ran through it over and over again, relishing it, until he realized abruptly what he was doing, what he was wishing, and he was almost physically ill.

All the excitement and fury drained out of him, leaving him shaken and sick. He'd always been a patient, peaceful man, perhaps too much so. He'd never been afraid to fight, but he'd always said that a man who couldn't talk his way out of most trouble was a fool. This sudden daydream lust for blood bothered him to the bottom of his soul. He'd seen plenty of death in 'Nam, and it hadn't affected him this way. It was the kids, he told himself. They drag everybody down to their own level. He kept seeing them inside his head all the way into Norridgewock—the thick, brutal faces, the hard reptile eyes, the contemptuously grinning mouths that seemed too full of teeth. The gypsy kids had changed over the years. The torrent of hippies and Jesus freaks had gradually run dry, the pluggers and the weeps had been all over the state for a few seasons, and then, slowly, they'd stopped coming too. The new crop of itinerant kids were—hard. Every year they became more brutal and dangerous. They didn't seem to care if they lived or died, and they hated everything indiscriminately—including themselves.

In Norridgewock, he delivered the stereo console to its owner, then went across town to pick up a malfunctioning 75-hp Johnson outboard motor. From the motor's owner, he heard that a town boy had beaten an elderly storekeeper to death that morning, when the storekeeper caught him shoplifting. The boy was in custody, and it was the scandal of the year for Norridgewock. Jacobs had noticed it before, but discounted it: the local kids were getting mean too, meaner every year. Maybe it was self-defense.

Driving back, Jacobs noticed one of the gypsy jeeps skewed up onto the road embankment. It was empty. He slowed, and stared at the jeep thoughtfully, but he did not stop.

A fire-rescue truck nearly ran him down as he entered Skowhegan. It came screaming out of nowhere and swerved onto Water Street, its blue blinker flashing, siren screeching in metallic rage, suddenly right on top of him. Jacobs wrenched his truck over to the curb, and it swept by like a demon, nearly scraping him. It left a frightened silence behind it, after it had vanished urgently from sight. Jacobs pulled back into traffic and continued driving. Just before the turnoff to his house, a dog ran out into the road. Jacobs had slowed down for the turn anyway, and he saw the dog in plenty of time to stop. He did not stop. At the last possible second, he yanked himself out of a waking dream, and swerved just enough to miss the dog. He had wanted to hit it; he'd liked the idea of running it down. There were too many dogs in the county anyway, he told himself, in a feeble attempt at justification. ''Big, ugly hound,'' he muttered, and was appalled by how alien his voice sounded—hard, bitterly hard, as if it were a rock speaking. Jacobs noticed that his hands were shaking.

Dinner that night was a fair success. Carol had turned out not to be particularly overjoyed that her husband had invited a horde of people over without bothering to consult her, but Jacobs placated her a little by volunteering to cook dinner. It turned out ''sufficient,'' as Everett put it. Everybody ate, and nobody died. Toward the end, Carol had to remind them to leave some for Dave Lucas, who had not arrived yet. The company did a lot to restore Jacobs' nerves, and, feeling better, he wrestled with curiosity throughout the meal. Curiosity won, as it usually did with him: in the end, and against his better judgment.

As the guests began to trickle into the parlor, Jacobs took Sussmann aside and asked him if he'd learned anything new about the abandoned car.

Sussmann seemed uneasy and preoccupied. ''Whatever it was happened to them seems to've happened again this afternoon. Maybe a couple of times. There was another abandoned car found about four o'clock, up near Athens. And there was one late yesterday night, out at Livermore Falls. And a tractor-trailer on Route Ninety-five this morning, between Waterville and Benton Station.''

''How'd you pry that out of Riddick?''

''Didn't.'' Sussmann smiled wanly. ''Heard about that Athens one from the driver of the tow truck that hauled it back—that one bumped into a signpost, hard enough to break its radiator. Ben, Riddick can't keep me in the dark. I've got more stringers than he has.''

''What d'you think it is?''

Sussmann's expression fused over and became opaque. He shook his head.

In the parlor, Carol, Everett's wife, Amy—an ample, gray woman, rather like somebody's archetypical aunt but possessed of a very canny mind—and Sussmann, the inveterate bachelor, occupied themselves by playing with Chris. Chris was two, very quick and bright, and very excited by all the company. He'd just learned how to blow kisses, and was now practicing enthusiastically with the adults. Everett, meanwhile, was prowling around examining the stereo equipment that filled one wall. "You install this yourself?" he asked, when Jacobs came up to hand him a beer.

"Not only installed it," Jacobs said, "I built it all myself, from scratch. Tinkered up most of the junk in this house. Take the beah 'fore it gets hot."

"Damn fine work," Everett muttered, absently accepting the beer. "Better'n my own setup, I purely b'lieve, and that set me back a right sma't piece of change. Jesus Christ, Ben—I didn't know you could do quality work like that. What the hell you doing stagnating out here in the sticks, fixing people's radios and washing machines, f'chrissake? Y'that good, you ought to be down in Boston, New York mebbe, making some real money."

Jacobs shook his head. "Hate the cities, big cities like that. C'n't stand to live in them at all." He ran a hand through his hair. "I lived in New York for a while, seven-eight yeahs back, 'fore settling in Skowhegan again. It was terrible theah, even back then, and it's worse now. People down theah dying on their feet, walking around dead without anybody to tell 'em to lie down and get buried decent."

"We're dying here too, Ben," Everett said. "We're just doing it slower, is all."

Jacobs shrugged. "Mebbe so," he said. " 'Scuse me." He walked back to the kitchen, began to scrape the dishes and stack them in the sink. His hands had started to tremble again.

When he returned to the parlor, after putting Chris to bed, he found that conversation had almost died. Everett and Sussmann were arguing halfheartedly about the Factory, each knowing that he'd never convince the other. It was a pointless discussion, and Jacobs did not join it. He poured himself a glass of beer and sat down. Amy hardly noticed him; her usually pleasant face was stern and angry. Carol found an opportunity to throw him a sympathetic wink while tossing her long hair back over her shoulder, but her face was flushed too, and her lips were thin. The evening had started off well, but it had soured somehow; everyone felt it. Jacobs began to clean his pipe, using a tiny knife to scrape the bowl. A siren went by outside, wailing eerily away into distance. An ambulance, it sounded like, or the fire-rescue truck again—more melancholy and mournful, less predatory than the siren of a police cruiser. ". . . brew viruses . . ." Everett was saying, and then Jacobs lost him, as if Everett were being pulled further and further away by some odd, local perversion of gravity, his voice thinning into inaudibility. Jacobs couldn't hear him at all now. Which was strange, as the parlor was only a few yards wide. Another siren. There were a lot of them tonight; they sounded like the souls of the dead, looking for home in the darkness, unable to find light and life. Jacobs found himself thinking about the time he'd toured Vienna, during "recuperative leave" in Europe, after hospitalization in 'Nam. There was a tour of the catacombs under the Cathedral, and he'd taken it, limping painfully along on his crutch, the wet, porous stone of the tunnel roof closing down until it almost touched the top of his head. They came to a place where an opening had been cut through the hard, gray rock, enabling the tourists to come up one by one and look into the burial pit on the other side, while the guide lectured calmly in alternating English and German. When you stuck your head through the opening, you looked out at a solid wall of human bones. Skulls, arm and leg bones, rib cages, pelvises, all mixed in helter-skelter and packed solid, layer after uncountable layer of them. The wall of bones rose up sheer out of the darkness, passed through the fan of light cast by a naked bulb at eye-level, and continued to rise—it was impossible to see the top, no matter how you craned your neck and squinted. This wall had been built by the Black Death, a haphazard but grandiose architect. The Black Death had eaten these people up and spat out their remains, as casual and careless as a picnicker gnawing chicken bones. When the meal was over, the people who were still alive had dug a huge pit under the Cathedral and shoveled the victims in by the hundreds of thousands. Strangers in life, they mingled in death, cheek by jowl, belly to backbone, except that after a while there were no cheeks or jowls. The backbones remained: yellow, ancient, and brittle. So did the skulls—upright, upside down, on their sides, all grinning blankly at the tourists.

The doorbell rang.

It was Dave Lucas. He looked like one of the skulls Jacobs had been thinking about—his face was gray and gaunt, the skin drawn tightly across his bones; it looked as if he'd been dusted with powdered lime. Shocked, Jacobs stepped aside. Lucas nodded to him shortly and walked by into the parlor without speaking. ". . . stuff about the Factory is news," Sussmann was saying, doggedly, "and more interesting than anything else that happens up here. It sells papers—" He stopped talking abruptly when Lucas entered the room. All conversation stopped. Everyone gaped at the old game warden, horrified. Unsteadily Lucas let himself down into a stuffed chair, and gave them a thin attempt at a smile. "Can I have a beah?" he said. "Or a drink?"

"Scotch?"

"That'll be fine," Lucas said mechanically.

Jacobs went to get it for him. When he returned with the drink, Lucas was determinedly making small talk and flashing his new dead smile. It was obvious that he wasn't going to say anything about what had happened to him. Lucas was an old-fashioned Yankee gentleman to the core, and Jacobs—who had a strong touch of that in his own upbringing—suspected why he was keeping silent. So did Amy. After the requisite few minutes of polite conversation, Amy asked if she could see the new paintings that Carol was working on. Carol exchanged a quick, comprehending glance with her, and nodded. Grim-faced, both women left the room—they knew that this was going to be bad. When the women were out of sight, Lucas said, "Can I have another drink, Ben?" and held out his empty glass. Jacobs refilled it wordlessly. Lucas had never been a drinking man.

"Give," Jacobs said, handing Lucas his glass. "What happened?"

Lucas sipped his drink. He still looked ghastly, but a little color was seeping back into his face. "A'n't felt this shaky since I was in the a'my, back in Korea," he said. He shook his head heavily. "I swear to Christ, I don't understand what's got into people in these pa'ts. Used t'be decent folk out heah, Christian folk." He set his drink aside, and braced himself up visibly. His face hardened. "Never mind that. Things change, I guess, c'n't stop 'em no way." He turned toward Jacobs. ''Remember that nighthunter I was after. Well we got 'im, went out with Steve Girard, Rick Barlow, few other boys, and nabbed him real neat—city boy, no woods sense at all. Well, we were coming back around the end of the pond, down the lumber road, when we heard this big commotion coming from the Gibson place, shouts, a woman screaming her head off, like that. So we cut across the back of their field and went over to see what was going on. House was wide open, and what we walked into—'' He stopped; little sickly beads of sweat had appeared all over his face. ''You remember the McInerney case down in Boston four-five yeahs back? The one there was such a stink about? Well, it was like that. They had a whatchamacallit there, a coven— the Gibsons, the Sewells, the Bradshaws, about seven others, all local people, all hopped out of their minds, all dressed up in black robes, and—blood, painted all over their faces. God, I—No, never mind. They had a baby there, and a kind of an altar they'd dummied up, and a pentagram. Somebody'd killed the baby, slit its throat, and they'd hung it up to bleed like a hog. Into cups. When we got there, they'd just cut its heart out, and they were starting in on dismembering it. Hell—they were tearing it apart, never mind that 'dismembering' shit. They were so frenzied-blind they hardly noticed us come in. Mrs. Bradshaw hadn't been able to take it, she'd cracked completely and was sitting in a corner screaming her lungs out, with Mr. Sewell trying to shut her up. They were the only two that even tried to run. The boys hung Gibson and Bradshaw and Sewell, and stomped Ed Patterson to death—I just couldn't stop 'em. It was all I could do to keep'em from killing the other ones. I shot Steve Girard in the arm, trying to stop 'em, but they took the gun away, and almost strung me up too. My God, Ben, I've known Steve Girard a'most ten yeahs. I've known Gibson and Sewell all my life.'' He stared at them appealingly, blind with despair. ''What's happened to people up heah?''

No one said a word.

Not in these pa'ts, Jacobs mimicked himself bitterly. *There are decent limits.*

Jacobs found that he was holding the pipe-cleaning knife like a weapon. He'd cut his finger on it, and a drop of blood was oozing slowly along the blade. This kind of thing—the Satanism, the ritual murders, the sadism—was what had driven him away from the city. He'd thought it was different in the country, that people were better. But it wasn't, and they weren't. It was bottled up better out here, was all. But it had been coming for years, and they had blinded themselves to it and done nothing, and now it was too late. He could feel it in himself, something long repressed and denied, the reaction to years of frustration and ugliness and fear, to watching the world dying without hope. That part of him had listened to Lucas's story with appreciation, almost with glee. It stirred strongly in him, a monster turning over in ancient mud, down inside, thousands of feet down, thousands of years down. He could see it spreading through the faces of the others in the room, a stain, a spider shadow of contamination. Its presence was suffocating: the chalky, musty smell of old brittle death, somehow leaking through from the burial pit in Vienna. Bone dust—he almost choked on it, it was so thick here in his pleasant parlor in the country.

And then the room was filled with sound and flashing, bloody light.

Jacobs floundered for a moment, unable to understand what was happening. He swam up from his chair, baffled, moving with dreamlike slowness. He stared in helpless confusion at the leaping red shadows. His head hurt.

"An ambulance!" Carol shouted, appearing in the parlor archway with Amy. "We saw it from the upstairs window—"

"It's right out front," Sussmann said.

They ran for the door. Jacobs followed them more slowly. Then the cold outside air slapped him, and he woke up a little. The ambulance was parked across the street, in front of the senior citizens' complex. The corpsmen were hurrying up the stairs of one of the institutional, cinderblock buildings, carrying a stretcher. They disappeared inside. Amy slapped her bare arms to keep off the cold. "Heart attack, mebbe," she said. Everett shrugged. Another siren slashed through the night, getting closer. While they watched, a police cruiser pulled up next to the ambulance, and Riddick got out. Riddick saw the group in front of Jacobs' house, and stared at them with undisguised hatred, as if he would like to arrest them and hold them responsible for whatever had happened in the retirement village. Then he went inside too. He looked haggard as he turned to go, exhausted, hagridden by the suspicion that he'd finally been handed something he couldn't settle with a session in the soundproofed back room at the sheriff's office.

They waited. Jacobs slowly became aware that Sussmann was talking to him, but he couldn't hear what he was saying. Sussmann's mouth opened and closed. It wasn't important anyway. He'd never noticed before how unpleasant Sussmann's voice was, how rasping and shrill. Sussmann was ugly too, shockingly ugly. He boiled with contamination and decay—he was a sack of putrescence. He was an abomination.

Dave Lucas was standing off to one side, his hands in his pockets, shoulders slumped, his face blank. He watched the excitement next door without expression, without interest. Everett turned and said something that Jacobs could not hear. Like Sussmann's, Everett's lips moved without sound. He had moved closer to Amy. They glanced uneasily around. They were abominations too.

Jacobs stood with his arm around Carol; he didn't remember putting it there—it was seeking company on its own. He felt her shiver, and clutched her more tightly in response, directed by some small, distanced, horrified part of himself that was still rational—he knew it would do no good. There was a thing in the air tonight that was impossible to warm yourself against. It hated warmth, it swallowed it and buried it in ice. It was a wedge, driving them apart, isolating them all. He curled his hand around the back of Carol's neck. Something was pulsing through him in waves, building higher and stronger. He could feel Carol's pulse beating under her skin, under his fingers, so very close to the surface.

Across the street, a group of old people had gathered around the ambulance. They shuffled in the cold, hawking and spitting, clutching overcoats and nightgowns more tightly around them. The corpsmen reappeared, edging carefully down the stairs with the stretcher. The sheet was pulled up all the way, but it looked curiously flat and caved-in—if there was a body under there, it must have collapsed, crumbled like dust or ash. The crowd of old people parted to let the stretcher

crew pass, then reformed again, flowing like a heavy, slug-
gish liquid. Their faces were like leather or horn: hard, dead,
dry, worn smooth. And *tired*. Intolerably, burdensomely tired.
Their eyes glittered in their shriveled faces as they watched
the stretcher go by. They looked uneasy and afraid, and yet
there was an anticipation in their faces, an impatience, almost
an envy, as they looked on death. Silence blossomed from a
tiny seed in each of them, a total, primordial silence, from the
time before there were words. It grew, consumed them, and
merged to form a greater silence that spread out through the
night in widening ripples.

The ambulance left.

In the hush that followed, they could hear sirens begin to
wail all over town.

Kids are afraid of a lot of things, from grown-ups to the world those grown-ups have given them. And well they should be; they have a talent for discovering the undiscoverable, for making real the fantastic, and for underscoring the idea that what scares them shouldn't automatically be dismissed simply because they supposedly don't know any better.

Jack Dann—editor, author, raconteur—has always been more comfortable with whisperings than with thunder, as this short-short illustrates. He is currently working on a new novel, and producing stories like . . .

A Cold Day
In the Mesozoic

by Jack Dann

JODY (which *is* a boy's name) purposely tarried in school so
he would miss the bus. His best friend Damon, who was two
years younger than Jody, begged him to ride the bus and trade
Bo Derek bubblegum cards, but Jody just wasn't ready to
face his Aunt Sophia, who was taking care of him while his
mother was in the hospital having a baby. As soon as he
walked into the house, she would fawn all over him and
pester him and ask him a million questions about what he had
done at school all day. She was a nice lady, he supposed, but
he couldn't stand her.

His green rubber boots crunched in the snow as he left the
empty schoolyard. It was uncomfortably cold, but Jody felt
exhilarated by the bite of the wind and the white-peppered
look of everything around him. A light snow had fallen and
then immediately froze into glitter.

He took a shortcut through a narrow stone underpass and
climbed a steep, slippery hill that led to the highway. From
this vantage he could see the city that was built around and
inside the raised highways and cloverleafs. He dashed across
the highway to the grassy median. As he walked along the
median the cars seemed to be rushing right at him, but Jody
liked that. His boots made squishing noises in the snow-

covered grass, and he was happy just walking and daydreaming and being alone.

Of course, Jody wasn't really walking home, for Route Seventeen stretched east and west, and Jody's house was on the south side of town.

When his face and ears began to burn from the cold, Jody worried a red-and-white woolen ski mask out of his coat pocket and pulled it over his head. Then he held his thumb and forefinger together and brought them toward his mouth, as if he were holding a cigarette. He exhaled a long stream of smoke: it was so cold that it seemed his breath would freeze into a cloud.

Ahead, the highway curved around a hill. A construction crew was working on the west side of the highway. There were large tractors and excavation equipment on the median and by the far side of the road, and a series of dented red-and-yellow cones indicated that cars had to merge into the right-hand lane. But what really interested Jody was a tarpaulin shaped like a great gray tent, which was situated on the edge of the construction site. It stood in the center of the median between Jody and the men who were busy digging noisily with jackhammers, operating steam shovels and tractors, and directing traffic. Jody had often seen these tarpaulin tents on highway medians when he took trips with his father— but never one quite as large as this—and he always wondered what was *inside* them.

Walking stiffly, as if to conserve his warmth, he trudged toward the tent. He was shivering and his teeth chattered as he sang a tune through them. He was careful not to be seen as he approached the tent, which looked to be about fifty feet tall at the two points where poles held it up teepee fashion. He kneeled beside the tent.

And he heard something breathing inside . . . something that was taking very long and very deep breaths.

He peeked under the heavy canvas. It was dim and warm and humid inside the tarpaulin. His eyes became used to the smoky grayness: light entered from the bottom edges of the tarp and around the poles at the top. Jody saw the enormous hulk of a beast that took up most of the tent. The beast's leathery skin looked green as a leaf. Slowly, as if just realizing it was being watched, the creature moved its long snake-like neck downward and Jody found himself looking into a huge yellow saurian eye.

Jody didn't move. He just stared back at the dinosaur, which was a brontosaurus. It was chewing on its cud like a cow.

It finally opened its mouth and exhaled a warm stream of air at Jody that smelled sickly sweet.

"Hey, get the hell outa there, kid," shouted a man's voice, and Jody scrambled back out into the freezing air. A construction worker wearing earmuffs and a hard hat said, "You should know better than to poke around where you don't belong. If you let the air in, the thing will catch cold and die. Is that what you want? Do you want it to die?"

Jody mumbled, "Nosir," and the man told him to get the hell home and never come back again. Jody turned and ran and didn't slow down until he had crossed the highway and climbed down the hill onto village property. He took a rest inside the old underpass. Then he hurried past the parts store and the shoe factories with all the tiny broken windows until he reached his house, which was surrounded by a white picket fence. His family lived on the first floor and rented out the second floor to students.

When he was inside, safe in the warm, delicious-smelling kitchen, his aunt hugged him and made a fuss. She was a dark, pretty, overweight woman. "Now what did you do *today*?" she asked brightly.

"Nothing . . ." Jody replied.

Trains these days are the target of much nostalgia, wonderful old-fashioned critters that justifiably provoke longing and excitement in those who have ridden them, and in those who would like to have ridden them when they were something more than aluminum-seeming trucks on wheels. But trains also travel from the real world to the fantastic, where there isn't much help when all the rules change.

William F. Nolan's latest is a massive and impressive, and scholarly in the best sense, biography of Steve McQueen. Yet he continues to find the time to propel his return to the field with such gems as the following. With Nolan, as with a train, you never know whether you'll make it to the station in one piece.

The Train

by William F. Nolan

Lonely train a' comin'
I can hear its cry
Lonely train from nowhere
Takin' me to die
—*folk ballad fragment, circa 1881*

AT BITTERROOT, VENTRY waited. Bone-cold, huddled on the
narrow wooden bench against the paint-blistered wall of the
depot, the collar of his heavy, fleece-lined coat turned up
against the chill Montana winds blowing in from the Plains,
he waited for the train.

Autumn was dying, and the sky over Bitterroot was gray
with the promise of winter. This would be the train's last run
before snow closed down the route. Ventry had calculated it
with consummate patience and precision. He prided himself
on his stubborn practicality, and he had earned a reputation
among his fellow ranchers as a hard-headed realist.

He had been unable to pinpoint the train's exact arrival, but
he was certain it would pass Bitterroot within a seven-day
period. Thus, he had brought along enough food and water to
last a week. His supplies were almost depleted now, but they

could be stretched through two more days and nights if need be; Ventry was not worried.

The train *would* be here.

It was lonely at Bitterroot. The stationmaster's office was boarded over, and bars covered the windows. The route into Ross Fork had been dropped from the rail schedule six months ago, and main-line trains bound for Lewistown no longer made the stop. Now the only trains that rattled past were desolate freights, dragging their endless rusted flatcars.

Ventry shifted the holstered ax pressing against his thigh, and unzipping a side pocket on his coat, he took out the thumb-worn postcard. On the picture side, superimposed over a multicolored panoramic shot of a Plains sunset, was the standard Montana salutation: GREETINGS FROM THE BIG SKY COUNTRY! And on the reverse, Amy's last words. How many times had he read her hastily scrawled message, mailed from this depot almost a year ago to the day?

> *Dear Paulie,*
> *I'll write a long letter, I promise, when I get to Lewistown, but the train came early so I just have time, dear brother, to send you my love. And don't you worry about your little kid sister because life for me is going to be super with my new job!*
> *Luv and XXXXXXX, Amy*

And she had added a quick P.S. at the bottom of the card:

> *You should see this beautiful old train! Didn't know they still ran steam locomotives like this one! Gotta rush—'cuz it's waiting for me!*
> A.

Ventry's mouth tightened, and he slipped the card back into his coat, thinking about Amy's smiling eyes, about how much a part of his life she'd been. Hell, she was a better sheep rancher than half the valley men on Big Moccasin! But, once grown, she'd wanted city life, a city job, a chance to meet city men.

"Just you watch me, Paulie," she had told him, her face

shining with excitement. "This lil' ole job in Lewistown is only the beginning. The firm has a branch in Helena, and I'm sure I can get transferred there within a year. You're gonna be real proud of your sis. I'll *make* you proud!"

She'd never had the chance. She'd never reached Lewistown. Amy had stepped aboard the train . . . and vanished.

Yet people don't vanish. It was a word Paul refused to accept. He had driven each bleak mile of the rail line from Bitterroot to Lewistown, combing every inch of terrain for a sign, a clue, a scrap of clothing. He'd spent two months along that route. And had found nothing.

Ventry posted a public reward for information leading to Amy's whereabouts. Which is when Tom Hallendorf contacted him.

Hallendorf was a game warden stationed at King's Hill Pass in the Lewis and Clark National Forest. He phoned Ventry, telling him about what he'd found near an abandoned spur track in the Little Belt range.

Bones. *Human* bones.

And a ripped, badly stained red leather purse.

The empty purse had belonged to Amy. Forensic evidence established the bones as part of her skeleton.

What had happened up there in those mountains?

The district sheriff, John Longbow, blamed it on a "weirdo." A roving tramp.

"Dirt-plain obvious, Mr. Ventry," the sheriff had said to him. "He killed her for what she had in the purse. You admit she was carryin' several hundred in cash. Which is, begging your pardon, a damn fool thing to do!"

But that didn't explain the picked bones.

"Lotta wild animals in the mountains," the lawman had declared. "After this weirdo done 'er in he just left her layin' there—and, well, probably a bear come onto 'er. It's happened before. We've found bones up in that area more than once. Lot of strange things in the Little Belt." And the sheriff had grinned. "As a boy, with the tribe, I heard me stories that'd curl your hair. It's wild country."

The railroad authorities were adamant about the mystery train. "No steamers in these parts," they told him. "Nobody runs 'em anymore."

But Ventry was gut-certain that such a train existed, and that Amy had died on it. Someone had cold-bloodedly murdered his sister and dumped her body in the mountains.

He closed down the ranch, sold his stock, and devoted himself to finding out who that someone was.

He spent an entire month at the main library in Lewistown, poring through old newspaper files, copying names, dates, case details.

A pattern emerged. Ventry found that a sizable number of missing persons who had vanished in this area of the state over the past decade had been traveling by *rail*. And several of them had disappeared along the same basic route Amy had chosen.

Ventry confronted John Longbow with his research.

"An' just who is this killer?" the sheriff asked.

"Whoever owns the steamer. Some freak rail buff. Rich enough to run his own private train, and crazy enough to kill the passengers who get on board."

"Look, Mr. Ventry, how come nobody's *seen* this fancy steam train of yours?"

"Because the rail disappearances have happened at night, at remote stations off the main lines. He never runs the train by daylight. Probably keeps it up in the mountains. Maybe in one of the old mine shafts. Uses off-line spur tracks. Comes rolling into a small depot like Bitterroot *between* the regular passenger trains and picks up whoever's on the platform."

The sheriff had grunted at this, his eyes tight on Paul Ventry's face.

"And there's a definite *cycle* to these disappearances," Ventry continued. "According to what I've put together, the train makes its night runs at specific intervals. About a month apart, spring through fall. Then it's hidden away in the Little Belt each winter when the old spur tracks are snowed over. I've done a lot of calculation on this, and I'm certain that the train makes its final run during the first week of November—which means you've still got time to stop it."

The sheriff had studied Paul Ventry for a long, silent moment. Then he had sighed deeply. "That's an interesting theory, Mr. Ventry, *real* interesting. But . . . it's also about as wild and unproven as any I've heard—and I've heard me a few. Now, it's absolute natural that you're upset at your sister's death, but you've let things get way out of whack. I figger you'd best go on back to your ranch and try an' forget about poor little Amy. Put her out of your mind. She's gone. And there's nothing you can do about that.''

"We'll see,'' Ventry had said, a cutting edge to his voice. "We'll see what I can do.''

Ventry's plan was simple. Stop the train, board it, and kill the twisted son of a bitch who owned it. Put a .45 slug in his head. Blow his fucking brains out—and blow his train up with him!

I'll put an end to this if no one else will, Ventry promised himself. And I've got the tools to do it.

He slipped the carefully wrapped gun rig from his knapsack, unfolded its oiled covering, and withdrew his grandfather's long-barreled frontier Colt from its worn leather holster. The gun was a family treasure. Its bone handle was cracked and yellowed by the years, but the old Colt was still in perfect firing order. His granddaddy had worn this rig, had defended his mine on the Comstock against claim jumpers with this gun. It was fitting and proper that it be used on the man who'd killed Amy.

Night was settling over Bitterroot. The fiery orange disc of sun had dropped below the Little Belt Mountains, and the sky was gray slate along the horizon.

Time to strap on the gun. Time to get ready for the train.

It's coming tonight! Lord God, I can feel it out there in the gathering dark, thrumming the rails. I can feel it in my blood and bones.

Well, then, come ahead, god damn you, whoever you are. I'm ready for you.

Ten P.M. Eleven. Midnight.

It came at midnight.

Rushing toward Bitterroot, clattering in fierce-wheeled thunder, its black bulk sliding over the track in the ash-dark Montana night like an immense, segmented snake—with a single yellow eye probing the terrain ahead.

Ventry heard it long before he saw it. The rails sang and

vibrated around him as he stood tall and resolute in midtrack, a three-cell silver flashlight in his right hand, his heavy sheepskin coat buttoned over the gun at his belt.

Have to flag it down. With the depot closed it won't make a stop. No passengers. It's looking for live game, and it doesn't figure on finding any here at Bitterroot.

Surprise! *I'm* here. *I'm* alive. Like Amy. Like all the others. Man alone at night. Needs a ride. Climb aboard, pardner. Make yourself to home. Drink? Somethin' to eat? What's your pleasure?

My pleasure is your death—and the death of your freak train, mister! *That's* my pleasure.

It was in sight now, coming fast, slicing a bright round hole in the night—and its sweeping locomotive beam splashed Paul Ventry's body with a pale luminescence.

The rancher swung his flash up, then down, in a high arc. Again. And again.

Stop, you bastard! *Stop!*

The train began slowing.

Sparks showered from the massive driving wheels as the train reduced speed. Slowing . . . slower . . . steel shrieking against steel. An easing of primal force.

It was almost upon him.

Like a great shining insect, the locomotive towered high and black over Ventry, its tall stack shutting out the stars. The rusted tip of the train's thrusting metal cowcatcher gently nudged the toe of his right boot as the incredible night mammoth slid to a final grinding stop.

Now the train was utterly motionless, breathing its white steam into the cold dark, waiting for him as he had waited for it.

Ventry felt a surge of exultation fire his body. He'd been right! It was here—and he was prepared to destroy it, to avenge his sister. It was his destiny. He felt no fear, only a cool and certain confidence in his ability to kill.

A movement at the corner of his eye. Someone was waving to him from the far end of the train, from the last coach, the train's only source of light. All of the other passenger cars were dark and blind-windowed; only the last car glowed hazy yellow.

Ventry eased around the breathing locomotive, his boots crunching loudly in the cindered gravel as he moved over the roadbed.

He glanced up at the locomotive's high, double-windowed cabin, but the engineer was lost behind opaque, soot-colored glass. Ventry kept moving steadily forward, toward the distant figure, passing along the linked row of silent, lightless passenger cars. The train bore no markings; it was a uniform, unbroken black.

Ventry squinted at the beckoning figure. Was it the killer himself, surprised and delighted at finding another passenger at this deserted night station?

He slipped the flash into his shouldered knapsack, and eased a hand inside his coat, gripping the warm bone handle of the .45 at his waist. You've had one surprise tonight, mister. Get ready for another.

Then, abruptly, he stopped, heart pounding. Ventry recognized the beckoning figure. Impossible! An illusion. Just *couldn't* be. Yet there she was, smiling, waving to him.

"Amy!" Ventry rushed toward his sister in a stumbling run.

But she was no longer in sight when he reached the dimly illumined car. Anxiously, he peered into one of the smoke-yellowed windows. A figure moved hazily inside.

"Amy!" He shouted her name again, mounting the coach steps.

The moment Ventry's boot touched the car's upper platform the train jolted into life. Ventry was thrown to his knees as the coach lurched violently forward.

The locomotive's big driving wheels sparked against steel, gaining a solid grip on the rails as the train surged powerfully from Bitterroot Station.

As Paul Ventry entered the coach, the door snap-locked behind him. Remote-control device. To make sure I won't leave by the rear exit. No matter. He'd expected that. He could get out when he had to, when he was ready. He'd come prepared for whatever this madman had in mind.

But Ventry had *not* been prepared for the emotional shock of seeing Amy. Had he *really* seen her? *Was* it his sister?

No. Of course not. He'd been tricked by his subconscious mind. The fault was his. A lapse in concentration, in judgment.

But *someone* had waved to him—a young girl who looked, at first sight, amazingly like his dead sister.

Where was she now?

And just where was the human devil who ran this train?

Ventry was alone in the car. To either side of the aisle the rows of richly upholstered green velvet seats were empty. A pair of ornate, scrolled gas lamps, mounted above the arched doorway, cast flickering shadows over antique brass fittings and handcarved wood ceiling. Green brocade draped the windows.

He didn't know much about trains, but Ventry knew this one *had* to be pre-1900. And probably restored by the rich freak who owned it. Plush was the word.

Well, it was making its last run; Ventry would see to that.

He pulled the flash from his shoulder pack, snapping on the bright beam as he moved warily forward.

The flashlight proved unnecessary. As Ventry entered the second car (door unlocked; guess he doesn't mind my going *forward*) the overhead gas lamps sputtered to life, spreading their pale yellow illumination over the length of the coach.

Again, the plush velvet seats were empty. Except for one. The last seat at the far end of the car. A woman was sitting there, stiff and motionless in the dim light, her back to Ventry.

As he moved toward her, she turned slowly to face him.

By Christ, it *was* Amy!

Paul Ventry rushed to her, sudden tears stinging his eyes. Fiercely, he embraced his sister; she was warm and solid in his arms. "Oh, Sis, I'm so glad you're *alive*!"

But there was no sound from her lips. No words. No emotion. She was rigid in his embrace.

Ventry stepped away from her. "What's wrong? I don't understand why you—"

His words were choked off. Amy had leaped from the seat, cat-quick, to fasten long pale fingers around his throat. Her thumbs dug like sharp spikes into the flesh of Ventry's neck.

He reeled back, gasping for breath, clawing at the incredibly strong hands. He couldn't break her grip.

Amy's face was changing. The flesh was falling away in gummy wet ribbons, revealing raw white bone! In the deep sockets of Amy's grinning skull her eyes were hot red points of fire.

Ventry's right hand found the butt of the Colt, and he dragged the gun free of its holster. Swinging the barrel toward Amy, he fired directly into the melting horror of her face.

His bullets drilled round, charred holes in the grinning skull, but Amy's fingers—now all raw bone and slick gristle—maintained their death grip at his throat.

Ax! Use the ax!

In a swimming red haze, Ventry snapped the short-handled woodsman's ax free of his belt. And swung it sharply downward, neatly removing Amy's head at shoulder level. The cleanly severed skull rolled into the aisle at his feet.

Yet, horribly, the bony fingers increased their deadly pressure.

Ventry's sight blurred; the coach wavered. As the last of his oxygen was cut off, he was on the verge of blacking out.

Desperately, he swung the blade again, missing the Amything entirely. The ax buried itself in thick green velvet.

The train thrashed; its whistle shrieked wildly in the rushing night, a cry of pain—and the seat rippled in agony. Oily black liquid squirted from the sliced velvet.

At Ventry's throat, the bony fingers dropped away.

In numbed shock, he watched his sister's rotting corpse flow down into the seat, melting and mixing with the central train body, bubbling wetly. . . .

Oh, sweet Jesus! Everything's moving! The whole foul train is alive!

And Ventry accepted it. Sick with horror and revulsion, he accepted it. He was a realist, and this thing was real. No fantasy. No dream.

Real.

Which meant he had to kill it. Not the man who owned it, because such a man did not exist. Somehow, the train itself, ancient and rusting in the high mountains, had taken on a sentient life of its own. The molecular components of iron and wood and steel had, over a slow century, transformed themselves into living tissue—and this dark hell-thing had rolled out onto the Montana plains seeking food, seeking flesh to sustain it, sleeping, sated, through the frozen winters, hibernating, then stirring to hungry life again as the greening earth renewed itself.

Lot of strange things in the Little Belt.

Don't think about it, Ventry warned himself. Just do what you came to do: *kill it!* Kill the foul thing. Blow it out of existence!

He carried three explosive charges in his knapsack, each equipped with a timing device. All right, make your plan! Set one here at the end of the train, another in a middle coach, and plant the final charge in the forward car.

No good. If the thing had the power to animate its dead victims it also had the power to fling off his explosive devices, to rid itself of them as a dog shakes leaves from its coat.

I'll have to go after it the way you go after a snake; to kill a snake, you cut off its head.

So go for the brain.

Go for the engine.

The train had left the main rail system now, and was on a rusted spur track, climbing steeply into the Little Belt range.

It was taking Ventry into the high mountains. One last meal of warm flesh, then the long winter's sleep.

The train was going home.

Three cars to go.

Ax in hand, Ventry was moving steadily toward the engine, through vacant, gas-lit coaches, wondering how and when it would attack him again.

Did it know he meant to kill it? Possibly it had no fear of him. God knows it was strong. And no human had ever harmed it in the past. Does the snake fear the mouse?

Maybe it would leave him alone to do his work; maybe it didn't realize how lethal this mouse could be.

But Ventry was wrong.

Swaying in the clattering rush of the train, he was halfway down the aisle of the final coach when the tissue around him rippled into motion. Viscid black bubbles formed on the ceiling of the car, and in the seats. Growing. Quivering. Multiplying.

One by one, the loathsome globes swelled and burst—giving birth to a host of nightmare figures. Young and old. Man, woman, child. Eyes red and angry.

They closed in on Ventry in the clicking interior of the hell coach, moving toward him in a rotting tide.

He had seen photos of many of them in the Lewistown library. Vanished passengers, like Amy, devoured and absorbed and now regenerated as fetid ectoplasmic horrors—literal extensions of the train itself.

Ventry knew that he was powerless to stop them. The Amy-thing had proven that.

But he still had the ax, and a few vital seconds before the train-things reached him, Ventry swung the razored blade left and right, slashing brutally at seat and floor, cutting deep with each swift blow. Fluid gushed from a dozen gaping wounds; a rubbery mass of coillike innards, like spilled guts, erupted from the seat to Ventry's right, splashing him with gore.

The train screamed into the Montana night, howling like a wounded beast.

The passenger-things lost form, melting into the aisle.

Now Ventry was at the final door, leading to the coal car directly behind the engine.

It was locked against him.

The train had reached its destination at the top of the spur, was rolling down a side track leading to a deserted mine. Its home. Its cave. Its dark hiding place.

The train would feast now.

Paul Ventry used the last of his strength on the door. Hacking at it. Slashing wildly. Cutting his way through.

Free! In a freezing blast of night wind, Ventry scrambled across the coal tender toward the shining black locomotive.

And reached it.

A heavy, gelatinous membrane separated him from the control cabin. The membrane pulsed with veined life.

Got to get inside . . . reach the brain of the thing. . . .

Ventry drove the blade deep, splitting the veined skin. And burst through into the cabin.

Its interior was a shock to Ventry's senses; he was assailed by a stench so powerful that bile rushed into his throat. He fought back a rising nausea.

Brass and wood and iron had become throbbing flesh. Levers and controls and pressure gauges were coated with a thick, crawling slime. The roof and sides of the cabin were moving.

A huge, red, heartlike mass pulsed and shimmered wetly in the center of the cabin, its sickly crimson glow illuminating Ventry's face.

He did not hesitate.

Ventry reached into the knapsack, pulled out an explosive charge, and set the device for manual. All he needed to do was press a metal switch, toss the charge at the heart-thing, and jump from the cabin.

It was over. He'd won!

But before he could act, the entire chamber heaved up in a bubbled, convulsing pincer movement, trapping Ventry like a fly in a web.

He writhed in the jellied grip of the train-thing. The explosive device had been jarred from his grasp. The ax, too, was lost in the mass of crushing slime-tissue.

Ventry felt sharp pain fire along his back. *Teeth!* The thing had sprouted rows of needled teeth and was starting to eat him alive!

The knapsack; he was still wearing it!

Gasping, dizzy with pain, Ventry plunged his right hand into the sack, closing bloodied fingers around the second explosive device. Pulled it loose, set it ticking.

Sixty seconds.

If he could not fight free in that space of time he'd go up with the train. A far better way to die than being ripped apart and devoured. Death would be a welcome release.

Incredibly, the train-thing seemed to *know* that its life was in jeopardy. Its shocked tissues drew back, cringing away from the ticking explosive charge.

Ventry fell to his knees on the slimed floor.

Thirty seconds.

He saw the sudden gleam of rails to his right, just below him, and he launched himself in a plunging dive through the severed membrane.

Struck ground. Searing pain. Right shoulder. Broken bone.

Hell with it! *Move, damn you, move!*

Ventry rolled over on his stomach, pain lacing his body. Pushed himself up. Standing now.

Five seconds.

Ventry sprawled forward. *Legs won't support me!*

Then *crawl!*

Into heavy brush. Still crawling—dragging his lacerated, slime-smeared body toward a covering of rocks.

Faster! No more time. . . . Too late!

The night became sudden day.

The explosion picked up Ventry and tossed him into the rocks like a boneless doll.

The train-thing screamed in a whistling death-agony as the concussion sundered it, scattering its parts like wet confetti over the terrain.

Gobbets of bleeding tissue rained down on Ventry as he lay in the rocks. But through the pain and the stench and the nausea his lips were curved into a thin smile.

He was unconscious when the Montana sun rose that morning, but when Sheriff John Longbow arrived on the scene he found Paul Ventry alive.

Alive and triumphant.

*What is sometimes more frightening than realizing what
we ourselves could do if we were pushed or tempted
strongly enough, is the realization of what others close
to us could do. We may be flawed, but our idols are
not. And when we learn that idols are not only flawed,
but considerably worse. . . .*

David Morrell, author of First Blood, The Totem,
*and others, is a genial man living in Iowa, gentle by all
accounts, and a professor whose students regularly fill
his classes in English. . . . A family man.*

The Dripping

by David Morrell

THAT AUTUMN WE live in a house in the country, my mother's house, the house I was raised in. I have been to the village, struck more by how nothing in it has changed, yet everything has, because I am older now, seeing it differently. It is as though I am both here now and back then, at once with the mind of a boy and a man. It is so strange a doubling, so intense, so unsettling, that I am moved to work again, to try to paint it.

So I study the hardware store, the grain barrels in front, the twin square pillars holding up the drooping balcony onto which seared wax-faced men and women from the old people's hotel above come to sit and rock and watch. They look the same aging people I saw as a boy, the wood of the pillars and balcony looks as splintered.

Forgetful of time while I work, I do not begin the long walk home until late, at dusk. The day has been warm, but now in my shirt I am cold, and a half mile along I am caught in a sudden shower and forced to leave the gravel road for the shelter of a tree, its leaves already brown and yellow. The rain becomes a storm, streaking at me sideways, drenching me; I cinch the neck of my canvas bag to protect my painting and equipment, and decide to run, socks spongy in my shoes, when at last I reach the lane down to the house and barn.

The house and barn. They and my mother, they alone have changed, as if as one, warping, weathering, joints twisted and strained, their gray so unlike the white I recall as a boy. The place is weakening her. She is in tune with it, matches its decay. That is why we have come here to live. To revive. Once I thought to convince her to move away. But of her sixty-five years she has spent forty here, and she insists she will spend the rest, what is left to her.

The rain falls stronger as I hurry past the side of the house, the light on in the kitchen, suppertime and I am late. The house is connected with the barn the way the small base of an L is connected to its stem. The entrance I always use is directly at the joining, and when I enter out of breath, clothes clinging to me cold and wet, the door to the barn to my left, the door to the kitchen straight ahead, I hear the dripping in the basement down the stairs to my right.

"Meg. Sorry I'm late," I call to my wife, setting down the water-beaded canvas sack, opening the kitchen door. There is no one. No settings on the table. Nothing on the stove. Only the yellow light from the sixty-watt bulb in the ceiling. The kind my mother prefers to the white of one hundred. It reminds her of candlelight, she says.

"Meg," I call again, and still no one answers. Asleep, I think. Dusk coming on, the dark clouds of the storm have lulled them, and they have lain down for a nap, expecting to wake before I return.

Still the dripping. Although the house is very old, the barn long disused, roofs crumbling, I have not thought it all so ill-maintained, the storm so strong that water can be seeping past the cellar windows, trickling, pattering on the old stone floor. I switch on the light to the basement, descend the wood stairs to the right, worn and squeaking, reach where the stairs turn to the left the rest of the way down to the floor, and see not water dripping. Milk. Milk everywhere. On the rafters, on the walls, dripping on the film of milk on the stones, gathering speckled with dirt in the channels between them. From side to side and everywhere.

Sarah, my child, has done this, I think. She has been

fascinated by the big wood dollhouse that my father made for me when I was quite young, its blue paint chipped and peeling now. She has pulled it from the far corner to the middle of the basement. There are games and toy soldiers and blocks that have been taken from the wicker storage chest and played with on the floor, all covered with milk, the doll-house, the chest, the scattered toys, milk dripping on them from the rafters, milk trickling on them.

Why has she done this, I think. Where can she have gotten so much milk? What was in her mind to do this thing?

"Sarah," I call. "Meg." Angry now, I mount the stairs into the quiet kitchen. "Sarah," I shout. She will clean the mess and stay indoors the remainder of the week.

I cross the kitchen, turn through the sitting room past the padded flower-patterned chairs and sofa that have faded since I knew them as a boy, past several of my paintings that my mother has hung up on the wall, bright-colored old ones of pastures and woods from when I was in grade school, brown-shaded new ones of the town, tinted as if old photographs. Two stairs at a time up to the bedrooms, wet shoes on the soft worn carpet on the stairs, hand streaking on the smooth polished maple bannister.

At the top I swing down the hall. The door to Sarah's room is open, it is dark in there. I switch on the light. She is not on the bed, nor has been; the satin spread is unrumpled, the rain pelting in through the open window, the wind fresh and cool. I have the feeling then and go uneasy into our bedroom; it is dark as well, empty too. My stomach has become hollow. Where are they? All in mother's room?

No. As I stand at the open door to mother's room I see from the yellow light I have turned on in the hall that only she is in there, her small torso stretched across the bed.

"Mother," I say, intending to add, "Where are Meg and Sarah?" But I stop before I do. One of my mother's shoes is off, the other askew on her foot. There is mud on the shoes. There is blood on her cotton dress. It is torn, her brittle hair disrupted, blood on her face, her bruised lips are swollen.

For several moments I am silent with shock. "My God, Mother," I finally manage to say, and as if the words are a spring releasing me to action I touch her to wake her. But I see that her eyes are open, staring ceilingward, unseeing though alive, and each breath is a sudden full gasp, then slow exhalation.

"Mother, what has happened? Who did this to you? Meg? Sarah?"

But she does not look at me, only constant toward the ceiling.

"For God's sake, Mother, answer me! Look at me! What has happened?"

Nothing. Eyes sightless. Between gasps she is like a statue.

What I think is hysterical. Disjointed, contradictory. I must find Meg and Sarah. They must be somewhere, beaten like my mother. Or worse. Find them. Where? But I cannot leave my mother. When she comes to consciousness, she too will be hysterical, frightened, in great pain. How did she end up on the bed?

In her room there is no sign of the struggle she must have put up against her attacker. It must have happened somewhere else. She crawled from there to here. Then I see the blood on the floor, the swath of blood down the hall from the stairs. Who did this? Where is he? Who would beat a gray, wrinkled, arthritic old woman? Why in God's name would he do it? I shudder. The pain of the arthritis as she struggled with him.

Perhaps he is still in the house, waiting for me.

To the hollow sickness in my stomach now comes fear, hot, pulsing, and I am frantic before I realize what I am doing—grabbing the spare cane my mother always keeps by her bed, flicking on the light in her room, throwing open the closet door and striking in with the cane. Viciously, sounds coming from my throat, the cane flailing among the faded dresses.

No one. Under the bed. No one. Behind the door. No one.

I search all the upstairs rooms that way, terrified, constantly checking behind me, clutching the cane and whacking into closets, under beds, behind doors, with a force that would certainly crack a skull. No one.

"Meg! Sarah!"

No answer, not even an echo in this sound-absorbing house.

There is no attic, just an overhead entry to a crawl space under the eaves, and that opening has long been sealed. No sign of tampering. No one has gone up.

I rush down the stairs, seeing the trail of blood my mother has left on the carpet, imagining her pain as she crawled, and search the rooms downstairs with the same desperate thoroughness. In the front closet. Behind the sofa and chairs. Behind the drapes.

No one.

I lock the front door, lest he be outside in the storm waiting to come in behind me. I remember to draw every blind, close every drape, lest he be out there peering at me. The rain pelts insistently against the windowpanes.

I cry out again and again for Meg and Sarah. The police. My mother. A doctor. I grab for the phone on the wall by the front stairs, fearful to listen to it, afraid he has cut the line outside. But it is droning. Droning. I ring for the police, working the handle at the side around and around and around.

They are coming, they say. A doctor with them. Stay where I am, they say. But I cannot. Meg and Sarah, I must find them. I know they are not in the basement where the milk is dripping—all the basement is open to view. Except for my childhood things, we have cleared out all the boxes and barrels and the shelves of jars the Saturday before.

But under the stairs. I have forgotten about under the stairs and now I race down and stand dreading in the milk; but there are only cobwebs there, already reformed from Saturday when we cleared them. I look up at the side door I first came through, and as if I am seeing through a telescope I focus largely on the handle. It seems to fidget. I have a panicked vision of the intruder bursting through, and I charge up to lock the door, and the door to the barn.

And then I think: if Meg and Sarah are not in the house they are likely in the barn. But I cannot bring myself to unlock the barn door and go through. *He* must be there as well. Not in the rain outside but in the shelter of the barn, and there are no lights to turn on there.

And why the milk? Did he do it and where did he get it? And why? Or did Sarah do it before? No, the milk is too freshly dripping. It has been put there too recently. By him. But why? And who is he? A tramp? An escapee from some prison? Or asylum? No, the nearest institution is far away, hundreds of miles. From the town then. Or a nearby farm.

I know my questions are for delay, to keep me from entering the barn. But I must. I take the flashlight from the kitchen drawer and unlock the door to the barn, force myself to go in quickly, cane ready, flashing my light. The stalls are still there, listing; and some of the equipment, churners, separators, dull and rusted, webbed and dirty. The must of decaying wood and crumbled hay, the fresh wet smell of the rain gusting through cracks in the walls. Once this was a dairy, as the other farms around still are.

Flicking my light toward the corners, edging toward the stalls, boards creaking, echoing, I try to control my fright, try to remember as a boy how the cows waited in the stalls for my father to milk them, how the barn was once board-tight and solid, warm to be in, how there was no connecting door from the barn to the house because my father did not want my mother to smell the animals in her kitchen.

I run my light down the walls, sweep it in arcs through the darkness before me as I draw nearer to the stalls, and in spite of myself I recall that other autumn when the snow came early, four feet deep by morning and still storming thickly, how my father went out to the barn to milk and never returned for lunch, nor supper. There was no phone then, no way to get help, and my mother and I waited all night, unable to make our way through the storm, listening to the slowly dying wind; and the next morning was clear and bright and blinding as we shoveled out to find the cows in agony in their stalls from not having been milked and my father dead, frozen rock-solid in the snow in the middle of the next field where he must have wandered when he lost his bearings in the storm.

There was a fox, risen earlier than us, nosing at him under the snow, and my father had to be sealed in his coffin before he could lie in state. Days after, the snow was melted, gone, the barnyard a sea of mud, and it was autumn again and my mother had the connecting door put in. My father should have tied a rope from the house to his waist to guide him back in case he lost his way. Certainly he knew enough. But then he was like that always in a rush. When I was ten.

Thus I think as I light the shadows near the stalls, terrified of what I may find in any one of them, Meg and Sarah, or him, thinking of how my mother and I searched for my father and how I now search for my wife and child, trying to think of how it was once warm in here and pleasant, chatting with my father, helping him to milk, the sweet smell of new hay and grain, the different sweet smell of fresh droppings, something I always liked and neither my father nor my mother could understand. I know that if I do not think of these good times I will surely go mad in awful anticipation of what I may find. Pray God they have not died!

What can he have done to them? To assault a five-year-old girl? Split her. The hemorrhaging alone can have killed her.

And then, even in the barn, I hear my mother cry out for me. The relief I feel to leave and go to her unnerves me. I do want to find Meg and Sarah, to try to save them. Yet I am relieved to go. I think my mother will tell me what has happened, tell me where to find them. That is how I justify my leaving as I wave the light in circles around me, guarding my back, retreating through the door and locking it.

Upstairs she sits stiffly on her bed. I want to make her answer my questions, to shake her, to force her to help, but I know it will only frighten her more, maybe push her mind down to where I can never reach.

"Mother," I say to her softly, touching her gently. "What has happened?" My impatience can barely be contained. "Who did this? Where are Meg and Sarah?"

She smiles at me, reassured by the safety of my presence. Still she cannot answer.

"Mother. Please," I say. "I know how bad it must have been. But you must try to help. I must know where they are so I can help them."

She says, "Dolls."

It chills me. "What dolls, Mother? Did a man come here with dolls? What did he want? You mean he looked like a doll? Wearing a mask like one?"

Too many questions. All she can do is blink.

"Please, Mother. You must try your best to tell me. Where are Meg and Sarah?"

"Dolls," she says.

As I first had the foreboding of disaster at the sight of Sarah's unrumpled satin bedspread, now I am beginning to understand, rejecting it, fighting it.

"Yes, Mother, the dolls," I say, refusing to admit what I know. "Please, Mother. Where are Meg and Sarah?"

"You are a grown boy now. You must stop playing as a child. Your father. Without him you will have to be the man in the house. You must be brave."

"No, Mother." I can feel it swelling in my chest.

"There will be a great deal of work now, more than any child should know. But we have no choice. You must accept that God has chosen to take him from us, that you are all the man I have left to help me."

"No, Mother."

"Now you are a man and you must put away the things of a child."

Eyes streaming, I am barely able to straighten, leaning wearily against the doorjamb, tears rippling from my face down to my shirt, wetting it cold where it had just begun to dry. I wipe my eyes and see her reaching for me, smiling, and I recoil down the hall, stumbling down the stairs, down, through the sitting room, the kitchen, down, down to the milk, splashing through it to the dollhouse, and in there, crammed and doubled, Sarah. And in the wicker chest, Meg. The toys not on the floor for Sarah to play with, but taken out so Meg could be put in. And both of them, their stomachs slashed, stuffed with sawdust, their eyes rolled up like dolls' eyes.

The police are knocking at the side door, pounding, calling out who they are, but I am powerless to let them in. They crash through the door, their rubber raincoats dripping as they stare down at me.

"The milk," I say.

They do not understand. Even as I wait, standing in the milk, listening to the rain pelting on the windows while they come over to see what is in the dollhouse and in the wicker chest, while they go upstairs to my mother and then return so

I can tell them again, "The milk." But they still do not understand.

"She killed them of course," one man says. "But I don't see why the milk."

Only when they speak to the neighbors down the road and learn how she came to them, needing the cans of milk, insisting she carry them herself to the car, the agony she was in as she carried them, only when they find the empty cans and the knife in a stall in the barn, can I say, "The milk. The blood. There was so much blood, you know. She needed to deny it, so she washed it away with milk, purified it, started the dairy again. You see, there was so much blood."

That autumn we live in a house in the country, my mother's house, the house I was raised in. I have been to the village, struck even more by how nothing in it has changed, yet everything has, because I am older now, seeing it differently. It is as though I am both here now and back then, at once with the mind of a boy and a man. . . .

Perhaps the ragman of this story is only a big-city fixture, but it's odd, isn't it, how our liberal, we-love-everyone attitudes somehow seldom include them. A true Christian should love them, a true humanitarian should pay attention to them, and a true liberal should march on their behalf. On the other hand. . . .

Leslie Horvitz's latest novel, Donors, *was a bestseller from New American Library. He has also recently completed a train trip from London to Hong Kong, has written some of the most popular stories in* The Twilight Zone, *and is working on a new thriller.*

The Ragman

by Leslie Alan Horvitz

SAM DRYSDALE HADN'T been married for very long—six months actually—when he was selected for the receipt of the first annual Llewellyn Award, "given in recognition of contributions to the stage in the previous twelve-month period." At the age of thirty Sam was already accustomed to prizes and awards, for his was an exceptional talent. Not only could he put words to paper in a manner calculated to entertain and, on occasion, provide an insight or two, but he had the knack of honing in on what the public wanted. It was as if he kept in his house a crystal ball by which he could predict what trend would next envelop America and get there—on paper and then on stage—before America could.

He was handsome the way certain soap opera actors are handsome; to look at his pictures one would not think that he spent long hours sequestered in a study. He was more often pictured in jogging shorts or knocking hell out of a ball on a squash court. It only stood to reason that he would eventually hitch up to a woman with suitable looks, attractive, warm, and open, with a smile so ready that there were some who believed it impossible for there to be any meaning in that smile—or intelligence in those big almond eyes of hers.

Her name was Morgan and when she married Sam she was

one day shy of her twenty-fourth birthday. She worked as a set designer and it was not unusual to see her walking hurriedly through the streets of New York on her way to a theater or an agent's midtown office, an oversized portfolio under her arm, an expression of immense preoccupation on her face.

When conducting business she favored skirts and crisp blouses, sometimes adorned with a thin black tie. At home in Connecticut she preferred flannel shirts and loose jeans that gave her a more down-to-earth appearance. She thought of herself as a pragmatist, but did not think of Sam as one. On the contrary, it was her conviction that disorder constantly threatened to take hold of Sam's life and that it was her responsibility to make certain that it didn't get the better of him.

But at the time the Llewellyn Award was announced there was no reason for Morgan to be concerned. Sam and she considered themselves to be happy and prosperous; the large two-story house, a spectacle of white in a forested landscape, attested to the good fortune of the Drysdales, for it was with proceeds from one of Sam's plays—"The Night Party"—that they'd purchased it.

The Llewellyn Award consisted of a small silver plaque and a check for one thousand dollars, part of a generous bequest by the Roger Banning Llewellyn estate, which had endowed several off-Broadway theaters in addition. It was to be presented to Sam at a ceremony at the Lincoln Center Theater Library. How many people were invited, and just what role they played in New York theater life, was something that Sam did not know. He was told that he could ask as many as a dozen friends if he wanted, but not more because there wasn't room enough to accommodate them all.

His friends, for the most part, still lived in New York. They hadn't enjoyed the sort of success he had to be able to afford a ten-room house in Westport and it was possible that they were in the process of becoming something other than friends—something less than friends—for this very reason.

Morgan was excited for him. She wasn't quite so used to his being honored by awards as he was. Even in elementary school he had received his share of prizes, one of the earliest for a Science Fair project (pertaining to the behavior of snails and garden plants) he'd contrived long before he turned to experimenting with words instead.

The ceremony was to begin at ten on the fifteenth of June following a reading by two actors and one actress of portions of Sam's second play, *The Road of Amber*.

For this occasion Morgan chose a chiffon blouse which suggested an image so respectable that she felt she needed to set it off with a pair of tight leather pants, stylish and sexy. As black as they were they tended to reflect a veritable rainbow of colors when any lights shone directly on them.

Sam, however, balked. "I don't think those are exactly appropriate, honey," he said on seeing them. He had put on a tie, and since he seldom wore one and felt as though this one was strangling him he decided that his wife, too, ought to make a concession to the formality of the affair.

It was one thing when he was dating her. Then he didn't mind what she wore nor was it his prerogative to say anything about it. But now, as much as he liked thinking of himself as still the renegade bohemian, he was forced to acknowledge a certain conservative streak taking root in him.

They were not used to bickering, certainly not to rancorous fights. They were definitely not prepared to start one now. That they did surprised them both. Morgan was stung by what Sam said. It was a relatively trivial matter, this business of what to wear, even she would admit, but anger seized hold of her and rather than try and resist it she went with it. For nearly an hour they fell to arguing. At one point Morgan said that Sam should go on his own and while he knew that deep down she wasn't serious about this, he had the uneasy sensation that he'd learned something he didn't want to find out this night. Something about her, about himself, about the ultimate fate of their marriage.

The sun was almost gone from the sky by the time they pulled out of their driveway. What they had managed wasn't a reconciliation, but more like a cessation of hostilities. She sat quietly, brooding, keeping her eyes straight ahead. Sam, tiring of the silence, hunted the radio waves for a station that might reward him with loud propulsive music, music he knew that Morgan didn't care for but which he needed nonetheless.

All she said was, "We're going to be late."

"I know, I know," he said, having already determined to violate the speed limit whenever he believed he could get away with it. "Worse comes to worse, we'll miss the reading, but there shouldn't be any problem getting there for the presentation."

He had half a mind to turn right around again and forget about the award, but people, his Manhattan-bound friends especially, were expecting him, and he couldn't very well disappoint them. And passing up the ceremony, he understood, would very likely be construed as an offensive gesture both by the Llewellyn Society and by the public. He didn't need that.

It was only when he reached the outskirts of New York City that he realized that he didn't know exactly where he was, that in his distracted state, he'd taken a wrong turnoff somewhere and was now making his way along an unfamiliar overpass.

"Why didn't you tell me when we hit the Bruckner?"

"You're the one doing the driving. I wasn't paying attention."

"Well, now we're lost."

"There'll be signs, don't worry. How can you lose Manhattan? It's not like we're looking for Worcester."

She'd gone to college in Worcester, which was why that name sprang so readily to her lips. There'd been a man, Sam knew, to whom she was engaged during that time, a man he suspected sometimes that she was still secretly in love with. Other ex-boyfriends she talked about with no hesitation, but not the one from Worcester. All she would tell him was that his name was Gerald Cocharan and that he was now married and living in Seattle working in the aerospace industry, Boeing maybe.

While Morgan might have thought there'd be signs, there were, in fact, very few, and those few were of no use since they directed Sam to places he neither had heard of nor in any case wanted to go to. He sped up for awhile, thinking that he would eventually get somewhere where the city would finally become recognizable, but this did not happen any time soon.

The streets they were proceeding through were for a stretch

filled with people, many of them listlessly eyeing their passage, others giving them accusatory looks, silently indicting them for the wealth their car represented and for the color of their skin. Several small children had turned on a fire hydrant and had succeeded in flooding a part of the street ahead of them. Water spattered their windshield, obscuring the view for several seconds until Sam got the wipers going.

Bottles kept smashing although they seldom saw this happen. They would just hear the shriek of breaking glass and the harsh cry of voices in response. On either side of them they had a view of tenements gone to hell: windows broken and the roofs fallen in. There were people in those dead windows, fanning themselves with folded newspapers and the flat of their hands.

"I'd suggest you roll up your windows, Morgan."

She looked as though she might say something, but then she only complied with his instruction and remained silent.

When people passed under the streetlights their skin seemed to pale and their faces became so filled with shadows that their bone structures assumed strange prominence, giving them all the look of people on their way to the grave. Many held bottles—cheap wine, cheap gin, Sam imagined—while others had the shambling, inattentive walk of addicts newly high.

The traffic lights were against them. Every few blocks they were forced to wait at empty intersections. Morgan glared at Sam, no doubt wondering why he felt so constrained by the law in a place where law had obviously abdicated its authority. A street sign said Vermilya Avenue. It meant nothing to either of them.

"Would you look in the glove compartment and see if you can find a map of the city?" Sam said.

"It's not here. We must have left it in the other car."

"*You* must have," he said. "I never touched that map."

"Just because you weren't looking where you were going is no reason to start blaming me for losing your goddamn map."

Now Sam again was forced to stop for a red light. Morgan was hunting for a classical station, WNCN or WQXR, and she was so absorbed in this task that she didn't register what Sam was saying.

She looked up suddenly and glared at him. "Were you swearing at me?"

"No, not at you. At him."

Now she saw what it was—rather, who it was—that had touched off Sam's indignation. A man had lumbered over to their car and now stood by Sam's door, his hands held out like a penitent. He looked only remotely human, as though he were a product of a species not yet evolved, a species that in its progress from the pre-Cambrian era to now had altered not at all, almost in defiance of Darwin. What Morgan first noticed about him was the way his skin coiled about most of his neck and jowls so that it formed a pulpy scabrous mass; it was darker in tone than the rest of his face and bore the unmistakable signs of disease and ravages of fire. Morgan wanted to look away but couldn't. She might as well have been under the thrall of some perverse compulsion. She was mesmerized.

The more she looked, the more she studied this sickening spectacle of misshapen flesh, the more she was convinced that she saw vermin crawling from out of ruptures in its surface. No, she thought, this cannot be, and by a difficult effort of will she closed her eyes. But upon opening them again, she found the man, the creature, whatever he was, still there, his eyes peering out of his desecrated face as from the bottom of a rain barrel fouled by rats and full of stale water. He seemed to have no nose, only a flap of skin that had slipped into its place and which, every so often, moved in response to air going in and out of the cavity.

He wrung his hands, then held them out again.

"Does he want money?" Her voice was reduced to a whisper.

The light had not changed or else it had changed and changed again and still they had not moved.

Sam seemed unable to find his voice. Like Morgan, he could not take his eyes off the man nor could he mobilize himself to take any action—of any sort.

"I don't know," he said at last. "I don't know."

He returned his eyes to the street that lay ahead of him in an attempt to ignore the man importuning him. Tension was visible in his eyes—Morgan rarely saw him get like this—and his jaw muscles had gone taut, drawing lines out of his skin that hinted of the old age that would one day come into his face. He made some uncharacteristic noise with his teeth, grating them together.

Again the man, with a gesture of a fretful washerwoman, thrust his hands together, but this time when he unclasped them, he had something in them: a dirty, damp rag. How he had done this, pulled a rag apparently out of thin air, was a mystery to both of them.

Morgan started to tell Sam to forget about the light and step on the gas, but the words wouldn't come to her. Her voice seemed lost.

Then it was too late. The man stepped in front of their car and began to wipe the windshield with this rag, making wide stroking motions that left the glass streaked and stained.

"Son of a bitch," Sam said, ramming the horn with his hand, revving the engine loudly, thinking that these disturbances might cause the man to abandon his enterprise. But the man seemed totally oblivious and kept right on with his work, spreading out his rag in such a way that he almost entirely blotted out Sam's view.

He was thinking at that moment that he was famous, and was about to become more famous, and that he was to be honored in an hour, and what was this bastard doing taking up his time and messing up his window on him? *This shouldn't have to be* was his thought. *This shouldn't have to be.*

"Is your door locked, Sam?"

"Yes, yes," he said edgily and honked once more. The din of it prompted his wife to put her hands over her ears.

Now Morgan realized that they were moving, Sam had his foot on the accelerator, and he was gently inching the BMW forward, though with the rag draping more than half the windshield, he would have no idea as to where he was going.

"Be careful, please, Sam," she urged.

"I'm not about to run him over, Morgan. . . ."

Abruptly he braked, then released the pressure of his foot, but the momentum was such that the car kept in motion. "I don't want to hurt him," he said, "just scare him the hell away."

"Where is he?" Morgan asked. She leaned to her right to peer out her side window, but could see no one. Maybe she was at the wrong angle.

"I don't know. I suspect he's gotten himself over the hood in some way."

Because he must have been there; the rag was still moving—counterclockwise—over the windshield. Curiously the rag seemed to become larger so that it began to encompass more and more of the glass until their view was totally obscured.

As much as Morgan strained to see him, as much as Sam did, they could catch not so much as a glimpse of the man. Neither of them was brave—or foolish—enough to dare roll down their windows and look out.

Morgan held herself stiffly. She thought she could smell her fear oozing out of her. Sam's hands, she observed, were trembling as he held onto the steering wheel.

But Sam was now leaning forward; he was growing angrier and when this happened his face grew red. His eyes were half-lidded; his breathing was shallow and came in fitful gasps. It was rare that he got like this and Morgan regarded him with interest, even fascination to see him this way.

"Damned if I'm going to let this son of a bitch intimidate me," he said. Shifting gears, he plunged his foot down on the gas, then propelled the BMW out into the intersection. Morgan could hear the whine of the tires as he did so.

She shut her eyes, waiting for the thud of impact as the man toppled from the hood. She could almost hear the tires as they drove into his flesh and muscle and bone. She expected at any moment to hear his plaintive wail as the life was snuffed out of him. She knew that when she looked again the windshield would be splattered with his blood.

But none of this happened. When she looked she could see nothing but the filthy rag still adhering to the glass.

Sam brought the car to a stop. Without saying a word, he got out and went to see what had become of him.

He picked the rag off the windshield first, holding it with just two fingers, suspecting that it was somehow contaminated and must be handled delicately. Then he dropped it to the ground. But of the man who'd held this rag there was no evidence, nothing.

He turned, scanning the empty street, Vermilya Avenue, but seeing nothing, he stooped down, thinking that maybe the man had gotten caught up by the tires and dragged underneath the car. With a growing look of bafflement on his face, he shrugged helplessly.

Back in the car he said, "Damndest thing, he's gone."

"You think he fell off?"

"I guess that's what must have happened."

"Did you hear anything?"

"Not a thing. Maybe with the noise of the car we just didn't hear him," he offered. His voice lacked conviction.

"But wouldn't we have seen him if he fell off?"

"I don't know. I've never had anything like this happen before. Well, it's over now. Let's try to find our way out of here."

And they did, soon enough. They located Broadway—or rather they stumbled on it as they continued west—and that was all the orientation they were in need of.

But still Morgan could not entirely escape the sensation that she hadn't seen the last of the man with the rag. And while she said nothing to Sam she continued to check the rearview mirror, half-suspecting that the fearsome spectacle of the ragman's face might be reflected there. That this did not occur failed to reassure her; it only meant that the moment they would—she would—see him again had been postponed, nothing more.

The reading of Sam's play was nearly over by the time they reached Lincoln Center. As many as sixty people were jammed into the room where the ceremony was being held. When Sam and Morgan entered they turned around in their seats and gave them inquisitive glances. Sam discovered that he was expected to take his place at the empty chair directly behind the rostrum where an actress was now concluding Act II of *The Road of Amber*. She was a middle-aged woman, beautiful in her prime, whose voice was resonant and even magical, endowing Sam's words with far more significance than they probably deserved.

There was sustained applause for her at the end of the reading, which carried over to the presentation. Awkwardly Sam stood to accept the plaque and the check for a thousand dollars. He knew he was supposed to say something; he had, in fact, already prepared a statement, but after what had happened on his way here, it had escaped his memory entirely. Looking out at the expectant audience all he could see was the man with the rag, his diseased skin coiled about his neck. He searched for his wife but he could not spot her. He sensed that people were growing impatient, that they could not comprehend why he was just standing there. Here was a playwright noted for his comic touch; surely they anticipated a display of wit, at the very least, a self-deprecating joke. He was almost about to say, "A funny thing happened to me on the way over here . . . ," but there as nothing funny about it at all.

At last he found his voice. He was saying something, and it seemed to be going over well. But he remained detached. It was as if he were hovering above the room, an astral presence, observing himself with indifference. He continued speaking and then, abruptly, he broke off. People were applauding, deciding that his sudden silence meant that he had concluded. He smiled graciously, shook hands with a venerable-looking gentleman who he supposed was a representative of the Llewellyn Foundation, who, for all he knew, might be a Llewellyn himself.

There was a party following, a comparatively informal affair with a single bartender and a selection of cheese, crackers, and chips with a tangy flavor to them. There was no point when he wasn't being congratulated or having his hand pumped. Morgan would come and go, occasionally taking a place by his side, then vanishing again. None of it was real to him.

Somebody asked him whether he was feeling all right.

"Sure, why do you ask?"

"I don't know, you seem a little pale."

"Work," he said. A wonderful, all-purpose explanation. Work could justify feverish looks and trembling hands. Work could excuse distracted behavior and inaudible replies.

As soon as he thought he could without offending anyone he found Morgan and suggested they leave. She seemed to be having a good time; she wasn't inclined to go. But she shrugged and said she was ready when he was. The dress she'd put on instead of the leather pants rustled when she moved. When the light struck it, the dress was revealed as practically transparent so that her legs were fully outlined. From what Sam could see, the dress was actually more provocative than the leather pants; it was just that he hadn't realized how much up until now.

Too many things occupying his mind at once, he thought. He felt edgy and angry in a way that he could not define. It required far more energy than he had to say all the good-byes that were necessary. He found himself the recipient of notes and business cards. He half-remembered promising people to have lunch or cocktails with them in the next few weeks. He did not know where he wanted to be, he knew only that he did not want to be here or even in New York City any longer.

Their car was parked five blocks uptown and one block to the east. For all the bad luck they'd had getting to their destination they still had managed to locate a parking place with surprising ease.

The car, Sam noticed now, was almost directly underneath a streetlight.

Halfway up the block Morgan stopped. An expression of horror came over her face.

"What is it?"

"Look, Sam, there!" She was pointing toward the car.

"I don't see anything. It doesn't look like anyone's broken into it or given us a parking ticket."

"No, the tires. Look at the tires."

He did. They were smeared with blood.

They both had the same thought; he saw it in her eyes, the fear that the end of the ragman wasn't in the dark streets far north of here after all.

Sam was looking under the car; it was almost as if he expected to see the ragman's body entangled in the body-work. There was no one there, of course.

"We should go back," he said.

"You can't be serious."

He wasn't. It was just something that seemed right to say.

"Well, at least we should report it to the police."

"Report what?"

He didn't know exactly what. That was the trouble. "I suppose that we struck someone."

He put his finger to the wall of the tires where the blood was particularly conspicuous in the glare of the streetlight. His eyes widened when he took away some of the blood on his finger. The blood should have dried after all this time, but it was as wet as if it had just come from a cut in his own skin.

Sam shuddered. He suspected a bad joke; he suspected other things, too, which he did not dare give voice to. He said to his wife, "Let's get out of here."

They drove in silence all the way out of New York. This time Sam was attentive to directions and signs. He got across the river, he got across the state line and into Connecticut with no trouble.

But coming into another state seemed to make no difference in the behavior they exhibited. They were sitting as far from each other as it was possible to get in the front seat of the car. They seemed to be in the mood to blame someone for what had happened—what might still be happening—and for Sam there was no one else but Morgan, and for Morgan no one else but Sam.

Yet there was another reason that accounted for their distance. They each held in their minds an impression of the ragman who'd accosted them; and as they approached their home the impression, rather than growing more diffuse and hazier, began on the contrary to grow stronger.

Morgan was petrified most of all of falling asleep and of having to see the disfigured face of the ragman in her dreams, while Sam worried that he might never be able to fall asleep at all with the memory of him.

But the man they remembered, the face they remembered, was not the same. Naturally they both recalled the burns, the way the skin coiled and wreathed about the face, the whole hideous spectacle of him. It was in the configuration of the contorted features that their recollections differed.

Sam was becoming convinced that what he'd seen—who he'd seen—did not exist. And while it was true that Morgan had registered the ragman's presence he still could not believe that the ragman had been of this world; rather he felt that he was some kind of apparition, a collaborative projection on his part and Morgan's, but a projection all the same. And the reason he was certain—almost certain—that this ragman owed its appearance to a conjuring trick of his imagination was because the ragman's face was his own, the face not that he owned right now, but the face that might very well one day be his.

Because this was what Sam feared: loss and death, loss of health, happiness, money, fame; loss of Morgan. And the kind of death that he feared was the kind that took forever to play itself out. He saw himself on street corners, a derelict, penniless, the old begrizzled boozer who sidles up to you in some dank saloon demanding you buy him a drink in exchange for his life story, a chronicle of applause and encomiums, a farce in other words that had all the makings of a tragedy without any ennobling virtues. He had gazed into the face of the ragman and, searching for the familiar in such a stranger, had come on the face of himself. It had not occurred to him until now. It was a recognition that had begun in the back of his mind and now, fifteen and a half miles into Connecticut, had penetrated to the front of it. He distrusted what he had, his talent, his money, his fame, his wife; he had always known how easily it could all slip away and he suspected that tonight, in the fever of ambition the Llewellyn Award had set burning in him, these many apprehensions of his had gathered together and produced the grotesque and spectral form of this ragman. The blood he didn't know about. It was so very real that he had (furtively, so that Morgan wouldn't see) tasted it.

And it had tasted real. Sweet and real.

The same mental process was occurring to Morgan. The memory of the ragman returned now with all the insistence of a commercial jingle you can't get out of your head, repeating itself over and over and over again. All she had to do was close her eyes to see him clearly: a face of such transcendent horror that it was almost possible to discover a beauty in it: the beauty of tarantulas, the beauty of slugs, the beauty of sulphuric creatures lifted from great depths out of the Pacific ocean.

●　　●　　●

The man she perceived in the ragman's face was not the face of her husband, not the face of Sam Drysdale. The face she saw now, with her eyes squeezed so tightly shut, was the face of a man she had once loved, Stephen Morrell. And Stephen Morrell had once loved her and for the love of her was dead.

Three and a half years they'd shared together, and in those three and a half years, she had had an intimation of what happiness could be like.

There was never any Gerald Cocharan, never any marriage or Seattle or Boeing job. It had all been invented by her, not to deceive Sam, but to keep her past and her love and the story of her love's ending far from him, for in a way that she could not quite comprehend herself, it was a sacred thing that she'd had with Stephen, and she couldn't bear to taint it by dredging up its memory with Sam, in Sam's bed. There was a part of her life that she would never divulge to Sam, for he had no right to it, he wouldn't understand it—but most of all he had no right to it.

They had planned to marry, they had planned to have children, and look what it had come to.

It had come to nothing.

She had not wanted to stay with him in the house he'd bought in Montana, a small town not far from Yellowstone; she had a life to lead in another place, a talent to discover. If she believed in herself she would have remained with him, but she did not, and had to go off to find out how one went about believing in oneself. He was old-fashioned, he did not know how to let go, it was an art lost on him. But alone, in the winter cold and snow of this small town in Montana, he'd despaired, spent hundreds of dollars he didn't have phoning her (for he was not a letter writer, he was anything but a letter writer, a guide, a huntsman, a lover, but not a letter writer). At last he decided he would go see her, try New York, try living with her wherever she wanted, and he had died in that flight coming to her, had sat in a plane that stalled out and careered into a white snow-covered valley in Midwestern America.

And so it was his face, Stephen's face, that Morgan had

beheld in the ragman's, his scorched and unhappy face, Stephen pursuing her past the barrier of death.

How surprised she was, surprised and not surprised, to touch her cheek and find so much moisture there. She was crying and Sam had not noticed.

Sam was speeding. The Connecticut cops were strict about speeding; they'd stop you for exceeding the limit by five, ten miles, and Sam was doing twenty over the fifty-five limit. Morgan didn't care; in fact, she almost welcomed the speed. She thought that her dead distant love was about to drive her mad; she had the feeling that madness was very close by, threatening like a panther poised for attack, but way above on an overhanging ledge where you couldn't so much as catch a glimpse of it. Love should not have the capacity to kill you like this, she thought.

The sky was charged. You could feel the currents in the air, the way the electricity surged across the sky, causing blue-white flashes of lightning to throw the whole of the horizon into stark relief. But there was only silence to accompany the lightning; it was too far away for the two of them, in the shelter of their BMW, to hear any thunder.

But clearly the rain had been in these parts, had come and gone, leaving in its wake the cement surface of the road slick and glistening and the bark of the neighboring trees with a black and porous look to it that it got when it was very wet. There were not many other cars on the road; those few that they spotted coming in the opposite direction had their windshield wipers still going as though their drivers had yet to understand that the storm had left them.

About nine or ten miles from their home, Sam saw up ahead, caught in the slash of his headlight beams, a car drawn off onto the shoulder of the road. All he could see of it was its rear, shimmering blue in the light of his lights and the light of a signal flare that flashed red every couple of seconds.

A man, hooded in a yellow rain jacket, was standing by the side of his car, attempting to wave them down. They could not immediately make out his face, and that was enough for them. Without saying a word to Morgan, Sam applied his foot to the gas and sped right by him.

Morgan twisted herself around in her seat so that she could

get a good look at the man while Sam settled for a glimpse of him in the rearview mirror. What they both saw was a middle-aged man—a suburban-looking man—gazing despondently after them. Who knew how many cars had passed him by that night.

Sam continued on for another hundred yards or so before suddenly braking. "Hell, we can't leave him stranded out here like this," he said and proceeded to back up.

"Thank God you stopped," said the man, coming up to Sam's window. "The battery's dead. All I need is a ride up to a gas station."

"I'm not sure one's open around here at this hour," Sam said.

"Well then, just to the nearest phone booth. I'm a member of the AAA."

"Get in, we'll see what we can do for you."

Again he voiced his gratitude and got into the backseat.

Up close he had the aspect of a lawyer who would never be made a partner in his firm; he was at a point in his life where he realized his opportunities were all in the past and that these were opportunities he had never had the imagination to take advantage of. He smelled a bit of men's cologne and of rain and of the car engine that had gone dead on him. Sam imagined a wife for him, sitting home and waiting up and wondering why he was so late; she would be unexceptional in looks and a willing buyer of faddish diet manuals once they appeared in paperback. They would have a son of twelve or thirteen—this man who now introduced himself as John Glower seemed to be in his early fifties—who would be impossible to control. An ordinary man in sum, sad and overworked and still vaguely hopeful about life.

"I was out there for half an hour, would you believe it?" he was saying.

Morgan had a taut expression on her face, almost pained. She did not like having this person intrude on their silence.

"There should be a Gulf station up here, we'll see if it's still open," Sam said, equally impatient to be rid of him.

"And I just had the car checked out and paid a whopping bill," said John Glower, "and it still screws up."

When neither Sam nor Morgan responded, he fell quiet

though Sam sensed that it was difficult for him not to speak. It was a nervous habit with him, talk, and he didn't like to be too long without it.

The Gulf station appeared to be open; its lights were blazing, but it was located on the other side of the highway, obliging Sam to take the next exit and find the entrance to the lanes going south.

But when they pulled into the station they saw that it was in fact closed. The lights seemed to be for effect because the office was locked and there was not a soul about.

Yet there was a phone booth right next to the soda machine and John Glower had said that a phone booth was all he needed.

"Have you got a dime?" Sam asked.

When he received no reply he turned around.

The man sitting in back was not John Glower. He might have been John Glower five minutes before, but he was John Glower no longer. Slowly he lowered the hood of his yellow rain jacket, exposing the full hideous sight of his face to them, so that they could look upon the burns and the rough ragged edges of skin that had never healed.

Morgan, too, turned and, seeing him, opened her mouth to let out a scream but the scream died in her throat and all she could produce was a muffled gargled sound.

For a single silent moment the ragman did nothing, looked hard at both of them, but did nothing.

Then he reached forward and, extending both his hands, took hold of Sam and Morgan by their necks.

His touch was warm, almost hot, as though a smoldering fire were in his palms and his fingers. He pressed closely, but not so that it hurt. His breath they could smell now and it smelled like food gone bad in a hot place.

Then he leaned forward, over the seat, and gave them each a kiss full on the lips, tender and loving and full of adoration.

What are you afraid of?

Dennis Etchison, the premier short story writer of the field, knows; and he's not always kind enough to keep it to himself.

DEATHTRACKS

by Dennis Etchison

ANNOUNCER:	Hey, let's go into this apartment and help this housewife take a shower!
ASSISTANT:	Rad!
ANNOUNCER:	Excuse me, ma'am!
HOUSEWIFE:	Eeek!
ANNOUNCER:	It's okay, I'm the New Season Man!
HOUSEWIFE:	You—you came right through my TV!
ANNOUNCER:	That's because there's no stopping good news! Have you heard about New Season Body Creamer? It's guaranteed better than your old-fashioned soap product, cleaner than water on the air! It's—
ASSISTANT:	Really rad!
HOUSEWIFE:	Why, you're so right! Look at the way New Season's foaming away my dead, unwanted dermal cells! My world has a whole new complexion! My figure has a glossy new paisley shine! The kind that men . . .
ANNOUNCER:	And women!
HOUSEWIFE:	. . . love to touch!
ANNOUNCER:	Plus the kids'll love it, too!
HOUSEWIFE:	You bet they will! Wait till my husband gets

up! Why, I'm going to spend the day spreading the good news all over our entire extended family! It's—

ANNOUNCER: It's a whole New Season!
HOUSEWIFE: A whole new reason! It's—
ASSISTANT: Absolutely RAD-I-CAL!

The young man fingered the edges of the pages with great care, almost as if they were razor blades. Then he removed his fingertips from the clipboard and tapped them along the luminous crease in his pants, one, two, three, four, five, four, three, two, one, stages of flexion about to become a silent drumroll of boredom. With his other hand he checked his watch, clicked his pen and smoothed the top sheet of the questionnaire, circling the paper in a cursive, impatient holding pattern.

Across the room another man thumbed a remote control device until the TV voices became silvery whispers, like ants crawling over aluminum foil.

"Wait, Bob." On the far side of the darkening living room a woman stirred in her beanbag chair, her hair shining under the black light. "It's time for *The Fuzzy Family*."

The man, her husband, shifted his buttocks in his own beanbag chair and yawned. The chair's Styrofoam filling crunched like cornflakes under his weight. "Saw this one before," he said. "Besides, there's no laughtrack. They use three cameras and a live audience, remember?"

"But it might be, you know, boosted," said the woman. "Oh, what do they call it?"

"Technically augmented?" offered the young man.

They both looked at him, as though they had forgotten he was in their home.

The young man forced an unnatural, professional smile. In the black light his teeth shone too brightly.

"Right," said the man. "Not *The Fuzzy Family*, though. I filtered out a track last night. It's all new. I'm sure."

The young man was confused. He had the inescapable feeling that they were skipping (or was it simply that he was missing?) every third or fourth sentence. *I'm sure*. Sure of what? That this particular TV show had been taped before an all-live audience? How could he be sure? And why would anyone care enough about such a minor technical point to bother to find out? Such things weren't supposed to matter to the blissed-out masses. Certainly not to AmiDex survey families. Unless . . .

Could he be that lucky?

The questionnaire might not take very long, after all.

This one, he thought, has got to work in the industry.

He checked the computer stats at the top of the questionnaire. MORRISON, ROBERT, AGE 54, UNEMPLOYED. Used to work in the industry, then. A TV cameraman, a technician of some kind, maybe for a local station? There had been so many layoffs in the last few months, with QUBE and Teletext and all the new cable licenses wearing away at the traditional network share. And any connection, past or present, would automatically disqualify this household. Hope sprang up in his breast like an accidental porno broadcast in the middle of *Sermonette*.

He flicked his pen rapidly between cramped fingers and glanced up, eager to be out of here and home to his own video cassettes. Not to mention, say, a Bob's Big Boy hamburger, heavy relish, hold the onions and add avocado, to be picked up on the way?

"I've been sent here to ask you about last month's Viewing Log," he began. "When one doesn't come back in the mail, we do a routine follow-up. It may have been lost by the post office. I see here that your phone's been disconnected. Is that right?"

He waited while the man used the remote selector. Onscreen, silent excerpts of this hour's programming blipped by channel by channel: reruns of *Cop City*, the syndicated version of *The Cackle Factory*, the mindless *Make Me Happy*, *The World As We Know It*, *T.H.U.G.S.*, even a repeat of that PBS documentary on Teddy Roosevelt, *A Man, A Plan, A Canal, Panama*, and the umpteenth replay of *Mork & Mindy*, this the infamous last episode that had got the series canceled, wherein Mindy is convinced she's carrying Mork's alien child and nearly ODs on a homeopathic remedy of Humphrey's Eleven tablets and blackstrap molasses. Still he waited.

"There really isn't much I need to know." He put on a friendly, stupid, shit-eating grin, hoping it would show in the purple light and then afraid that it would. "What you watch is your own business, naturally. AmiDex isn't interested in influencing your viewing habits. If we did, I guess that would undermine the statistical integrity of our sample, wouldn't it?"

Morrison and his wife continued to stare into their flickering 12-inch Sony portable.

If they're so into it, I wonder why they don't have a bigger set, one of those new picture-frame projection units from Mad Man Muntz, for example? I don't even see a Betamax. What was Morrison talking about when he said he'd taped *The Fuzzy Family*? The man had said that, hadn't he?

It was becoming difficult to concentrate.

Probably it was the black light, that and the old Day-Glow posters, the random clicking of the beaded curtains. Where did they get it all? Sitting in their living room was like being in a time machine, a playback of some Hollywood Sam Katzman or Albert Zugsmith version of the sixties; he almost expected Jack Nicholson or Luanna Anders to show up. Except that the artifacts seemed to be genuine, and in mint condition. There were things he had never seen before, not even in catalogues. His parents would know. It all must have been saved out of some weird prescience, in anticipation of the current run on psychedelic nostalgia. It would cost a fortune to find practically *any* original black light posters, however primitive. The one in the corner, for instance, "Ship of Peace," mounted next to "Ass Id" and an original Crumb "Keep on Truckin' " from the Print Mint in San Francisco, had been offered on the KCET auction just last week for $450, he remembered.

He tried again.

"Do you have your Viewing Log handy?" Expectantly he paused a beat. "Or did you—misplace it?"

"It won't tell you anything," said the man.

"We watch a lot of oldies," said the woman.

The young man pinched his eyes shut for a moment to clear his head. "I know what you mean," he said, hoping to put them at ease. "I can't get enough of *The Honeymooners*, myself. That Norton." He added a conspiratorial chuckle. "Sometimes I think they get better with age. They don't make 'em like that anymore. But, you know, the local affili-ates would be very interested to know what you're watching.''

"Not that old," said the woman. "We like the ones from the sixties. And some of the new shows, too, if—"

Morrison inclined his head toward her, so that the young man could not see, and mouthed what may have been a warning to his wife.

Suddenly and for reasons he could not name, the young man felt that he ought to be out of here.

He shook his wrist, pretending that his collector's item Nixon-Agnew watch was stuck. "What time is it getting to be?" Incredibly, he noticed that his watch had indeed stopped. Or had he merely lost track of the time? The hands read a quarter to six. Where had they been the last time he looked? "I really should finish up and get going. You're my last interview of the day. You folks must be about ready for dinner."

"Not so soon," said the woman. "It's almost time for *The Uncle Jerry Show*."

That's a surprise, he thought. It's only been on for one season.

"Ah, that's a new show, isn't it?" he said, again feeling that he had missed something. "It's only been on for . . ."

Abruptly the man got up from his beanbag chair and crossed the room.

He opened a cabinet, revealing a stack of shipment cartons from the Columbia Record Club. The young man made out the titles of a few loose albums, "greatest hits" collections from groups which, he imagined, had long since disbanded. Wedged into the cabinet, next to the records, was a state-of-the-art audio frequency equalizer with graduated slide con-trols covering several octaves. This was patched into a small black accessory amplifier box, the kind that are sold for the purpose of connecting a TV set through an existing home stereo system. Morrison leaned over and punched a sequence of preset buttons, and without further warning a great hissing filled the room.

"This way we don't miss anything," said the wife.

The young man looked around. Two enormous Voice-of-the Theatre speakers, so large they seemed part of the walls, had sputtered to life on either side of the narrow room. But as yet there was no sound other than the unfathomable, rolling hiss of spurious signal-to-noise output, the kind of distortion he had heard once when he set his FM receiver between stations and turned the volume up all the way.

Once the program began, he knew, the sound would be deafening.

"So," he said hurriedly, "why don't we wrap this up, so I can leave you two to enjoy your evening? All I need are the answers to a couple of quick questions, and I'll be on my way."

Morrison slumped back into place, expelling a rush of air from his beanbag chair, and thumbed the remote control selector to a blank station. A pointillist pattern of salt-and-pepper interference swarmed the 12-inch screen. He pushed up the volume in anticipation, so as not to miss a word of *The Uncle Jerry Show* when the time came to switch channels again, eyed a clock on the wall over the Sony—there was a clock, after all, if only one knew where to look amid the glowing clutter—and half-turned to his visitor. The clock read ten minutes to six.

"What are you waiting to hear?" asked Morrison.

"Yes," said the wife, "why don't you tell us?"

The young man lowered his eyes to his clipboard, seeking the briefest possible explanation, but saw only the luminescence of white shag carpeting through his transparent vinyl chair—another collector's item. He felt uneasy circulation twitching his weary legs, and could not help but notice the way the inflated chair seemed to be throbbing with each pulse.

"Well," trying one more time, noting that it was coming up on nine minutes to six and still counting, "your names were picked by AmiDex demographics. Purely at random. You represent twelve thousand other viewers in this area. What you watch at any given hour determines the rating points for each network."

There, that was simple enough, wasn't it? No need to go into the per-minute price of sponsor ad time buys based on the overnight share, sweeps week, the competing services each selling its own brand of accuracy. Eight-and-a-half minutes to go.

"The system isn't perfect, but it's the best way we have so far of—"

"You want to know why we watch what we watch, don't you?"

"Oh no, of course not! That's really no business of ours. We don't care. But we do need to tabulate viewing records, and when yours wasn't returned—"

"Let's talk to him," said the woman. "He might be able to help."

"He's too young, can't you see that, Jenny?"

"I beg your pardon?" said the young man.

"It's been such a long time," said the woman, rising with a whoosh from her chair and stepping in front of her husband. "We can try."

The man got slowly to his feet, his arms and torso long and phosphorescent in the peculiar mix of ultraviolet and television light. He towered there, considering. Then he took a step closer.

The young man was aware of his own clothing unsticking from the inflated vinyl, crackling slightly, a quick seam of blue static shimmering away across the back of the chair; of the snow pattern churning on the untuned screen, the color tube shifting hues under the black light, turning to gray, then brightening in the darkness, locking on an electric blue, and holding.

Morrison seemed to undergo a subtle transformation as details previously masked by shadow now came into focus. It was more than his voice, his words. It was the full size of him, no longer young but still strong, on his feet and braced in an unexpectedly powerful stance. It was the configuration of his head in silhouette, the haunted pallor of the skin, stretched taut, the large, luminous whites of the eyes, burning like radium. It was all these things and more. It was the reality of him, no longer a statistic but a man, clear and unavoidable at last.

The young man faced Morrison and his wife. The palms of his hands were sweating coldly. He put aside the questionnaire.

Six minutes to six.

''I'll put down that you—you declined to participate. How's that? No questions asked.''

He made ready to leave.

''It's been such a long time,'' said Mrs. Morrison again.

Mr. Morrison laughed shortly, a descending scale ending in a bitter, metallic echo that cut through the hissing. ''I'll bet it's all crazy to you, isn't it? This *stuff*.''

''No, not at all. Some of these pieces are priceless. I recognized that right away.''

''Are they?''

''Sure,'' said the young man. ''If you don't mind my saying so, it reminds me of my brother Jack's room. He threw out most of his underground newspapers, posters, that sort of thing when he got drafted. It was back in the sixties—I can barely remember it. If only he'd realized. Nobody saved anything. That's why it's all so valuable now.''

''We did,'' said Mrs. Morrison.

''So I see.''

They seemed to want to talk, after all—lonely, perhaps—so he found himself ignoring the static and actually making an effort to prolong his exit. A couple of minutes more wouldn't hurt. They're not so bad, the Morrisons, he thought. I can see that now. Could be I remind them of their son. I guess I should be honored.

''Well, I envy you. I went through a Marvel Comics phase when I was a kid. Those are worth a bundle now, too. My mother burned them all when I went away to college, of course. It's the same principle. But if I could go back in a time machine . . .'' He shook his head and allowed an unforced smile to show through.

''These were our son's things,'' said Mrs. Morrison.

''Oh?''

''Our son David,'' said Mr. Morrison.

''I see.'' There was an awkward pause. The young man felt vaguely embarrassed. ''It's nice of him to let you hold his collection. You've got quite an investment here.''

The minute hand of the clock on the wall ground through its cycle, pressing forward in the rush of white noise from the speakers.

"David Morrison." Her voice sounded hopeful. "You've heard the name?"

David Morrison, David Morrison. Curious. Yes, he could almost remember something, a magazine cover or . . .

"It was a long time ago. He—our son—was the last American boy to be killed in Vietnam."

It was four minutes to six and he didn't know what to say.

"When it happened, we didn't know what to think," said Mrs. Morrison. "We talked to people like us. Mostly they wanted to pretend it never happened."

"They didn't understand, either," said Mr. Morrison.

"So we read everything. The magazines, books. We listened to the news commentators. It was terribly confusing. We finally decided even they didn't know any more than we did about what went on over there, or why."

"What was it to them? Another story for *The Six O'Clock News*, right, Jenny?"

Mrs. Morrison drew a deep, pained breath. Her eyes fluttered as she spoke, the television screen at her back lost in a grainy storm of deep blue snow.

"Finally the day came for me to clear David's room. . . ."

"Please," said the young man, "you don't have to explain."

But she went ahead with it, a story she had gone over so many times she might have been recalling another life. Her eyes opened. They were dry and startlingly clear.

It was three minutes to six.

"I started packing David's belongings. Then it occurred to us that *he* might have known the reason. So we went through his papers and so forth, even his record albums, searching. So much of it seemed strange, in another language, practically from another planet. But we trusted that the answer would be revealed to us in time."

"We're still living with it," said Morrison. "It's with us when we get up in the morning, when we give up at night. Sometimes I think I see a clue there, the way *he* would have seen it, but then I lose the thread and we're back where we started.

"We tried watching the old reruns, hoping they had something to tell. But they were empty. It was like nothing important was going on in this country back then."

"Tell him about the tracks, Bob."

"I'm getting to it. . . . Anyway, we waited. I let my job go, and we were living off our savings. It wasn't much. It's almost used up by now. But we had to have the answer. *Why*? Nothing was worth a damn, otherwise. . . ."

"Then, a few months ago, there was this article in *TV Guide*. About the television programs, the way they make them. They take the tracks—the audience reactions, follow? —and use them over and over. Did you know that?"

"I—I had heard . . ."

"Well, it's true. They take pieces of old soundtracks, mix them in, a big laugh here, some talk there—it's all taped inside a machine, an audience machine. The tapes go all the way back. I've broken 'em down and compared. Half the time you can hear the same folks laughing from twenty, twenty-five years ago. *And from the sixties*. That's the part that got to me. So I rigged a way to filter out everything— dialogue, music—except for the audience, the track."

"Why, he probably knows all about that. Don't you, young man?"

"A lot of them, the audience, are gone now. It doesn't matter. They're on tape. It's recycled, 'canned' they call it. It's all the same to TV. Point is, this is the only way left for us to get through, or them to us. To make contact. To listen, eavesdrop, you might say, on what folks were doing and thinking and commenting on and laughing over back then. . . .

"I can't call 'em up on the phone, or take a poll, or stop people on the street, 'cause they'd only act like nothing happened. Today, it's all passed on. Don't ask me how, but it has.

"They're passed on now, too, so many of 'em."

"Like the boys," said Mrs. Morrison softly, so that her voice was all but lost in the hiss of the swirling blue vortex. "So many beautiful boys, the ones who would talk now, if only they could."

"Like the ones on the tracks," said Mr. Morrison.

"Like the ones who never came home," said his wife. "*Dead now, all dead, and never coming back.*"

One minute to six.

"Not yet," he said aloud, frightened by his own voice.

Jack, I loved you, did you know that? You were my broth-er. I didn't understand, either. No one did. There was no time. But I told you, didn't I? Didn't I?

As Mr. Morrison cranked up the gain and turned back to his set, the young man hurried out. As Mrs. Morrison opened her ears and closed her eyes to all but the laughtrack that rang out around her, he tried in vain to think of a way to reduce it all to a few simple marks in a now pointless language on sheets of printed paper. And as the Morrisons listened for the approving bursts of laughter and murmuring and applause, separated out of an otherwise meaningless echo from the past, he closed the door behind him, leaving them as he had found them. He began to walk fast, faster, and finally to run.

The questionnaire crumpled and dropped from his hand.

He passed other isolated houses on the block, ghostly living rooms turning to flickering beacons of cobalt blue against the night. The voices from within were television voices, muffled and anonymous and impossible to decipher unless one were to listen too closely, more closely than life itself would seem to want to permit, to the exclusion of all else, as to the falling of a single blade of grass or the unseen whisper of an approaching scythe. And it rang out around him then, too, through the trees and into the sky and the cold stars, the sound of the muttering and the laughter, the restless chorus of the dead, spreading rapidly away from him across the city and the world.

Parents are easy targets for revenge tales, easier still for daydreams. What isn't so easy is doing something about them, without them doing something in return. A parent good or evil is a special sort of creature, "special" and "creature" being used advisedly.

Al Sarrantonio continues to appear in magazines and anthologies with increasing regularity. He has just given up his post as an editor for Doubleday and is now writing full time, his first novel completed and his stories either marvelously sick or unrelentingly grim. Your choice.

Father Dear

by Al Sarrantonio

HE NEVER BEAT me, but told me stories about what would happen to me if I did certain things.

"The crusts of bread," he told me, cutting the crusts off his own bread instructively and throwing them into the waste bin, "gather inside you. If you eat bread with the crusts still on, you will digest the bread but your body will not digest the crusts. They will build up inside you until . . ." Here he made an exploding gesture with his hands, close by my face. He smiled. I smiled. I was four years old, and cut the crusts off of my bread.

"The yellow pulpy material left after an orange is peeled," he told me another day, a bright sunny one as I remember, with thick slats of sunshine falling on the white kitchen table between us; I recall the sound of a cockatoo which flitted by outside, and the vague visual hint of green and the smell of spring that came in through the bottom of the window which he had opened a crack (I believe now that he opened it that crack for effect, to accentuate the brightness of spring outside with the stuffy dreariness of our indoor habitation—he told me other things about dust and about the indoors), "will make your teeth yellow if you ingest it. With the eating of oranges, which, by the way, you must eat, Alfred, for your condition, any specks of this pulp will be caught in a receptacle just to the back of your throat, just out of sight, and will creep up like an army of ants at night to stain your teeth. In time, your teeth will become the deep shade of a ripe banana; perhaps, someday, that of a bright lemon just picked.'' How I remember the hours I spent whisking those orange fruits clean of pulp, examining my fingernails afterward to make sure no bits had adhered to them; O, how many other hours did I lay awake at night in my bedroom, hating him and at the same time believing him (no, that's not right; the hate came later, much later; there was only love then, and if not that at least a respect for his knowledge, for the things he was so gently trying to save me from—no, it was Love after all) and waiting, with a dry ticking at the back of my tongue where the saliva had dried as I lay fearfully waiting for those tiny insect bits of pulp to march up my mouth, dousing my gums and teeth with yellow spray from their bucketlike tails; O! How many hours did I spend in front of a mirror, trying to see, my mouth as wide as my jaw would allow it, that ''receptacle'' where those lemon-ants waited!

I hate him now; came to hate him slowly, inexorably, and, in time, I have come to love that hate, to relish and enjoy it since it is the only thing I have in this world that I am not afraid of.

He taught me nothing of value. He taught me to hate books, to hate what was in them and the men who wrote them; taught me to, above all, hate the world, everyone in it; everything it stood for. ''It is a corrupt place, Alfred,'' he lectured endlessly, ''filled with useless people possessed of artificial sensibilities, people who respect and cherish nothing. They live like animals, all of them, huddled into cities chockablock one on top of the other; they are of different colors, and speak different languages until all their words mix in one jumbled whirr and none of them understand what any of the others are saying. I know, I come from that world, Alfred. They don't know what life is. They don't know what's *safe*. But you know what's safe, don't you?''

I remember grinning eagerly up at him at times like this, like a puppy; he always bent down over me, his hands behind his straight tall back, and I remember at times reaching up to him with my tiny hands, begging him, "Pick me up, pick me up, swing me, please!"

"Swinging you will make your stomach move in your body," he answered, smiling wanly, "and once moved, at your delicate age, it will stay in that new spot, perhaps where your lungs or pancreas should be, and will make you sick for the rest of your life. It may even turn you into a hunchback, or make you slur your words if it moves, on the high arc of your swing, into your vocal cavity. You *do* understand, don't you?"

My arms lowered slowly, tentatively, to my sides.

I was not allowed to play on the swings on the grounds, either, but would stare at them for hours through my bedroom window.

The grounds, naturally, were beautiful, wooded and sprawling. No one, I heard it whispered among the servants, had grounds like this anymore; no one, I once heard a Chinese servant say, *deserved* to have such grounds. The world, he whispered to mute Mandy, my sometimes guardian (when He was away), was still far too crowded for this type of thing to crop up again; there were too many other problems to be solved without one man shutting himself up in such a way. I am sure that Mandy went straight to my father after this bit of sacrilege had been imparted, and the man, if I remember correctly, was gone the following day. Another servant, of course, was in place instantly.

The grounds, as I say, were sprawling, but I was not allowed to make use of that sprawl. There were too many opportunities to be "hurt." The swinging motion I have already described could, of course, be accomplished to dire effect by the swing set just beyond the Italian-tiled patio; there was also at that spot a set of monkey bars which "would upset the balance of your hormones if you were to use it, since hanging upside down by a boy of your delicate constitution would only lead your body to hormone imbalance. The features of your face would begin to move about by the action of the blood rushing to your head, and you would end up looking something like this." He made an extremely grotesque—and terribly funny—face then, and I laughed along with him until I abruptly began to cry. If my memory serves me correctly, I ran and threw my arms around him, thanking him for saving me and asking him to promise never to leave or send me away; and, yes, I remember pointedly and now as clearly as if the moment were again occurring that my teary eyes were staring at his hands, still behind his back, and I was willing them to move around toward me, to show me anything parental and physical. I believe that may be the moment when I thought something was not right between us; for a fleeting second I entertained the thought that maybe he didn't love me after all but then quickly dismissed it, knowing that it must have been me, that I may already have been in danger of contracting some vile disease, something transmitted by a touch of the hands to the head, something transmitted by a loving hold, and that he was merely, as lovingly as he could, trying to avoid exposing me to it. He was saving me from himself. I threw myself from him, aching with apology for what I had almost accomplished. I don't remember if he thanked me or just went away.

"If you gaze at the sky too long," he said, after catching me leaning out of an upper story window at the moon overhead, "your head is very liable to fall off or stay locked in that position at least. Never look up in the daytime."

"Not even to watch a bird fly overhead?"

"Never. How old are you now?"

"Seven."

"Never look up again, Alfred. Up until now you have been lucky, but with the age of reason comes a severity of life that you will only too soon realize."

I never looked up.

"If you sit in a chair for more than five minutes, your feet will begin to lose their circulation and may never get it back. If you stand for more than five minutes, too much blood will rush to the bottom of your body and your feet will become heavy, as if filled with lead." I crouched when I walked.

"Meat will cause you to turn red."

I did not eat meat.

"Vegetables will cause you to turn their own color—yellow, green, orange."

I only ate vegetables when desperate.

"Chocolate will cause you to turn black. Wheat you may

take, and potatoes, and you may drink water in moderation after boiling, cooling and then boiling again. Do not drink milk: it will make you white as paper."

He showed me a book with these things in it, or rather read to me from one. The book, I later discovered, was *Moby Dick*. Such a thick book, such thick lies.

And yet I followed his instructions and thanked him for it.

I grew. I grew fat. Wheat and potatoes were my diet, and teenagehood found me stout and ugly. I wore glasses thick with mottled glass, because he told me a lucid pair would cause my eyes to change color and shape. My teeth hurt, and he scolded, saying that I had eaten something, possibly so long ago I could not remember, something that had gone against his wishes and was now catching up with me.

I will kill him when I find him.

He left abruptly; abandoned that massive estate in the dead of night when I was fifteen years old. There was only one hint that this would happen. Late in December of the winter he left, during the coldest part of a cold month, Mandy, the ghostly mute, took to her bed believing she would die. She was attended to by other of the staff, and even my father occasionally visited her. I was told never to go into her bedroom. I had once had a peek into that room—enormous and cluttered, with a high sculpted ceiling (there were paintings on it, clouds and blue sky which made me fearful lest my eyes and neck lock on it) and deep brown carved wooden walls. A huge bed, with high spikes at the four corners. A green-and-yellow coverlet. This was all I remembered. In the very last days of December, when it was made known with the usual whispering (whispers were what filled that manse, whispers and lies) that she would die before the night was gone, I went in to see her.

I knew she was alone. There were statues on that floor, as on every floor, behind which I had often hidden and which I had no neuroses about since my father did not know or had never caught me at it. There was one particular statue, a golden, tiny wood goddess with bow, set prominently high on a pedestal just to the left of the wide winding staircase (I used to occasionally slide down that staircase railing also, until He found me at it one day and told me that my genitals would be forced back into my body by the pressure of the railing if I continued) which gave an excellent view of Mandy's sickroom entrance. Shortly after supper I secreted myself there, watching the comings and goings of the servants, the dour doctor who came from somewhere and departed again to it, and, finally and surprisingly, my father, who came quietly out of the door somewhere just before midnight. He had no reason to check on my whereabouts, since he had made sure I was tucked solidly into my bedchamber just after dinner and had no reason to believe I would be anywhere else (he told me as a baby of the "things that were abroad after dark") but this was one of the few of his lies that I had managed to outgrow, even though at times on my nightly sojourns I thought I spied one of his "beasties of the night"—more likely optical illusions of the night. It occurs to me that he was neglectful in this, but why quibble; I seem to recall he was getting a little old by this time and had forgotten to reinforce some of the foul walls he had built, brick by blood red brick, around me for my fifteen years. Anyway, here I was when he hobbled off (he *was* getting old, and I remember him making use of a cane just before he left the next month) to his own voluptuous quarters somewhere to the other side of the building and one flight up (I had seen those quarters once, too, and they made Mandy's into a tent) and, probably, to one of his live-in paramours, servant-man or woman or possibly someone from outside who was occasionally flown in, usually around the holiday season (which was not, naturally, celebrated, in this household).

I waited a full ten minutes, crouched in my hiding spot and beginning to balance the two fears—fear of discovery by leaving the shadow of that statue too soon and fear of my legs being lost to me since I could feel numbness setting into them—before slowly moving out toward the door in a rabbit's crouch.

The lock ticked open easily. The room was not as big as I had remembered, but the bed seemed even bigger. Grey moonlight suffused the room, throwing a pale line of light across the bottom half of the bed; there was also a low-wattage bulb set into the wall over the bedstead, illuminating the upper half.

All I could see was a pile of pillows and that same green-and-yellow comforter which looked as flat as if no one were under it. At first I thought that this might be the case; perhaps they had moved her without my seeing; perhaps she had died and they had lowered her from the window into the waiting arms of the dour doctor to be carted off for burial or burning; perhaps this had all been a setup to lure me to this spot so that my hiding place behind that wood goddess could be uncovered and I could be mind-tortured further. I whirled quickly around but saw no one at the doorway behind me and no one, seemingly, in the corners of the room ready to jump out.

By this time I had moved close enough to see that, yes, she was in bed after all. Barely there, what was left of her. There was a head above the line of the quilt that looked like the head of a monkey, shriveled and nut brown; and below that the coverlet stretched as flat as I had imagined it did, scarcely revealing the outline of an evaporated body.

I leaned down over her, wanting very badly to peel up her eyelids as I had seen once on television (before He had decided that this pleasure, too, should be denied me for my own good) when her eyes opened of their own and she stared straight into my face.

She tried to scream, but nothing came out. Her features contorted, her lips pulling back over her teeth, making her look even more like a monkey. It was now that I saw why she was mute: her tongue ended in a surgically sharp line at the back of her throat, giving her nothing to articulate with. Or so I thought.

After a moment she ceased trying to scream, and a curious calm descended on her. She looked at me for a few moments, apparently recognizing me now. Why had she tried to scream? Possibly she had thought I was someone else. But now, recognizing me as she did, her eyes brightened and she tried desperately to say something.

"What?" I asked, leaning down close with my ear to her mouth, wanting to draw back because of the disease she might impart to me but overcome with a violent compulsion, for the first time in my life, to explore a mystery on my own.

"I can't hear you."

She was muttering something, so far under her breath and with such obvious effort that I hushed my own breathing, concentrating doubly hard to pick up her faint, insect's voice.

"Mo . . ." she was saying. "Mot . . ."

"What?" I rasped at her, impatient and now with one eye on the door lest someone hear the faint struggle going on in here.

"Mot . . ."

"Mot? What do you mean, mot?"

"Mot . . . Mother," she said, so far in the back of her throat that it was like listening to an echo off somewhere in a cave.

My body became ice. I nearly grabbed her by the mouth to make her repeat that word; but her eyes had filmed over and her lips were slack. For a moment I thought she had died there before me, but as I watched her eyes cleared again and once more she looked straight into me, through me.

I said nothing, and then I whispered, "You are my mother?"

Her mouth said nothing, but it formed the word, yes.

"*Oh*," I said, my throat gagging. I threw myself from the bed, instinctively going for the window and then pushing myself away from it when I looked up to see the full moon staring down at me from above. I fell to the floor. My throat would not work; I lay gasping for air like a reefed fish. My head was on fire, too; I thought for a moment that one of the terrible things my father had warned me about for so many years had come true, that the moon, or my disobedience in being out of my room, or my visit to this chamber, or the sight of this woman or what she had said, had triggered one of those ugly reactions which had for so long hung above me like a sword. I had eaten too many crusts when a baby, I thought desperately; possibly it was lemons; or bananas, or my brains had blown up to balloon size from hanging upside down, or not hanging upside down, or from bumping into a doorjamb, or not—

With a Herculean effort I staggered to my feet, to the door, into the hallway past the Hunter Goddess (her bow for a moment as I came out of the room pointed straight at my head) and into my own room, clawing my way into bed and so far under the covers that everything—the light, the evening, myself—was extinguished and a sudden darkness dropped upon me . . .

Only to rise again into dim light later, much later, when the first tepid hints of spring were manifesting themselves, and when my father was long departed, my mother long dead. My father brought most of the staff (at least those he had comported with) with him, leaving only a skeleton klatch of indifferent menials to attend to me, supplemented by his own horrid ghost, hanging in the air, usually in dusty corners, wherever I went in that house, reminding me of what I was and what he had made me and, in his absence, daring me to be anything else.

For the next twenty years I listened to that ghost.

Haunted, bloated by shame, starch and nightmares, I lurched from room to room (save one, of course) in that mansion, trying once again to be an infant by following my father's twisted directions on life. I was not rational; I was nothing but a bundle of neuroses held together by muscle and bone matter. I shouted much, screamed much, cried much except when I remembered what he had told me about crying: "If you weep, Alfred, the water reserves in your body will never be filled again. Recall that you are born with a certain amount of tear-water in you; that all other water which you take in is used for other purposes or expelled; and recall that once that tear-matter is depleted it can never be restored and you will never be able to cry again. Your body will try, throwing you into horrid convulsions, but nothing will come out of your eyes. Eventually your tear ducts will take the liquid they so crave from your eyeballs themselves, turning them into dry, paperlike orbs. Needless to say, you will go blind."

I tried to go blind. I cried incessantly, half-waiting for (and not caring about) the coming moment when there would be a cracking sound from deep within my eyesockets signalling the end of vision and the beginning of physical darkness. It never came, and after many months (years?—there is much about those twenty summers, winters, springs and falls that memory does not serve) I came slowly to realize that here was one of His major lessons that turned out not to be history but fiction. Might there be others? I began to explore.

Carefully, of course. The litany of my fears was a long one, and there were some areas where I would not tread—those fears were so deep-rooted. But there were many—"You must *always*, Alfred, walk with a measured step, throwing one foot out in front of the other, pausing before letting it touch the ground, and then letting it down in two phases, heel and then toe, *two separate stages*, heel then toe, or the feet will become flat and useless and hurt you incessantly"—that I was able, with patient years of self-imposed physical and mental therapy, to be rid of. I never, when speaking, doubled the letter "a" when using it as an article anymore (He had assured me it would prevent further stuttering, an offering to the Stutter Gods, I suppose). I didn't knock my knees together when standing up anymore. I didn't blink consciously before looking at something close up (to adapt the eyes to closeness).

And so, at age thirty-five, I was ready to find and kill Him.

It must have appeared quite comical, this fat (though by now not so bloated since I had learned that my diet could be expanded to include a healthier assortment of food; I had also discovered vitamins, something He had never spoken of), squinting (I had done away with the glasses, learning that they were not needed, were actually destroying my eyesight; I would squint with or without them now), white-haired (is it any wonder my hair had turned snow white—actually it was that way after I came to my senses after my mother's death) middle-aged man with enough tics, bad habits and eccentricities to fill two thick volumes, fumbling his way into the world beyond his little castle (I made it a point to pass by those monkey-bars, even swinging once upon them, pulling myself upside down and screaming my father's name at the deepest of blue skies that was evident that day) and out onto the Road of Vengeance, a road I, this abnormal specimen of man, knew nothing about, cared to know nothing about, begging only that it lead him through the maze of the terrible big world to the front door of the man-monster who had caused him to hate not only it (the world) but also his father and himself. Curiously, I had come to love one thing: the image of my mother on her deathbed: a deep and mysterious totem she became for me since I really knew so little about her; any of the servants who were left after my father's abandonment knew nothing of her, and my own recollections were so dim—she took care of me, I seemed to recall, in those odd periods when my father was ill in bed or occupied with one of his paramours. Never saying anything, she was hardly noticed. She had become safe, become, in fact, much larger than life. She was my mother; she had nurtured me, brought me into the world, possibly even loved me secretly, had certainly done nothing to harm me directly; and so, she became Sacred. She became the image I could hold up to Him; and when I found him I fully intended to flay him alive—peeling the flesh from his now ancient bones, as many strips for Her as for myself.

I found him easily.

Almost too easily; I admitted a little disappointment that the chase did not go on longer because the scent was so strong. The City was a strange place but not all so horrible; I had heard him speak about it to me for so long in revulsive tones ("You must *never*, Alfred, I repeat *never* go into the outside world, the vile City waiting out there, for it would be your end"); I found it somewhat less than my imagination had made it out to be. It seemed merely too many people pressed into too small a space; but they were, after all, people, and did not frighten me or revolt me as I had expected they would.

I had fully expected the Hunt to go on for some time, and so found myself immensely surprised when the most discreet inquiries as to my father's whereabouts led to his discovery. He seemed to be someone of import; I had never had doubt as to his monetary worth since the very fact that we had resided on such a vast expanse of land, at a time (you'll remember the comments of the servants as to this) when no one seemed to live this way, but I was duly shocked to find him so readily known *outside* of our isolated manse.

I was careful in approaching him. He resided in the most well-to-do building in the most well-to-do part of the City (naturally), holding an entire floor in a dreamlike blue metal and glass monstrosity; it overlooked the river, which, in its flowing blueness, hurt the eyes with all that visual concentration at one far end of the spectrum (he had once told me the color blue would hurt me; would make me, he said, "see nothing but blue until you are driven mad and want to tear your eyes out"). I had also been told, by one overly cautious individual who had easily succumbed to bribery for information (he insisted that we meet in a series of brief encounters in a park, where he imparted, on a bench by an ice cream custard stand—once, even, in the bushes by a children's zoo—tiny snatches of information that, when added together, gave a picture of a man of immense power in the last throes of life. This hurt me terribly, because if He were already dying he would be that much less horrified by my appearance, never mind my actions, and would probably already be faced toward the last dark precipice which I would gleefully tumble him over. I didn't want him to die. I wanted to kill him.

I made my way to Him with the utmost caution. Ironically, and to my delight, there was in the entrance to his entire 14th floor a statue remarkably like that wood goddess in our manse which I remembered with so much fondness and which, in a way, was the catalyst to my new life; with her arrow she had pointed me in the direction of Salvation and Revenge and had, in her smooth and godlike way, brought me to this delicious point.

I hid behind this statue, distinct from that other only in that this one was clothed, and I methodically, patiently mapped the comings and goings to His suite. I did this for days, managing to hide myself from the watchful (or half-watchful— he was not very attentive to his job) orbs of the guard who seemed always to be present. There were visitors, all during the day—men with briefcases, dull brown suits always buttoned, grim grey faces; but I noticed that in the evening there were never any visitors, and that somewhere around nine o'clock the bored guard usually slipped off for a cigarette no doubt shared with other bored guards on other floors of the building. He invariably stayed away a half-hour, and no one ever checked on him, so after a week of this surveillance I quietly slipped from behind my lair (knocking my knees together once as I rose—damn Him!) and stole my way into his metal manse.

If possible, this abode of his was even more regally attired than the other; the richness of the furnishings—velvet-covered furniture in blacks, reds and greens, tapestries, oiled wood walls and floors and antique ceramics—not to mention the other artworks, paintings and, yes, sculpture everywhere—that I began to gag in reaction to it. He had been a Pig before; but the realization that he was now an even greater one, a *public* one—this was all too much. I fingered the blade in my overcoat pocket—I had searched long and hard through the manse for just the right instrument, finally settling on one that, if the little blurbs often found in museums next to art treasures are to be believed, was once used for ritual sacrifice in Celtic Ireland. Oh, yes, I would use it again for just such a purpose, reviving a custom. . . .

Room after room of nauseating ostentation passed before me, until the hairs on the back of my head ("Don't ever let the hairs on the back of your head rise in fright, Alfred: it will cause you, in time, to lose your hairs as they are pulled into the back of your skull by the action of forced straightening") (!!!) stood on end and I knew that the richly carved, heavy-hinged door (hares and hunters on that door, how delightfully appropriate!) before which I stood was the last in the apartment and would lead to his bedroom. And indeed it did, for as I edged it open I heard a faint but unmistakable voice call out questioningly, "Grace? Grace?"

I was going to answer that no, it was not Grace and that the state of grace was what I hoped he possessed for the journey he would soon take, but when I saw that the room was so completely black dark that he would not see me until I stood just over his bed I decided to slip through that oily darkness and do just that. He called out again, very faintly, and then lapsed into a ragged, even breathing that told me he had slipped into sleep.

In a stealthy moment I was at his bedside, and leaning over him to turn on the Tiffany lamp by his bed.

At the instant I turned on that lamp he awoke.

"No!" was all he said, hoarsely. He tried to mouth my name, but I knew at that moment that he had suffered a stroke at this very instant of nirvana and would have trouble saying anything at all. I drew my blade out slowly, running it over my nails in front of his straining red face; he was gulping for air like a blowfish out of water.

"Alfred," I said slowly, quietly, completing for him what he was trying so hard to say. He shook his head from side to side, his eyes never leaving my face.

"Yes, Father, it is I. Are you surprised?"

He was puffing hard, and I lowered my ear (as I had done so long ago for my dear mute mother!) to hear him say, "Go . . . back."

I laughed. I pulled my head back and spat laughter, and then I put my face close to his.

"I don't think so, Father."

Again he was straining.

"Must," he said.

"Why? To keep me away from you? Don't you want me by your living side?" I lowered my wide eyes just inches from his, and brought the blade up close to his straining, yellow nostrils. "Would you rather I didn't speak? Would you rather I cut my own tongue out, make myself mute like my mother?"

His eyes went very wide and he shook his head violently from side to side.

"What, Father? What is it you want to say?"

I pulled him up by the shoulders, a little frightened by how light and frail he was, and pressed his lips to my ear.

"No . . ." he said.

"Speak, damn you!"

"Did it . . . herself . . ."

"Did what?"

"Cut her . . . own . . . tongue out . . ."

I pushed him back down into his pile of silken pillows. "*Liar!*" I said, raising my fist to strike him.

"No!" he said, suddenly finding his voice from somewhere down deep before it cracked off into a whisper again. "True . . ."

Calming abruptly, or rather moving off beyond rage to a calmer, more clear, more vicious place, I once again lowered my ear to his lips.

"Why did you leave, Father?"

There was a gurgle in his throat, and then, ". . . her . . . house . . ."

"What do you mean, 'Her house'?"

". . . kept me there. Gave me everything to keep me silent. Made me . . ."

"Made you what?" My voice was regaining its edge.

"Made me . . ." He was breathing very unevenly, and said with great effort, with what a fool could have taken to be pleading in his eyes, "You."

My voice was very calm now, and I made sure he could see me drawing the blade through my fingers, letting it glint off the weak light from the amber reading lamp.

"You're lying," I said. "You're lying like you always have to me. Your life is a lie from beginning to this, the end. You twisted my mind from as early as I can remember. It's a sewer now, Father. It always will be. I am scared to death just to be outside that mansion. Just coming here made me tremble and sweat. My life is a catalog of unnameable things, sick things, tics and neuroses that I can't escape. I fear everything. Except you." I brought the blade down slowly, delicately toward his old man's chicken neck.

"Did it for you, go back," he croaked, looking at my eyes, not at the blade. "Hybrid. She . . . hated you. Only way to keep you alive. Statue," he said, his face suddenly getting very red, blood pumping into it from the ruptured machine in his chest and making his eyes nearly pop out of his face. His voice became, for a moment, very loud and clear. "Alfred! She was from the woods, not like us! Go back, save your life!" He grabbed at me with his spindly arms, his twiglike fingers. He tried to pull himself up, tried to clasp his vile body to mine. ". . . back . . ."

His grasp loosened then, and he slipped, like a flat rock into a pool of water, down into death.

I sat up, panting, and looked down at him; the blade felt sharp in my hand and I entertained for a moment the notion of carving him up anyway, of taking the pound of flesh I had come for and at least giving to my mother the sacrifice I had vowed. But instead I lowered it into my coat and stood up. He was pitifully dead, and in death he appeared much less the object of hate; the soul had left, leaving only meat behind.

It was then, when I was leaving his bedroom and passing the massive, gilded mirror over the dresser by the doorway, that I saw something that made me stop.

My skin had turned red. I thought immediately of the meat I had eaten in the past months, of the bounteous meat I had eaten in the past days in the City. I shook my head to clear it, turned on the bright lamp on the dresser and once again my color was correct. I smiled knowingly at myself: for a chilly moment my teeth looked yellow and I thought of all the oranges I had eaten—the back of my throat became uncontrollably dry and it felt as though something tiny was ticking around back there—but then this passed too.

"Fool," I said, and left the apartment in haste, throwing a fleeting glance at the statue in the foyer before passing on.

Everything outside was blue.

Overhead, there was a fat full moon, and as I looked up at it it turned indigo and my neck began to ache, giving me trouble in lowering it.

I sat down on a bus and then a train, and my feet went numb.

I now felt, inside me, the movement of my organs and the gathering of bread crusts as they pressed out through my ribs, hernialike.

Somehow, I made it back to the grounds of the manse. I think a servant found me outside the front gates in the morning, curled up like a gnarled root, my face pointed at the killing sky. I don't know how he recognized me, since as they carried me in I passed a looking glass and saw that the features of my face had rearranged themselves, grotesquely mimicking that funny face my father had made at me so long ago.

They placed me in my father's old bedroom; the dour doctor came and went, and from the look on his dour face I knew that he would not return from the woods from which he was summoned.

I don't know what color I am now—red, black, blue, green, bone white. I do know that the pulp-ants are active this morning and that therefore my teeth must be a particular shade of yellow. Lemon yellow, perhaps. My genitals have retracted into my body. My head feels as though it will shortly fall off my shoulders.

I have had the statue of my mother moved into my new

bedroom and placed in my line of sight. The arrow in her bow points directly at my forehead and I now see a look of lust and self-loathing on her features that I didn't see before. I want to look at that statue; I want to look at it hard and long.

I think often of my father.

I know that soon my tear ducts will rob the liquid they need so desperately from my eyeballs, turning them into crackly paper orbs, and that, naturally, I will go blind.

You look around you, whether in a small town or a good-sized city, and you wonder where in hell all these people come from? Especially the ones you feel somewhat nervous about passing on the street, and the ones you see watching you from doorways and alleys, and the ones you think you know but of course it can't be him because he . . . well, it just can't be.

Peter Pautz lives in New Jersey, is married to artist Andrea Pautz, and is currently expanding his freelance business to include professional photography and writing for computers. Unlike the old saw, he is both Jack of all trades and master of many as well.

As Old As Sin

by Peter D. Pautz

A CENTURY AGO the old woman would have been wearing rags, carrying a coarse burlap sack slung over her shoulder filled with dams and iron cookware and memories older than her ancient line. But the children, Carla Hensler knew, would have been no different. Even her eight-year-old Davey became a taunting little monster, she thought as she watched the scene through the plastic sheeting that covered her windows.

Those three blocks from the corner market to the woman's ramshackle home must have been like running a gauntlet. More like crawling it at her age, Carla thought, although she was never quite sure what a knight's iron glove had to do with it. Just the image of something that hard and jagged was enough to make her cringe. It was almost the same image she had of Mike, at least from before he had deserted them. Since his return appearance two months ago, however, she had begun to think of him as anything but hard. Jagged still, yes. His temper flared for no more reason than it ever had, yet the only part of him that was hard anymore was his mind. He had become fixated on two thoughts since he had come back. His son and his sexuality.

Not that he was any great stud. At the most, he barely went through the motions, much as she had until he'd taken a

145

three-year leave of them. It had taken her half that time to convince herself that she was no longer *his*. She could go out if she wanted, date, dance, drink. All on her say-so alone. When he came home, though, he was demanding service in ways she had never dreamed of in her life. And if she hesitated even for a moment, he would simply go elsewhere. She wondered if the others found any part of him hard. She never did.

He was different with Davey. Trying to become a "pal" again, he played ball with his son, took him fishing, hiking. All the things he had just never bothered with before. There was hardly a free moment when they weren't together. On occasion, Davey had to avoid him just to do something alone with his friends. A couple of times, they had even invited Mike into a wild game of football or soccer and when the man began to tire out, they would run him all the more, until he dropped. Then they'd take off without a word, excitement and triumph lighting their eyes, having tested their power and won.

Now, the sounds of the catcalls drew her attention outside again. The ancient battle was joined, and she wondered what the strategy would be this time. Weeks ago, the old woman had tried threatening the more violent ones with her cane as they raced past her, hardly an inch away with their skateboards. Later she had tried to ignore them. Carla had seen her walk half the block with her eyes closed tightly so she would not flinch. Yet the verbal abuse worsened. The older children had found out somehow that the wizened old lady's name was Mother Corbin. For a while Carla had used that, telling them that she must have been a nun, retired now, and should be left alone. When she saw their angry looks and sniggering whispers about to turn toward her, however, she retreated, and over time heard the cries of "Hey, Mother," turn to "Hey, you mother," and finally drag down completely to some filthy obscenity that made even Carla blush.

She watched as the shuddering old woman passed in front of her house, the yelling children framed for a moment in the crumbling bare wood of the porch. Davey was with them, a little farther away than most, but she could still hear him calling with the others. "Hey! When you gonna dry up and blow away, huh?"

Carla didn't move.

Then, one of the older boys from down the street, Jeff Morton, ran right in front of the woman. As he passed her, he faked a stumble on her cane and came up cursing. "You old bitch. Why don't you go drop dead in a sandbox or something."

Mother Corbin showed not a flicker of an eye that she'd heard him. Slowly she continued her way on home. Jeff jumped to his feet and moved in front of her, blocking the path. "Hey," he yelled, waving his arms wildly at his sides. "Hey, what are you deaf, too?"

There was no way around him without stepping into the street, and the two of them froze. The boy stared into the old woman's face while she seemed to be concentrating on a spot ten feet beyond him.

Behind the snapping plastic, Carla·sighed. She would have to do something. She had seen Mike take that stance too many times not to know what was going to happen. Quickly she stepped to the door, pulled it open, and strode to the porch rail. She took a deep breath.

"Jeffrey Morton," she called, "you leave her alone this instant. Do you hear me?"

He didn't answer, didn't move.

"I said, do you hear me, Jeffrey?" This time she dared to hint of anger.

For another long moment he remained still, then he glanced at Carla and quickly back at the old woman before him. "Yeah," he said, smiling. Covering his ears with his hands, he ran off yelling, "Jeez, I could hear you if I was in China."

The others sped off after him. Davey hesitated for a moment and turned to follow, but too late.

"Davey, you come here right now."

He stopped, turning sulking eyes toward her. "Ah, Mom."

"Never mind 'Ah, Mom.' " She crossed her arms. "You get in here. Your father will be home soon and I've got to start dinner. You," she said pointedly, "can peel the potatoes."

She could not make out what she heard him mumble, but slowly he shuffled past her and into the house. She stood a moment longer on the porch, letting the autumn wind cut into her, wondering what it would be like to be old, trying to remember what it was like to be young. Under her folded arms, she could feel the sagging plasticity of her breasts.

Inside, the phone rang. And, for a while, age was forgotten.

By the time Mike had pulled his new Shelby on to the bare patch of yard beside the house, Carla had managed to stop crying, though her eyes were still raw. It was the same effect her sister's phone calls always had on her, and she was surprised she didn't feel worse.

Margie lived way down south, in Houston. She had escaped from their family's rotting little trailer outside Trenton the day she had turned eighteen. Their father had cried for months, whimpering in his corner chair about "my little Margie," a phrase he'd picked up standing on the street in front of some store window. For six months he had cried, then a valve blew in his heart, dropping him all splotched in red-and-white patches to the floor, where Carla found him just before she turned sweet sixteen. When her mother called Margie to tell her, the conversation could not have lasted for more than three minutes.

When Mike came through the door, the sharp crack of the bare wood made her jump. She gazed at him for a minute, wondering if she dared show him the tears, but the glare in his eyes made her stiffen immediately.

"What the hell's the matter with you?"

Carla dabbed once at her eyes and shoved the tissue down the side of the seat cushion. "Margie called," she said.

"What for?" He moved across the dark room and dropped onto the couch. "She have to tell you about every wheeze and moan your old lady made this week?"

"Mom died last night." She kept her voice steady. "The funeral's on Tuesday."

"So?"

"So, she wants me to come down and help out for a few days," Carla said. When he did not respond, she continued,

"There's just enough in the savings account for me to take one of those People's flights down tomorrow."

She watched wearily as Mike inhaled deeply and let it slide out.

"We can't afford it," he said flatly. "Besides, you've got a family to take care of right here."

"Now, I do," she replied sharply.

"What's that supposed to mean?"

"You know damned well what it's supposed to mean!"

"Carla, look. Your mother and your sister couldn't give a damn about you. Margie's probably just all set up to play the grieving daughter and that damned accountant husband of hers is too cheap to hire some help. She just wants you to come housekeep for her, while she sucks up all the attention. She doesn't give a squat about your mother."

"She cared enough to take her in when I couldn't."

"The only damned reason she took her in is because she's still feeling guilty about killing your old man, and you know it."

"Margie did not kill daddy. He had a heart attack, that's all."

"Yeah, like the one you're trying to give me." He stood up, finished with her and the problem. "Where's Davey?"

"In the kitchen," she said, resigned, leaning back into her chair. "He's peeling the potatoes."

"He's what? Oh, Christ." He stomped out of the room.

A few seconds later she heard the screen door in the kitchen slam and the Shelby start up. She knew the potatoes would be left half-done in the sink. They'd be back in an hour, expecting supper to be hot and on the table.

Spreading her hands over the tough, damp fabric of the arms of the chair, she scraped her palms back and forth. Silently, she raised herself to her feet and headed toward the kitchen. Thinking about Mother Corbin.

A light drizzle fell during dinner and when it disappeared a sheen lay on the streets and buildings. Mike and Davey pushed from the table without a word. As they left the kitchen, Davey began running up the steps to his room but Mike called him back.

"Hey, why don't you just sit and talk with the old man for a while?"

As she filled the sink with dishes, Carla could hear the boy clump back down the few stairs, sighing heavily. The running water drowned out the sounds of their harsh whispers, but once the washing was done, she could hear them, their voices louder, lulled into false privacy by her apparent absence.

"She's just an old bitch," Davey was saying.

"Yeah, I know what you mean." Mike was laying it on heavy with his best buddy-buddy drawl. "We had an old crow like that used to live up the street from us when I was a kid, too. My mother kept warning us about her. 'She's as old as sin,' she'd say, 'and twice as dangerous.' And ten times as ugly, we'd tell her. She used to give us hell, until we fried her cat in a garbage can one Halloween. You should have heard the racket it put up. The lousy old bitch called the cops on us, too. You can't get away from them; they're all over the damned place. They must grow them out of prunes or something."

"Yeah, she's always messing up our fun."

"How do you mean?"

"Well, you know all that long grass she has growing down from the steps in front of her house?" Davey asked, slyly falling into his father's rhythms. "That real long stuff, ain't been cut in a coon's age?"

Mike said, "Uh-huh," though he didn't sound too sure.

"It's great rolling down and hiding in it, playing jungle and kind of like that. Well, every time we try, one of her windows opens up and a bucket of water gets chucked out at us." Carla could hear Davey slap the arm of the couch in indignation. "It always stinks, too. Like piss-water."

"So do something about it."

"Whadda ya mean? Do what?" the boy asked, leaning forward now, anxious.

"Give her a shot of her own medicine." Mike was grinning, you could hear it in his voice. "Drop some burning dog shit on her porch. Just wrap it in waxed paper, light it, drop it in front of her door, ring the bell, and run like hell."

"What'll that do?"

"She'll try to stamp it out, bonehead."

"Yeah," Davey screamed, and laughed. "What else can we do?"

Carla immediately grew more nervous at the word "we."

"I'll show you." Old springs creaked as Mike stood up. "You go get your pals and I'll meet you down the corner in a couple of minutes. Here's a buck; go to Housemann's and get a dozen eggs."

"We gonna egg her? That's nothing."

"When we suck them and load them with ink and ammonia it will be."

"Great!"

The door slammed and Davey was gone, whooping down the wet street.

Mike stepped into the kitchen, where Carla was just finishing up the drying, and started rummaging around in the cabinets under the sink.

"Mike, why don't you just leave the old lady alone. The kids'll get in trouble."

"Oh, shut up, will ya? They're only boys."

"You're not."

"You got dishes to do?" he said sharply.

"Hmm." She turned back to face the wall, rubbing the last plate harder than ever.

"Well, do them then. Christ, don't you remember what it was like being a kid?"

Then he was gone, too.

It was after ten when the police brought them home. And one of Davey's little friends, Paul Scarborough, was dead.

Although Mike and Davey had been gone for almost four hours, Carla wasn't too worried. It would not have been the first time she'd misread Mike's intentions. Often he would change his plans at the last minute, keeping Davey out to watch a meteor shower or taking him to an R-rated movie, even on a school night. There was just no consistency to her life anymore.

After scrubbing and rescrubbing the kitchen floor, she decided to settle down and watch a movie on their new cable tv. If they couldn't come home at a decent hour, she thought, they could damn well turn down their own beds. It was easy to be brave, to refuse them her services as homemaker and chief doormat. Especially when they weren't home. But she knew fully well she'd start the cycle all over again the minute she heard them on the steps.

When the lights atop the police car tore their way through the windows, however, that was all the spurring she needed. Struggling momentarily with the door, she burst from the house only to freeze before she reached the sidewalk. The driver was bent over, leaning into the opened rear door of the squad car, shifting legs, guiding arms. Davey stood by the fender behind him. His head was bowed and his hands were clasped at his elbows.

The officer emerged, pulling Mike erect and leading him by the arm to the porch. Carla ran past them, squatted down by her son and threw her arms around him.

"Honey, are you all right?" The words hurt her throat, but she could see that he was crying exhaustedly, as if the worst of it was long gone yet the ghost of some terrible memory would linger forever behind those soft, wide eyes.

Davey sniveled and nodded his head.

She wrapped her arm around his back—he was far too old for her to carry him, though her inability pained her now—and walked him slowly to the house, her body hovering over him like a willow.

As they came into the living room, the officer was lowering Mike onto the ratty couch. He set the older man down carefully and turned to Carla.

"Your son's all right, Mrs. Hensler." He took a handkerchief from his back pocket and wiped his forehead, then waved it toward Mike. "He's in a bit of bad shape, though. The doctor's given him a shot, said to keep him quiet and rested for the next few days. He's had one hell of a shock."

Carla stared at the young man, with his cropped red hair and spotty complexion, heard him sounding so knowledge-able, yet she could tell he was only mouthing someone else's words.

"Thank you," she said automatically. "Thank you, offi-cer. I'll take care of him."

He hesitated a moment and she thought he was about to say something she would not want to hear, so she turned away.

"Yes, ma'am," he said finally. "Goodnight." Then he stepped gently around her and moved quickly out the door to his car. After a few seconds, the flashing lights blinked off and she heard him pull away.

Gazing briefly at her husband, she led Davey upstairs to his bedroom, changed him into his pajamas, slid him snugly under the covers, then messed them up immediately as she held and rocked him until he fell into a deep sleep. An hour later she left the room quietly on the balls of her feet and crept back down to the living room.

Mike sat on the couch where the policeman had left him. Not a muscle had moved. He looked as if he hadn't even shut his eyes for a second. Lightly, she touched his arm.

"Mike?" He did not respond. "Mike, honey."

He turned his head slowly. For the first time she saw how strained and red his eyes were. His mouth flapped obscenely as he tried to say something, but no sound emerged. Just a slight wheeze, like an old man's.

The shot the doctor had given him eventually took effect enough that Carla managed to get him up to their room and into bed. His body—or was it his mind? she wondered briefly—seemed to be fighting the drug. His muscles relaxed and his eyelids fluttered, but he would not sleep. He struggled fiercely to stay awake, to talk. And by the early morning he had told her everything.

It had only taken Davey about ten minutes to round up three of his best friends and meet his father down at Housemann's Market, the same store where Mother Corbin did her shopping. He had tried to get that wise-ass, Jeff Morton, to come too, but Jeff wasn't about to do anything with "a bunch of kids and their old man." So Davey had said the hell with him, and by the time Mike arrived, he and his friends were waiting expectantly outside the store. Davey held a brown paper bag in his hands, clutching the top closed and patting it.

When Mike walked up to them with a paper sack of his own "goodies," Davey quickly said. "Dad, aren't you going to show us how to get old Mother Corbin good? Didn't you say that, Dad?"

"Come off it, Davey." Joey Spratz obviously did not believe anyone's father would do such a thing. "My dad would whip our behinds good if he caught us doing something like that."

"Not my dad!" Davey looked proudly at his father.

"That's right, boy," Mike said to Joey. "Old ladies are always fair game, even after you grow up."

Ralph Brokaw, a lanky towhead, nodded in agreement.

"Just don't marry one," Mike said, then broke into laughing. The boys made retching sounds and laughed, too.

"My father . . ." began a short lad standing behind Davey, but the words stopped immediately.

Mike stared at him and the boy squirmed. "That's Paul, Dad," Davey said. "He's my best friend at school." He put his arm around his friend's shoulder and brought him up next to him.

"Paul, huh?" Mike inspected him closely.

"Yes, sir," Paul said bravely, bolstered by Davey's confidence. "Paul Scarborough."

"Okay, boys. Let's go get her."

They took off screaming in the direction of the old lady's house, but Mike called them back. "Hey, we've got to be quiet about this. Surprising them's half the fun. Besides, we've got to make plans first."

He led them to a vacant lot down the street. The tall grass was still damp but it was only a block over from where Davey said Mother Corbin's house was. Mike began to remember it. It was a miniature mansion, complete with turrets, built about sixty years ago but trying desperately to look like it should be over a hundred years old. Narrow steps led up to a porch that ran along the entire front and swept around one side. A wide, humped lawn lay before it, sloping steeply down to the sidewalk. It crouched in on its neighbors' yards, cut off only by a spiked wrought iron fence that crept around the sides and back of the house only a few feet from the walls.

The usual buggy old house, Mike thought. There'd be newspapers moldering in the downstairs rooms and a dozen cats making the whole place smell like an open sewer. The attic—not to mention those great turrets—would be completely unused for the last thirty years at least; the old bitch too tired to climb the steep stairs anymore. All in all, it was just another old lady's house, going to waste, falling down around her ears, not worth anything to her. Fixed up it might be nice, but you could never pry the old bitch out. Even when they died it seemed another ancient hag just took their place, as if they circulated from town to town.

In the lot, he sat before the boys on a crate and asked Davey for his Swiss army knife. Then each of them took three eggs, and following his instructions, opened a crack in the small end and began sucking out part of the white.

"You leave the yellow in," he said. "Stinks like hell when it dries up in the sun. Even worse than the ammonia."

Mike dumped the contents of his bag on the ground and carefully began filling the partially hollowed shells. Once filled with the mixture of yolk, ammonia, and India ink, he sealed the tiny cracks with pieces of electrical tape. He was just about finished with his three when he noticed that Paul hadn't even begun to suck out his first egg yet. Mike nudged his son and nodded toward the kid.

"Come on, Paul," Davey said. "You gotta suck them before we can fill them."

"I don't want to. I'll use them just like this."

"Oh, grow the hell up, will you?" Mike jibed.

Paul just stared at him.

"Pauley's afraid." Ralph laughed.

"I am not," he shouted. "I . . . I just don't throw very good." He turned to Davey.

"That's right," he said. "We don't want to waste them." He took the fragile grenades from Paul's hands and gave one to each of the others.

"Well, what's he going to do then?" asked Joey Spratz.

Mike started to tell him to go the hell home, but Davey piped up in defense of his friend. "He can be our lookout."

"Yeah," Paul agreed quickly. "I got real good eyes."

Anxious to get on with it, they all agreed.

"Okay," Mike said. "You can climb up on top of the porch and look in the windows to let us know where she is."

Ten minutes later the street was dark and they surrounded the house. No light shone downstairs and Mike boosted Paul up to the rain gutter around the porch and watched as the boy clung tightly to the loose, rotting shingles.

"Okay," he whispered up to the boy, "crawl up to those windows and see if you can see where she is."

Paul swiveled his head and looked up the inclined roof, then back down at Mike with pleading eyes.

"Get going," Mike said through gritted teeth. "We haven't got all night." And slowly the boy inched his way up the slope.

Mike ran around the house, asking the other kids, "Anybody see anything?"

They'd all shook their heads.

"She can't be downstairs or we would've seen her, Dad."

"Right. Let's get back around front and see what Paul's doing."

Gathering together, they moved around the house and stared up at Paul. He was standing at the very top of the porch roof, hugging the wall of the second floor beside a corner window. He did not speak, but pointed sharply around his body to the glass. After a second, he brought his arm back and pressed tightly into the wall, not looking down.

Davey shot him an okay-sign and grinned at his father.

"All right," Mike asked. "You guys ready?"

They nodded.

Just as they were all about to throw, Paul thrust out his hands and they stopped.

"Let me down first." His voice was a harsh whisper, caught between fear and panic.

"No, stay there," Mike called up. "We don't want to lose her. Just move around to the other side."

Paul stared at him in disbelief.

"Go on!"

As quickly as he could, the boy slid to the corner of the building and let his hand swim around the edge, still hugging tightly to the wall above the slanted roof. But as he came to the edge, Mike yelled, "Now!" and two eggs smashed through the window. Another splattered near Paul's outstretched hand.

"Again," Mike ordered. And the missiles launched.

A second after they landed, two more flying through the

shattered glass, a terrible screeching burst from the room, and a bucket of water flew from the jagged hole. Then Mother Corbin herself was hanging out the window, screaming and banging on the sill with the bucket.

The boys started to run, but Mike took aim and threw one more doctored egg. It missed its target and hit Paul square in the mouth.

The boy staggered against the wall, clawing at his face. His foot shot backward as he spun and he flopped onto his back, bouncing down the sharp incline.

Mike ran to the side to catch him, but before he got there Paul pitched off the roof and landed on two of the filed points of the iron fence. The black spears drove through the back of his chest and neck. He hung there, bent backward and staring into Mike's eyes.

As he started to scream, a small hand took his and led him away. In a quickly closing portion of his mind, he heard a whimpering voice saying over and over again, "Daddy . . . Daddy . . ."

Carla watched him finally fall asleep as the last words blurred from his lips. She was horrified. For the first time, she realized how much she actually hated that rotten maggot of a man lying beside her. She rose from the bed and left him drifting off. She'd sleep on the couch tonight, and tomorrow . . . well, tomorrow she'd see, but either way she was through with him, now and forever.

As she closed the door behind her and silently paced down the hall, she noticed a rhythmic thumping coming from Davey's room. Gently, she touched the knob, opened the door, and peered in.

Davey was sitting upright in the middle of his bed. His eyes stared blankly ahead but she could tell he was seeing nothing in his room. In his hand was the Swiss army knife Mike had bought him when he'd returned last September. He was plunging it into the pillow on his lap, over and over again, tearing it to shreds.

That Wednesday Davey did not go to school. Instead he accompanied his mother to the cemetery for Paul's burial.

He was a bit more animated that day. He'd taken to long walks and somehow they seemed to prevent the nightmares and hysterics of the previous Sunday night. As they drove with the procession from the church to the graveyard, his eyes flew over every sidewalk and house they passed. Squinting against the sunlight he inspected every passerby, every shaded porch, but with no sign of recognition.

When they arrived home, he asked for permission to go outside for a while, and sat neatly on the front steps, leaning against the bare, splintering rail.

Carla went up to see if Mike had gotten out of bed yet. He had not moved since the accident and had barely spoken in the three days either. She tried the knob and found it locked.

"Mike?"

Something creaked against the inside of the door.

"Mike, open this door." She'd lost all patience with him two days before. He refused to acknowledge the terrible thing he had done. The Scarboroughs were even thinking of bringing charges against him, but all he did was holler that he wanted to be left alone. Whenever Carla was in the room with him, he scrutinized her every move. He did not even ask her why she was sleeping on the couch now; the situation seemed to suit him just fine. But this was getting ridiculous.

Carla began pounding on the door.

"Mike! Open up, goddamnit!"

"Go away!" He sounded worse than ever. His words came out cracking and hoarse and so weak she could barely hear them.

"Mike, it's Carla. Open the door."

"Carla?" Oh my God, she thought, he's whimpering.

A shrill wooden screech came through the door and the lock turned. Mike opened it slightly and peeked around the edge. Behind him Carla saw he was using their heavy oak bedframe as a barricade.

"Carla," he said again. "Are you alone?"

"Of course, I'm alone. The cops probably won't be here to take you to jail for at least another hour." She wanted to be cruel, but this seemed only to excite him.

"Really," he said, hope shining in his eyes like a fever. "Do you really think they'll come take me to jail?"

"For Christ's sake." She squeezed through the doorway, driving him back into the room. "Will you stop all this and come downstairs for a while? You should talk with Davey. You haven't said a word to him since Sunday night, and he's confused as hell."

"He's confused," Mike replied bitterly, the light fading from his eyes. "Well, fuck the little bastard! He's confused. Oh, I love that. He's the one who got me into this and now *she's* after me and all you can think about is that the little bastard's confused. Oh, Jesus."

Carla stepped warily back toward the door. "Who's after you? What are you talking about?"

"Her! That old bitch!"

"Mother Corbin?"

"It's not Mother anything." He was shouting at the top of his lungs. "I don't know what you call her, but that old bitch in the house is Mrs. Ferguson! I know. She looked right at me."

"Who?"

"Who? Who?" He was mocking her. "The old lady with the cats. My God, it's been over twenty years. How the hell did she find me?"

"What the hell are you talking about?"

He turned on her quickly, his voice almost gone with his screaming. "Get out!"

Carla moved out into the hall and closed the door, praying he'd lock it again. She could hear him talking weakly to himself.

"Won't get me . . . none of them." Then his soft, boyish laugh. "Yeah, must hatch them out of prunes."

The sun was going down as Carla descended the stairs. She'd have to take Davey away. She did not know where, but they had to get out of that house, and now. There was no telling what Mike might do.

"Davey," she called, stepping out on to the porch. He was no longer sitting against the rail. "Davey," she cried louder. She gazed up and down the street, but he was nowhere to be seen.

She waited a moment, listening, then called his name once more.

A voice came from behind her.

"Where is he?"

It was Mike.

She did not wait for him to ask again. Jumping from the porch she ran down the street, screaming her son's name.

"I know where he is, Carla," Mike called after her from the front door. "I know. I know. I know." And just before she rounded the corner, she heard him say, "They won't give me a goddamn chance, not one!"

By the time Carla decided to check Mother Corbin's house, it had grown late. The moon showed only its first quarter and the wind had gone cold.

As she approached the old house, she could see a few wavering lights in the upstairs windows. Candle flames, she thought. But why would an old lady use candles? Most elderly people were terribly afraid of even the slightest risk of fire. The front window on the second floor had a sheet of heavy plastic covering it. It flapped in the wind, making a harsh snapping sound like a teacher's wooden ruler.

Climbing the path past the undulating lawn, she noticed that the front door was open. She moved to it, stuck her head in, rapped on the jamb a few times, and called, "Hello?"

There was no answer. But after a minute she began to make out a low moaning coming from somewhere upstairs, apparently from the room where she had seen the lights.

"Mother Corbin, are you all right?"

She waited a few more minutes but still no one responded. Worrying that the old woman might be hurt—and with burning candles around yet—Carla stepped carefully inside and moved up the stairs to the second floor. The old woman had been through so much, she thought, pitying her. It must be terrible to be old and unwanted, to have even the children hate you.

As she reached the upper landing, a door opened before her and a familiar voice said, "Come in, Carla. We're almost finished with them."

She seemed to have lost control of herself, for she stepped over the threshold and entered the room, while her mind urged her to run, to hide, but the voice pulled her too powerfully.

In the center of the room Mike sat in a wheelchair. Several bent, crumpled figures dressed all in old browns and blacks encircled him. The low moaning she had heard from downstairs came from these haggard creatures, and suddenly she realized that they were singing. And gradually, as she watched, Mike began issuing a soft, canting wail that rose and fell with their rhythm.

Then she saw Davey, standing in a corner next to a table, and ran to him. He was dazed, unmoving. As she hugged him tightly to her chest, she saw a few, relatively small tatters of shriveled meat lying on the table behind him. There was a little blood but not much more. Bending to look into his eyes, she reached for his hands and found his army knife, clutched tightly and slick with drying blood. Yet, somehow, she did not scream; from somewhere a memory peeked from behind a mound in her brain and she was not afraid. Concerned for her son, yes, but not afraid.

Behind her she could hear clothes rustling, and the squeaking of the wheels from the old wheelchair. One of the figures broke from the circle and came to her, rested a weak, gnarled hand on her shoulder.

"It's all right, Carla," she heard her mother say. "Take Davey home. He's safe from us now. So are you."

Carla nodded her head in thanks, but could not bring herself to look at the women around her as she moved toward the door with her son. She wanted desperately to take him home, but before she reached the staircase, she forced one last blazing glare back at what had been her husband.

His clothes were gone, lying in a ragged pile on the floor. A ratty brown housedress was being pulled down over his narrowed shoulders, black support stockings rolled up his now hairless legs. A dozen tiny blades swirled around his face and arms and hands, carving deep bloodless folds, etching his shrunken skin with coarse wrinkles.

And all the while the old women were cackling to him, "Leave me alone . . . I'm just an old woman . . . my heart's not good. . . ."

They clasped one of his hands around the shawl they had draped over his shoulders and held it tightly against his frail chest.

"Leave me alone," he said in his new, indistinguishable old voice. "I'm just an old woman . . . my heart's not good. . . ."

A flashback to Ray Bradbury here, though with an underlying shadow considerably darker than Bradbury ever used. Which unnerves you more—staying in the here and now and continuing to continue coping, or escaping to some other time/place where the grass may be greener, but it may also be dying.

Joe Lansdale lives and writes in Texas, has a lovely wife and a son, has done several novels, both mysteries and westerns, and is becoming a welcome regular in The Twilight Zone and other fantasy-oriented markets.

Fish Night

by Joe R. Lansdale

IT WAS A bleached-bone afternoon with a cloudless sky and a monstrous sun. The air trembled like a mass of gelatinous ectoplasm. No wind blew.

Through the swelter came a worn, black Plymouth, coughing and belching white smoke from beneath its hood. It wheezed twice, backfired loudly, died by the side of the road.

The driver got out and went around to the hood. He was a man in the hard winter years of life, with dead brown hair and a pot belly riding his hips. His shirt was open to the navel, the sleeves were rolled up past his elbows. The hair on his chest and arms was grey.

A younger man climbed out on the passenger side, went around front too. Yellow sweat explosions stained the pits of his white shirt. An unfastened, striped tie was draped over his neck like a pet snake that had died in its sleep.

"Well?" the younger man asked.

The old man said nothing. He opened the hood. A calliope note of steam blew out from the radiator in a white puff, rose to the sky, turned clear.

"Damn," the old man said, and he kicked the bumper of the Plymouth as if he were kicking a foe in the teeth. He got little satisfaction out of the action, just a nasty scuff on his brown wingtip and a jar to his ankle that hurt like hell.

"Well?" the young man repeated.

"Well what? What do you think? Dead as the can opener trade this week. Deader. The radiator's chickenpocked with holes."

"Maybe someone will come by and give us a hand."

"Sure."

"A ride anyway."

"Keep thinking that, college boy."

"Someone is bound to come along," the young man said.

"Maybe. Maybe not. Who else takes these cutoffs? The main highway, that's where everyone is. Not this little no account shortcut." He finished by glaring at the young man.

"I didn't make you take it," the young man snapped. "It was on the map. I told you about it, that's all. You chose it. You're the one that decided to take it. It's not my fault. Besides, who'd have expected the car to die?"

"I did tell you to check the water in the radiator, didn't I? Wasn't that back as far as El Paso?"

"I checked. It had water then. I tell you, it's not my fault. You're the one that's done all the Arizona driving."

"Yeah, yeah," the old man said, as if this were something he didn't want to hear. He turned to look up the highway.

No cars. No trucks. Just heat waves and miles of empty concrete in sight.

They seated themselves on the hot ground with their backs to the car. That way it provided some shade—but not much. They sipped on a jug of lukewarm water from the Plymouth and spoke little until the sun fell down. By then they had both mellowed a bit. The heat had vacated the sands and the desert chill had settled in. Where the warmth had made the pair snappy, the cold drew them together.

The old man buttoned his shirt and rolled down his sleeves while the young man rummaged a sweater out of the backseat. He put the sweater on, sat back down. "I'm sorry about this," he said suddenly.

"Wasn't your fault. Wasn't anyone's fault. I just got to yelling sometime, taking out the can opener trade on everything but the can openers and myself. The days of the door to door salesman are gone, son.''

"And I thought I was going to have an easy summer job," the young man said.

The old man laughed. "Bet you did. They talk a good line, don't they?''

"I'll say!''

"Make it sound like found money, but there ain't no found money, boy. Ain't nothing simple in this world. The company is the only one ever makes any money. We just get tireder and older with more holes in our shoes. If I had any sense I'd have quit years ago. All you got to make is this summer—''

"Maybe not that long.''

"Well, this is all I know. Just town after town, motel after motel, house after house, looking at people through screen wire while they shake their heads No. Even the cockroaches at the sleazy motels begin to look like little fellows you've seen before, like maybe they're door to door peddlers that have to rent rooms too.''

The young man chuckled. "You might have something there.''

They sat quietly for a moment, welded in silence. Night had full grip on the desert now. A mammoth gold moon and billions of stars cast a whitish glow from eons away.

The wind picked up. The sand shifted, found new places to lie down. The undulations of it, slow and easy, were reminiscent of the midnight sea. The young man, who had crossed the Atlantic by ship once, said as much.

"The sea?" the old man replied. "Yes, yes, exactly like that. I was thinking the same. That's part of the reason it bothers me. Part of why I was stirred up this afternoon. Wasn't just the heat doing it. There are memories of mine out here," he nodded at the desert, "and they're visiting me again.''

The young man made a face. "I don't understand.''

"You wouldn't. You shouldn't. You'd think I'm crazy.''

"I already think you're crazy. So tell me.''

The old man laughed pleasantly. "All right, but you can't laugh.''

"Okay."

A moment of silence moved between them. Finally the old man said, "It's fish night, boy. Tonight's the full moon and this is the right part of the desert if memory serves me, and the feel is right—I mean, doesn't the night feel like its made up of some soft fabric, that it's different from other nights, that it's like being inside a big dark bag, the sides of which are sprinkled with glitter, a spotlight at the top, at the open mouth, to serve as a moon?"

"You lost me."

The old man sighed. "But it feels different. Right? You can feel it too, can't you?"

"I suppose. Sort of thought it was just the desert air. I've never camped out in the desert before, and I guess it's just different."

"Different all right. You see, boy, this is the road I got stranded on twenty years back. I didn't know it at first, least not consciously. But down deep in my gut I must have known it, and that's why I got fried today. Maybe I knew all along I was taking this road, tempting fate, offering it, as the football people say, an instant replay."

"I still don't understand about fish night. What do you mean you were here before?"

"Not this exact spot, somewhere along in here. This was even less of a road back then than it is now. The Navajos were about the only ones who traveled it. My car conked out, like this one today, and I started walking instead of waiting. As I walked the fish came out. Swimming along in the starlight pretty as you please. Lots of them. All the colors of the rainbow. Small ones, big ones, thick ones, thin ones. You call it and they were there. Swam right up to me . . . *right through me!* Fish just as far as you could see. High up and low down to the ground.

"Hold on, boy. Don't start looking at me like that. Listen: You're a college boy, you know something about these things. I mean, about what was here before we were, before we crawled out of the sea and changed enough to call ourselves men. Weren't we once just slimy things, brothers to the things that swim?"

"I guess, but—"

"Millions and millions of years ago this was the sea bottom. Maybe even the birthplace of man. Who knows? I read that in some science books, boy, and I believe it. And I got to thinking this: If the ghost of people who have lived can haunt houses, why can't the ghost of creatures long dead haunt where they lived, float about in a ghostal sea?"

"Fish with a soul?"

"Don't go small mind on me, boy. Look here: Some of the Indians I've talked to up North tell me about a thing they call the manitou. That's a spirit. They believe everything has one. Rocks, trees, you name it. Even if the rock wears to dust or the tree gets cut to lumber, the manitou of it is still around."

"Then why can't you see these fish all the time?"

"Why can't we see ghosts all the time? Why do some of us never see them? Time's not right, that's why. It's a precious situation, and I figure its like some fancy time lock—like the banks use. The lock clicks open at the bank, and *tada*! money. Here it ticks open and we get the fish of a world long gone."

"Well, it's something to think about," the young man managed.

The old man grinned at him. "I don't blame you for thinking what you're thinking. But this happened to me twenty years ago and I've never forgotten it. I saw those fish for a good hour before they disappeared. A Navajo came along in an old pickup right after and I bummed a ride into town with him. I told him what I'd seen. He just looked at me and grunted. But I could tell he knew what I was talking about. I bet he'd seen it too, and probably not for the first time.

"I've heard that Navajos don't eat fish for some reason or another, boy, and I just bet it's the fish in the desert that keep them from it. Maybe they hold them sacred. And why not? It was like being in the presence of the creator; like crawling back inside your Mom and being unborn again, just kicking around in the liquids with no cares in the world."

"I don't know. That sounds sort of . . ."

"Fishy?" The old man laughed. "It does, it does. So this Navajo drove me to town and I got off. Next day I got my car fixed and went on. I've never taken that cutoff again—until today, and I think that was more than accident. My subconscious was driving me. That night scared me, boy, and I don't mind admitting it. But it was wonderful too, and I've never been able to get it out of my mind.''

The young man didn't know what to say.

The old man looked at him and smiled. ''I don't blame you,'' he said. ''Not even a little bit. Maybe I am crazy.''

They sat awhile longer with the desert night, and the old man took his false teeth out and poured some of the warm water on them to clean them of coffee and cigarettes.

''I hope we don't need that water,'' the young man said.

''You're right. Stupid of me! We'll sleep awhile, start walking before daylight. It's not too awful far to the next town. Ten miles at best.'' He put his teeth back in. ''We'll be just fine.''

The young man nodded.

No fish came. They did not discuss it. They crawled inside the car, the young man in the front seat, the old man in the back. They used their spare clothes to bundle under, to pad out the cold fingers of the night.

Long about midnight the old man came awake suddenly and lay with his hands behind his head and looked up and out the window opposite him, studied the crisp desert sky.

And a fish swam by.

Long and lean and speckled with all the colors of the world, flicking its tail as if in good-bye. Then it was gone.

The old man sat up. Outside, all about, were the fish—all sizes, colors and shapes.

''Hey, boy, wake up,'' the old man called.

The younger man moaned.

''Wake up.''

The young man, who had been resting face down on his arms, rolled over. ''What's the matter? Time to go?''

''The fish.''

''Not again.''

''Look!''

The young man sat up. His mouth fell down. His eyes bloated. Around and around the car, faster and faster in whirls of dark color, swam all manner of fish.

''Well, I'll be. . . . There's no water. How?''

''I told you, I told you.''

The old man reached for the door handle, but before he could pull it a fish swam lazily through the back window glass, swirled about the car, once, twice, passed through the old man's chest, whipped up and went out through the roof.

The old man cackled, jerked open the door. He bounced around beside the road. Leaped up to swat his hands through the spectral fish. "Like soap bubbles," he said. "No. Like smoke!"

The young man, his mouth still dangling, opened his door and got out. Even high up he could see the fish. Strange fish, like nothing he'd ever seen pictures of or imagined. They flittered and skirted about like flashes of light.

As he looked up, he saw, nearing the moon, a big dark cloud. The only cloud in the sky. That cloud tied him to reality suddenly, and he thanked the heavens for it. Normal things still happened. The whole world had not gone insane.

After a moment the old man quit hopping among the fish and came to lean on the car and hold his hand to his fluttering chest.

"Feel it, boy? Feel the presence of the sea? Doesn't it feel like the beating of your own mother's heart while you float inside the womb?"

And the younger man had to admit that he felt it, that inner rolling rhythm that is the tide of life and the pulsating heart of the sea.

"How?" the young man said. "Why?"

"The time lock, boy. The locks clicked open and the fish are free. Fish from a time before man was man. Before all this culture was weighing us down. Suddenly, I know it's true. The truth's been in me all the time. It's in us all."

"It's like time travel," the young man said. "From the past to the future, they've come all that way."

"Yes, yes, that's it. . . . Why, if they can come to our world, why can't we go to theirs? Release that spirit inside of us, tune into their time?"

"Now wait a minute."

"My God, that's it! They're pure, boy, pure. Clean and free of civilization's trappings. That must be it! They're pure and we're not. We're weighted down with technology. These clothes. That car."

The old man started removing his clothes.

"Hey!" the young man said. "You'll freeze."

"If you're pure, if you're completely pure," the old man mumbled, "that's it . . . yeah, that's the key."

"You've gone crazy."

"I won't look at the car," the old man yelled, running across the sand, trailing the last of his clothes behind him. He bounded about the desert like a jackrabbit. "God, God, nothing is happening, nothing," he moaned. "This isn't my world. I'm of that world. I want to float free in the belly of the sea, away from can openers and cars and—"

The young man called the old man's name. He did not seem to hear.

"I want to leave here," the old man yelled. "Leave this. . . ." Suddenly the old man was springing about again. "The teeth," he yelled. "It's the teeth. Dentist, science, foo." He punched a hand into his mouth, plucked the teeth free, tossed them over his shoulder, high and wide.

Even as the teeth fell the old man rose. He began to stroke. To swim up and up and up, moving like a pale pink seal among the fish.

In the light of the moon the young man could see the pouched jaws of the old man, holding the last of the future's air. Up went the old man, up, up, up, swimming strong in the long lost waters of a time gone by.

The young man began to strip his clothes. Maybe he could nab him, pull him down, put his clothes on him. Something . . . God, something . . . But, what if he couldn't come back? And there were the fillings in his teeth, the metal rod in his back from a motorcycle accident. No, unlike the old man, this was his world and he was tied to it. There was nothing he could do.

A great shadow weaved in front of the moon, made a wriggling slat of darkness that caused the young man to quit his shirt buttons and look up.

A big black rocket of a shape moved through the invisible sea; the granddaddy of all sharks, the seed for all of man's fears of the deeps.

It had the old man in its mouth, was swimming upward toward the golden light of the moon. The old man dangled from the creature's mouth like a ragged rat from a house cat's jaws. Blood blossomed out of him, weaved and coiled darkly in the invisible sea.

The young man trembled. Hastily rebuttoned his shirt. "Oh God," he said once.

Then along came that thick dark cloud, rolling right smack across the face of the moon.

Momentary darkness.

And when the cloud passed there was light once again, and an empty sky.

No fish.

No shark.

And no old man.

Just the night, the moon and the stars.

The past is past; let it lie. People who do not study history are doomed to repeat it. On the personal, as well as the global, scale, what we've done with and in our lives isn't always as important as whether or not we did it well enough to keep it where it belongs—in the past.

George R. R. Martin is a multiple award winner, known primarily for his finely-tuned and humane science fiction. He does, however, cross over now and then, as with this piece, and his latest novel, Fevre Dream (Poseidon Books), *without losing a thing in translation.*

Remembering Melody

by George R. R. Martin

TED WAS SHAVING when the doorbell sounded. It startled him so badly that he cut himself. His condominium was on the thirty-second floor, and Jack the doorman generally gave him advance warning of any prospective visitors. This had to be someone from the building, then. Except that Ted didn't know anyone in the building, at least not beyond the trade-smiles-in-the-elevator level.

"Coming," he shouted. Scowling, he snatched up a towel and wiped the lather from his face, then dabbed at his cut with a tissue. "Shit," he said loudly to his face in the mirror. He had to be in court this afternoon. If this was another Jehovah's Witness like the one who'd gotten past Jack last month, they were going to be in for a very rough time indeed.

The buzzer buzzed again. "Coming, dammit," Ted yelled. He made a final dab at the blood on his neck, then threw the tissue into the wastebasket and strode across the sunken living room to the door. He peered through the eyehole carefully before he opened. "Oh, hell," he muttered. Before she could buzz again, Ted slid off the chain and threw open the door.

"Hello, Melody," he said.

She smiled wanly. "Hi, Ted," she replied. She had an old suitcase in her hand, a battered cloth bag with a hideous

177

red-and-black plaid pattern, its broken handle replaced by a length of rope. The last time Ted had seen her, three years before, she'd looked terrible. Now she looked worse. Her clothes—shorts and a tie-dyed T-shirt—were wrinkled and dirty, and emphasized how gaunt she'd become. Her ribs showed through plainly; her legs were pipestems. Her long stringy blond hair hadn't been washed recently, and her face was red and puffy, as if she'd been crying. That was no surprise. Melody was always crying about one thing or another.

"Aren't you going to ask me in, Ted?"

Ted grimaced. He certainly didn't *want* to ask her in. He knew from past experience how difficult it was to get her out again. But he couldn't just leave her standing in the hall with her suitcase in hand. After all, he thought sourly, she was an old and dear friend. "Oh, sure," he said. He gestured. "Come on in."

He took her bag from her and set it by the door, then led her into the kitchen and put on some water to boil. "You look as though you could use a cup of coffee," he said, trying to keep his voice friendly.

Melody smiled again. "Don't you remember, Ted? I don't drink coffee. It's no good for you, Ted. I used to tell you that. Don't you remember?" She got up from the kitchen table and began rummaging through his cupboards. "Do you have any hot chocolate?" she asked. "I like hot chocolate."

"I don't drink hot chocolate," he said. "Just a lot of coffee."

"You shouldn't," she said. "It's no good for you."

"Yeah," he said. "Do you want juice? I've got juice."

Melody nodded. "Fine."

He poured her a glass of orange juice and led her back to the table, then spooned some Maxim into a mug while he waited for his kettle to whistle. "So," he asked, "what brings you to Chicago?"

Melody began to cry. Ted leaned back against the stove and watched her. She was a very noisy crier, and she produced an amazing amount of tears for someone who cried so often. She didn't look up until the water began to boil. Ted poured some into his cup and stirred in a teaspoon of sugar. Her face was redder and puffier than ever. Her eyes fixed on him accusingly. "Things have been real bad," she said. "I need help, Ted. I don't have any place to live. I thought maybe I could stay with you awhile. Things have been real bad."

"I'm sorry to hear that, Melody," Ted replied, sipping at his coffee thoughtfully. "You can stay here for a few days, if you want. But no longer. I'm not in the market for a room-mate." She always made him feel like such a bastard, but it was better to be firm with her right from the start.

Melody began to cry again when he mentioned roommates. "You used to say I was a *good* roommate," she whined. "We used to have fun, don't you remember? You were my friend."

Ted set down his coffee mug and looked at the kitchen clock. "I don't have time to talk about old times right now," he said. "I was shaving when you rang. I've got to get to the office." He frowned. "Drink your juice and make yourself at home. I've got to get dressed." He turned abruptly and left her weeping at the kitchen table.

Back in the bathroom, Ted finished shaving and tended to his cut more properly, his mind full of Melody. Already he could tell that this was going to be difficult. He felt sorry for her—she was messed up and miserably unhappy, with no one to turn to—but he wasn't going to let her inflict all her troubles on him. Not this time. She'd done it too many times before.

In his bedroom, Ted stared pensively into the closet for a long time before selecting the gray suit. He knotted his tie carefully in the mirror, scowling at his cut. Then he checked his briefcase to make sure all the papers on the Syndio case were in order, nodded, and walked back into the kitchen.

Melody was at the stove, making pancakes. She turned and smiled at him happily when he entered. "You remember my pancakes, Ted?" she asked. "You used to love it when I made pancakes, especially blueberry pancakes, you remember? You didn't have any blueberries, though, so I'm just making plain. Is that all right?"

"Jesus," Ted muttered. "Dammit, Melody, who said you should make *anything?* I told you I had to get to the office. I don't have time to eat with you. I'm late already. Anyway, I don't eat breakfast. I'm trying to lose weight.''

Tears began to trickle from her eyes again. ''But—but these are my special pancakes, Ted. What am I going to do with them? What am I going to *do?*''

''Eat them,'' Ted said. ''You could use a few extra pounds. Jesus, you look terrible. You look like you haven't eaten for a month.''

Melody's face screwed up and became ugly. ''You bastard,'' she said. ''You're supposed to be my *friend.*''

Ted sighed. ''Take it easy,'' he said. He glanced at his watch. ''Look, I'm fifteen minutes late already. I've got to go. You eat your pancakes and get some sleep. I'll be back around six. We can have dinner together and talk, all right? Is that what you want?''

''That would be nice,'' she said, suddenly contrite. ''That would be real nice.''

''Tell Jill I want to see her in my office, right away,'' Ted snapped to the secretary when he arrived. ''And get us some coffee, will you? I really need some coffee.''

''Sure.''

Jill arrived a few minutes after the coffee. She and Ted were associates in the same law firm. He motioned her to a seat and pushed a cup at her. ''Sit down,'' he said. ''Look, the date's off tonight. I've got problems.''

''You look it,'' she said. ''What's wrong?''

''An old friend showed up on my doorstep this morning.''

Jill arched one elegant eyebrow. ''So?'' she said. ''Reunions can be fun.''

''Not with Melody they can't.''

''Melody?'' she said. ''A pretty name. An old flame, Ted? What is it, unrequited love?''

''No,'' he said, ''no, it wasn't like that.''

''Tell me what it was like, then. You know I love the gory details.''

''Melody and I were roommates back in college. Not just us—don't get the wrong idea. There were four of us. Me and a guy named Michael Englehart, Melody and another girl,

Anne Kaye. The four of us shared a big run-down house for two years. We were—friends.''

"Friends?" Jill looked skeptical.

Ted scowled at her. "Friends," he repeated. "Oh, hell, I slept with Melody a few times. With Anne, too. And both of them balled Michael a time or two. But when it happened, it was just kind of—kind of *friendly*, you know? Our love lives were mostly with outsiders. We used to tell each other our troubles, swap advice, cry on one another's shoulders. Hell, I know it sounds weird. It was 1970, though. I had hair down to my ass. Everything was weird." He sloshed the dregs of his coffee around in the cup and looked pensive. "They were good times, too. Special times. Sometimes I'm sorry they had to end. The four of us were close, really close. I loved those people."

"Watch out," Jill said. "I'll get jealous. My roommate and I cordially despised each other." She smiled. "So what happened?"

Ted shrugged. "The usual story," he said. "We graduated, drifted apart. I remember the last night in the old house. We smoked a ton of dope and got very silly. Swore eternal friendship. We weren't ever going to be strangers, no matter what happened, and if any of us ever needed help, well, the other three would always be there. We sealed the bargain with—well, kind of an orgy."

Jill smiled. "Touching," she said. "I never dreamed you had it in you."

"It didn't last, of course," Ted continued. "We tried, I'll give us that much. But things changed too much. I went on to law school, wound up here in Chicago. Michael got a job with a publishing house in New York City. He's an editor at Random House now, been married and divorced, two kids. We used to write. Now we trade Christmas cards. Anne's a teacher. She was down in Phoenix the last I heard, but that was four, five years ago. Her husband didn't like the rest of us much, the one time we had a reunion. I think Anne must have told him about the orgy."

"And your house guest?"

"Melody," he sighed. "She became a problem. In college, she was wonderful: gutsy, pretty, a real free spirit. But afterwards, she couldn't cut it. She tried to make it as a painter for a couple of years, but she wasn't good enough. Got nowhere. She went through a couple of relationships that turned sour, then married some guy about a week after she'd met him in a singles bar. That was terrible. He used to get drunk and beat her. She took about six months of it, and finally got a divorce. He still came around to beat her up for a year, until he finally got frightened off. After that, Melody got into drugs—bad. She spent some time in an asylum. When she got out, it was more of the same. She can't hold a job or stay away from drugs. Her relationships don't last more than a few weeks. She's let her body go to hell." He shook his head.

Jill pursed her lips. "Sounds like a lady who needs help," she said.

Ted flushed and grew angry. "You think I don't know that? You think we haven't tried to help her? *Jesus!* When she was trying to be an artist, Michael got her a couple of cover assignments from the paperback house he was with. Not only did she blow the deadlines, but she got into a screaming match with the art director. Almost cost Michael his job. I flew to Cleveland and handled her divorce for her, gratis. Flew back a couple of months later and spent quite a while there trying to get the cops to give her protection against her ex-hubby. Anne took her in when she had no place to live, got her into a drug rehabilitation program. In return, Melody tried to seduce her boyfriend—said she wanted to *share* him, like they'd done in the old days. All of us have lent her money. She's never paid back any of it. And we've listened to her troubles, God but we've listened to her troubles. There was a period a few years ago when she'd phone every week, usually collect, with some new sad story. She cried over the phone a lot. If *Queen for a Day* was still on TV, Melody would be a natural!"

"I'm beginning to see why you're not thrilled by her visit," Jill said dryly. "What are you going to do?"

"I don't know," Ted replied. "I shouldn't have let her in. The last few times she's called, I just hung up on her, and that seemed to work pretty well. Felt guilty about it at first, but that passed. This morning, though, she looked so pathetic that I didn't know how to send her away. I suppose eventually I'll have to get brutal and go through a scene. Nothing else works. She'll make a lot of accusations, remind me of what good friends we were and the promises we made, threaten to kill herself. Fun times ahead.''

"Can I help?" Jill asked.

"Pick up my pieces afterwards," Ted said. "It's always nice to have someone around afterwards to tell you that you're not a son of a bitch even though you just kicked an old dear friend out into the gutter."

He was terrible in court that afternoon. His thoughts were full of Melody, and the strategies that most occupied him concerned how to get rid of her most painlessly, instead of the case at hand. Melody had danced flamenco on his psyche too many times before; Ted wasn't going to let her leech off him this time, nor leave him an emotional wreck.

When he got back to his condo with a bag of Chinese food under his arm—he'd decided he didn't want to take her out to a restaurant—Melody was sitting nude in the middle of his conversation pit, giggling and sniffing some white powder. She looked up at Ted happily when he entered. "Here," she said. "I scored some coke."

"*Jesus*," he swore. He dropped the Chinese food and his briefcase, and strode furiously across the carpet. "I don't *believe* you," he roared. "I'm a *lawyer*, for Chrissakes. Do you want to get me disbarred?"

Melody had the coke in a little paper square and was sniffing it from a rolled-up dollar bill. Ted snatched it all away from her, and she began to cry. He went to the bathroom and flushed it down the toilet, dollar bill and all. Except it wasn't a dollar bill, he saw as it was sucked out of sight. It was a twenty. That made him even angrier. When he returned to the living room, Melody was still crying.

"Stop that," he said. "I don't want to hear it. And put some clothes on." Another suspicion came to him. "Where did you get the money for that stuff?" he demanded. "Huh, *where?*"

Melody whimpered. "I sold some stuff," she said in a timid voice. "I didn't think you'd mind. It was good coke."

She shied away from him and threw an arm across her face, as if Ted was going to hit her.

Ted didn't need to ask whose stuff she'd sold. He knew; she'd pulled the same trick on Michael years before, or so he'd heard. He sighed. "Get dressed," he repeated wearily. "I brought Chinese food." Later he could check what was missing and phone the insurance company.

"Chinese food is no good for you," Melody said. "It's full of monosodium glutamate. Gives you headaches, Ted." But she got to her feet obediently, if a bit unsteadily, went off towards the bathroom, and came back a few minutes later wearing a halter top and a pair of ratty cutoffs. Nothing else, Ted guessed. A couple of years ago she must have decided that underwear was no good for you.

Ignoring her comment about monosodium glutamate, Ted found some plates and served up the Chinese food in his dining nook. Melody ate it meekly enough, drowning everything in soy sauce. Every few minutes she giggled at some private joke, then grew very serious again and resumed eating. When she broke open her fortune cookie, a wide smile lit her face. "Look, Ted," she said happily, passing the little slip of paper across to him.

He read it. OLD FRIENDS ARE THE BEST FRIENDS, it said. "Oh, shit," he muttered. He didn't even open his own. Melody wanted to know why. "You ought to read it, Ted," she told him. "It's bad luck if you don't read your fortune cookie."

"I don't want to read it," he said. "I'm going to change out of this suit." He rose. "Don't do anything."

But when he came back, she'd put an album on the stereo. At least she hadn't sold that, he thought gratefully.

"Do you want me to dance for you?" she asked. "Remember how I used to dance for you and Michael? Real sexy . . . You used to tell me how good I danced. I could of been a dancer if I'd wanted." She did a few dance steps in the middle of his living room, stumbled, and almost fell. It was grotesque.

"Sit down, Melody," Ted said, as sternly as he could manage. "We have to talk."

She sat down.

"Don't cry," he said before he started. "You understand that? I don't want you to cry. We can't talk if you're going to cry every time I say anything. You start crying and this conversation is over."

Melody nodded. "I won't cry, Ted," she said. "I feel much better now than this morning. I'm with you now. You make me feel better."

"You're *not* with me, Melody. Stop that."

Her eyes filled up with tears. "You're my friend, Ted. You and Michael and Anne, you're the special ones."

He sighed. "What's wrong, Melody? Why are you here?"

"I lost my job, Ted," she said.

"The waitress job?" he asked. The last time he'd seen her, three years ago, she'd been waiting tables in a bar in Kansas City.

Melody blinked at him, confused. "Waitress?" she said. "No, Ted. That was before. That was in Kansas City. Don't you remember?"

"I remember very well," he said. "What job was it you lost?"

"It was a shitty job," Melody said. "A factory job. It was in Iowa. In Des Moines. Des Moines is a shitty place. I didn't come to work, so they fired me. I was strung out, you know? I needed a couple days off. I would have come back to work. But they fired me." She looked close to tears again. "I haven't had a good job in a long time, Ted. I was an art major. You remember? You and Michael and Anne used to have my drawings hung up in your rooms. You still have my drawings, Ted?"

"Yes," he lied. "Sure. Somewhere." He'd gotten rid of them years ago. They reminded him too much of Melody, and that was too painful.

"Anyway, when I lost my job, Johnny said I wasn't bringing in any money. Johnny was the guy I lived with. He said he wasn't gonna support me, that I had to get some job, but I couldn't. I *tried*, Ted, but I couldn't. So Johnny talked to some man, and he got me this job in a massage parlor, you know. And he took me down there, but it was crummy. I didn't want to work in no massage parlor, Ted. I used to be an art major."

"I remember, Melody," Ted said. She seemed to expect him to say something.

Melody nodded. "So I didn't take it, and Johnny threw me out. I had no place to go, you know. And I thought of you, and Anne, and Michael. Remember the last night? We all said that if anyone ever needed help . . ."

"I remember, Melody," Ted said. "Not as often as you do, but I remember. You don't ever let any of us forget it, do you? But let it pass. What do you want this time?" His tone was flat and cold.

"You're a lawyer, Ted," she said.

"Yes."

"So, I thought—" Her long, thin fingers plucked nervously at her face. "I thought maybe you could get me a job. I could be a secretary, maybe. In your office. We could be together again, every day, like it used to be. Or maybe—" She brightened visibly, "—maybe I could be one of those people who draw pictures in the courtroom. You know. Like of Patty Hearst and people like that. On TV. I'd be good at that."

"Those artists work for the TV stations," Ted said patiently. "And there are no openings in my office. I'm sorry, Melody. I can't get you a job."

Melody took that surprisingly well. "All right, Ted," she said. "I can find a job, I guess. I'll get one all by myself. Only—only let me live here, okay? We can be roommates again."

"Oh, Jesus," Ted said. He sat back and crossed his arms. "No," he said flatly.

Melody took her hand away from her face and stared at him imploringly. "Please, Ted," she whispered. "Please."

"No," he said. The word hung there, chill and final.

"You're my *friend*, Ted," she said. "You *promised*."

"You can stay here a week," he said. "No longer. I have my own life, Melody. I have my own problems. I'm tired of dealing with yours. We all are. You're nothing but problems. In college, you were fun. You're not fun any longer. I've helped you and helped you and helped you. How goddam much do you want out of me?" He was getting angrier as he talked. "Things change, Melody," he said brutally. "People change. You can't hold me forever to some dumb promise I made when I was stoned out of my mind back in college. I'm not responsible for your life. Tough up, dammit. Pull yourself together. I can't do it for you, and I'm sick of all your shit. I don't even like to see you anymore, Melody, you know that?''

She whimpered. ''Don't say that, Ted. We're friends. You're special. As long as I have you and Michael and Anne, I'll never be alone, don't you see?''

''You *are* alone,'' he said. Melody infuriated him.

''No, I'm not,'' she insisted. ''I have my friends, my special friends. They'll help me. You're my *friend*, Ted.''

''I used to be your friend,'' he replied.

She stared at him, her lip trembling, hurt beyond words. For a moment he thought that the dam was going to burst, that Melody was finally about to break down and begin one of her marathon crying jags. Instead, a change came over her face. She paled perceptibly, and her lips drew back slowly, and her expression settled into a terrible mask of anger. She was hideous when she was angry. ''You bastard,'' she said.

Ted had been this route too. He got up from the couch and walked to his bar. ''Don't start,'' he said, pouring himself a glass of Chivas Regal on the rocks. ''The first thing you throw, you're out on your ass. Got that, Melody?''

''You scum,'' she repeated. ''You were never my friend. None of you were. You lied to me, made me trust you, used me. Now you're all so high and mighty and I'm nothing, and you don't want to know me. You don't want to help me. You never wanted to help me.''

''I did help you,'' Ted pointed out. ''Several times. You owe me something close to two thousand dollars, I believe.''

''Money,'' she said. ''That's all you care about, you bastard.''

Ted sipped at his scotch and frowned at her. ''Go to hell,'' he said.

''I could, for all you care.'' Her face had gone white. ''I cabled you, two years ago. I cabled all three of you. I needed you, you promised that you'd come if I needed you, that you'd be there, you promised that and you made love to me and you were my friend, but I cabled you and you didn't come, you bastard, you didn't come, none of you came, none of you came.'' She was screaming.

Ted had forgotten about the telegram. But it came back to him in a rush. He'd read it over several times, and finally he'd picked up the phone and called Michael. Michael hadn't been in. So he'd reread the telegram one last time, then crumbled it up and flushed it down the toilet. One of the others could go to her this time, he remembered thinking. He had a big case, the Argrath Corporation patent suit, and he couldn't risk leaving it. But it had been a desperate telegram, and he'd been guilty about it for weeks, until he finally managed to put the whole thing out of his mind. "I was busy," he said, his tone half-angry and half-defensive. "I had more important things to do than come hold your hand through another crisis."

"It was *horrible*," Melody screamed. "I needed you and you left me all *alone*. I almost *killed* myself."

"But you didn't, did you?"

"I could have," she said, "I could have killed myself, and you wouldn't even of cared."

Threatening suicide was one of Melody's favorite tricks. Ted had been through it a hundred times before. This time he decided not to take it. "You could have killed yourself," he said calmly, "and we probably wouldn't have cared. I think you're right about that. You would have rotted for weeks before anyone found you, and we probably wouldn't even have heard about it for half a year. And when I did hear, finally, I guess it would have made me sad for an hour or two, remembering how things had been, but then I would have gotten drunk or phoned up my girlfriend or something, and pretty soon I'd have been out of it. And then I could have forgotten all about you."

"You would have been sorry," Melody said.

"No," Ted replied. He strolled back to the bar and freshened his drink. "No, you know, I don't think I would have been sorry. Not in the least. Not guilty, either. So you might as well stop threatening to kill yourself, Melody, because it isn't going to work."

The anger drained out of her face, and she gave a little whimper. "Please, Ted," she said. "Don't say such things. Tell me you'd care. Tell me you'd remember me."

He scowled at her. "No," he said. It was harder when she was pitiful, when she shrunk up all small and vulnerable and whimpered instead of accusing him. But he had to end it once and for all, get rid of this curse on his life.

"I'll go away tomorrow," she said meekly. "I won't bother you. But tell me you care, Ted. That you're my friend. That you'll come to me. If I need you."

"I won't come to you, Melody," he said. "That's over. And I don't want you coming here anymore, or phoning, or sending telegrams, no matter what kind of trouble you're in. You understand? Do you? I want you out of my life, and when you're gone I'm going to forget you as quick as I can, 'cause lady, you are one hell of a bad memory."

Melody cried out as if he had struck her. "*No!*" she said. "No, don't say that, remember me, you *have* to. I'll leave you alone, I promise I will, I'll never see you again. But say you'll remember me." She stood up abruptly. "I'll go right now," she said. "If you want me to, I'll go. But make love to me first, Ted. Please. I want to give you something to remember me by." She smiled a lascivious little smile and began to struggle out of her halter top, and Ted felt sick.

He set down his glass with a bang. "You're crazy," he said. "You ought to get professional help, Melody. But I can't give it to you, and I'm not going to put up with this anymore. I'm going out for a walk. I'll be gone a couple of hours. You be gone when I get back."

Ted started for the door. Melody stood looking at him, her halter in her hand. Her breasts looked small and shrunken, and the left one had a tattoo on it that he'd never noticed before. There was nothing even vaguely desirable about her. She whimpered. "I just wanted to give you something to remember me by," she said.

Ted slammed the door.

It was midnight when he returned, drunk and surly, resolved that if Melody was still there, he would call the police and that would be the end of that. Jack was behind the desk, having just gone on duty. Ted stopped and gave him hell for having admitted Melody that morning, but the doorman denied it vehemently. "Wasn't nobody got in, Mr. Cirelli. I don't let in anyone without buzzing up, you ought to know that. I been here six years, and I never let in nobody without buzzing up." Ted reminded him forcefully about the Jehovah's Witness, and they ended up in a shouting match.

Finally Ted stormed away and took the elevator up to the thirty-second floor.

There was a drawing taped to his door.

He blinked at it furiously for a moment, then snatched it down. It was a cartoon, a caricature of Melody. Not the Melody he'd seen today, but the Melody he'd known in college: sharp, funny, pretty. When they'd been roommates, Melody had always illustrated her notes with little cartoons of herself. He was surprised that she could still draw this well. Beneath the face, she'd printed a message.

I LEFT YOU SOMETHING TO REMEMBER ME BY.

Ted scowled down at the cartoon, wondering whether he should keep it or not. His own hesitation made him angry. He crumpled the paper in his hand and fumbled for his keys. At least she's gone, he thought, and maybe for good. If she left the note, it meant that she'd gone. He was rid of her for another couple of years at least.

He went inside, tossed the crumpled ball of paper across the room towards a wastebasket, and smiled when it went in. "Two points," he said loudly to himself, drunk and self-satisfied. He went to the bar and began to mix himself a drink.

But something was wrong.

Ted stopped stirring his drink and listened. The water was running, he realized. She'd left the water running in the bathroom.

"Christ," he said, and then an awful thought hit him: maybe she hadn't gone after all. Maybe she was still in the bathroom, taking a shower or something, freaked out of her mind, crying, whatever. *"Melody!"* he shouted.

No answer. The water was running, all right. It couldn't be anything else. But she didn't answer.

"Melody, are you still here?" he yelled. "Answer, dammit!" Silence.

He put down his drink and walked to the bathroom. The door was closed. Ted stood outside. The water was definitely running. "Melody," he said loudly, "are you in there? Melody?"

Nothing. Ted was beginning to be afraid.

He reached out and grasped the doorknob. It turned easily in his hand. The door hadn't been locked.

Inside, the bathroom was filled with steam. He could hardly see, but he made out that the shower curtain was drawn. The shower was running full blast, and judging from the amount of steam, it must be scalding. Ted stepped back and waited for the steam to dissipate. "Melody?" he said softly. There was no reply.

"Shit," he said. He tried not to be afraid. She only talked about it, he told himself; she'd never really do it. The ones who talk about it never do it, he'd read that somewhere. She was just doing this to frighten him.

He took two quick strides across the room and yanked back the shower curtain.

She was there, wreathed in steam, water streaming down her naked body. She wasn't stretched out in the tub at all; she was sitting up, crammed in sideways near the faucets, looking very small and pathetic. Her position seemed half-fetal. The needle spray had been directed down at her, at her hands. She'd opened her wrists with his razor blades and tried to hold them under the water, but it hadn't been enough; she'd slit the veins crosswise, and everybody knew the only way to do it was lengthwise. So she'd used the razor elsewhere, and now she had two mouths, and both of them were smiling at him, smiling. The shower had washed away most of the blood; there were no stains anywhere, but the second mouth below her chin was still red and dripping. Trickles oozed down her chest, over the flower tattooed on her breast, and the spray of the shower caught them and washed them away. Her hair hung down over her cheeks, limp and wet. She was smiling. She looked so happy. The steam was all around her. She'd been in there for hours, he thought. She was very clean.

Ted closed his eyes. It didn't make any difference. He still saw her. He would always see her.

He opened them again; Melody was still smiling. He reached across her and turned off the shower, getting the sleeve of his shirt soaked in the process.

Numb, he fled back into the living room. God, he thought, God. I have to call someone, I have to report this, I can't deal with this. He decided to call the police. He lifted the phone, and hesitated with his finger poised over the buttons. The police won't help, he thought. He punched for Jill.

When he had finished telling her, it grew very silent on the other end of the phone. "My God," she said at last, "how awful. Can I do anything?"

"Come over," he said. "Right away." He found the drink he'd set down, took a hurried sip from it.

Jill hesitated. "Er—look, Ted, I'm not very good at dealing with corpses. Why don't you come over here? I don't want to—well, you know. I don't think I'll ever shower at your place again."

"Jill," he said, stricken. "I need someone right now." He laughed a frightened, uncertain laugh.

"Come over here," she urged.

"I can't just *leave* it there," he said.

"Well, don't," she said. "Call the police. They'll take it away. Come over afterwards."

Ted called the police.

"If this is your idea of a joke, it isn't funny," the patrolman said. His partner was scowling.

"Joke?" Ted said.

"There's nothing in your shower," the patrolman said. "I ought to take you down to the station house."

"Nothing in the shower?" Ted repeated, incredulous.

"Leave him alone, Sam," the partner said. "He's stinko, can't you tell?"

Ted rushed past them both into the bathroom.

The tub was empty. Empty. He knelt and felt the bottom of it. Dry. Perfectly dry. But his shirt sleeve was still damp. "No," he said. "No." He rushed back out to the living room. The two cops watched him with amusement. Her suitcase was gone from its place by the door. The dishes had all been run through the dishwasher—no way to tell if anyone had made pancakes or not. Ted turned the wastebasket upside down, spilling out the contents all over his couch. He began to scrabble through the papers.

"Go to bed and sleep it off, mister," the older cop said. "You'll feel better in the morning."

"C'mon," his partner said. They departed, leaving Ted still pawing through the papers. No cartoon. No cartoon. No cartoon.

Ted flung the empty wastebasket across the room. It caromed off the wall with a ringing metallic clang.

He took a cab to Jill's.

It was near dawn when he sat up in bed suddenly, his heart thumping, his mouth dry with fear.

Jill murmured sleepily. "Jill," he said, shaking her.

She blinked up at him. "What?" she said. "What time is it, Ted? What's wrong?" She sat up, pulling up the blanket to cover herself.

"Don't you hear it?"

"Hear what?" she asked.

He giggled. "Your shower is running."

That morning he shaved in the kitchen, even though there was no mirror. He cut himself twice. His bladder ached, but he would not go past the bathroom door, despite Jill's repeated assurances that the shower was not running. Dammit, he could *hear* it. He waited until he got to the office. There was no shower in the washroom there.

But Jill looked at him strangely.

At the office, Ted cleared off his desk, and tried to think. He was a lawyer. He had a good analytical mind. He tried to reason it out. He drank only coffee, lots of coffee.

No suitcase, he thought. Jack hadn't seen her. No corpse. No cartoon. No one had seen her. The shower was dry. No dishes. He'd been drinking. But not all day, only later, after dinner. Couldn't be the drinking. Couldn't be. No cartoon. He was the only one who'd seen her. No cartoon. I LEFT YOU SOMETHING TO REMEMBER ME BY. He'd crumpled up her cable and flushed her away. Two years ago. Nothing in the shower.

He picked up his phone. "Billie," he said, "get me a newspaper in Des Moines, Iowa. Any newspaper, I don't care."

When he finally got through, the woman who tended the morgue was reluctant to give him any information. But she softened when he told her he was a lawyer and needed the information for an important case.

The obituary was very short. Melody was identified only as a "massage parlor employee." She'd killed herself in her shower.

"Thank you," Ted said. He set down the receiver. For a long time he sat staring out of his window. He had a very good view; he could see the lake and the soaring tower of the Standard Oil building. He pondered what to do next. There was a thick knot of fear in his gut.

He could take the day off and go home. But the shower would be running at home, and sooner or later he would have to go in there.

He could go back to Jill's. If Jill would have him. She'd seemed awfully cool after last night. She'd recommended a shrink to him as they shared a cab to the office. She didn't understand. No one would understand . . . unless . . . He picked up the phone again, searching through his circular file. There was no card, no number; they'd drifted that far apart. He buzzed for Billie again. "Get me through to Random House in New York City," he said. "To Mr. Michael Englehart. He's an editor there."

But when he was finally connected, the voice on the other end of the line was strange and distant. "Mr. Cirelli? Were you a friend of Michael's? Or one of his authors?"

Ted's mouth was dry. "A friend," he said. "Isn't Michael in? I need to talk to him. It's . . . urgent."

"I'm afraid Michael's no longer with us," the voice said. "He had a nervous breakdown, less than a week ago."

"Is he . . . ?"

"He's alive. They took him to a hospital, I believe. Maybe I can find you the number."

"No," Ted said, "no, that's quite all right." He hung up.

Phoenix directory assistance had no listing for an Anne Kaye. Of course not, he thought. She was married now. He tried to remember her married name. It took him a long time. Something Polish, he thought. Finally it came to him.

He hadn't expected to find her at home. It was a school day, after all. But someone picked up the phone on the third ring. "Hello," he said. "Anne, is that you? This is Ted, in Chicago. Anne, I've got to talk to you. It's about Melody. Anne, I need help." He was breathless.

There was a giggle. "Anne isn't here right now, Ted," Melody said. "She's off at school, and then she's got to visit her husband. They're separated, you know. But she promised to come back by eight."

"Melody," he said.

"Of course, I don't know if I can believe her. You three were never very good about promises. But maybe she'll come back, Ted. I hope so.

"I want to leave her something to remember me by."

Fear isn't something that always vanishes when the dream is over. There are those of us who hoard fears, as well, against the time when, paradoxically, we hope they'll give us strength. Unfortunately, for some, the dream doesn't end.

Pat Cadigan is the award-winning coeditor (with husband Arnie Fenner) of Shayol, *and has rapidly made an enviable reputation for herself as one of the field's brightest new stars.*

The Pond

by Pat Cadigan

THE POND was evil.

That was a sad, silly thought to have on such a beautiful May afternoon with the trees whispering in the fresh wind and the distant sounds of insects buzzing and birds singing coming to her dreamily from the small woods that cupped the pond like protective hands. The pond itself was lovely, smooth and untroubled today, reflecting the surrounding trees like dark glass. Occasionally ripples appeared here and there on its surface, spreading out from tiny points where something had pricked the water. It should have been an idyllic spot.

Paula Stromsted leaned back on her palms and looked at her five year old daughter Richie, who was trying unsuccessfully to weave a garland of the flowers and leaves wilting in a pile between her folded legs. She had seen a picture of fairies dancing with wreaths of flowers around their heads in a storybook and the idea had captivated her. The girl worked meticulously with the tremendous concentration only the very young seemed capable of. After a few moments, she felt her mother's gaze on her and looked up.

"Mommy, I just can't get them to go in a circle like in the book. They won't stay." She wrapped two daisy stems around each other and grimaced when they fell apart. "See?"

Paula sat up, brushing her hands on her jeans. "Well, what do you say we head back to Grandma's house for something cold to drink? We've been down here for almost an hour and I'm getting thirsty."

"Do we *have*ta?" Richie looked longingly at the pond. "It's so nice here. This is my favoritest spot in the whole world."

"I thought Funland was your favoritest spot in the whole world."

"It's a different favoritest," Richie said seriously. "Can't we stay one more mimit?"

"Minute."

"Minute. Please, Mommy?"

She sighed. "Just one. Then we go back to the house and no arguments. OK?"

"Well, OK." The girl got up and went looking for more flowers, bending over with her hands on her knees in a perfect imitation of her grandmother inspecting the vegetable garden. Paula felt a little guilty. How was a little girl to understand the way she felt about the pond? To Richie, it was what it was—a pretty lake, a place to play and daydream, a welcome change from their cramped apartment in the city and the tiresomely cheerful daycare center where she spent the hours Paula was at work. For Paula, it was something else.

Dare you. Double dare you.

Darers go first.

She closed her eyes. That day twenty-five years ago had been warm and beautiful, too, when she and her cousin Jeffrey had come down to the pond to play Robin Hood. She and Jeff didn't always get along very well—there was something cold and mean in the bright blue eyes that grown-ups were always exclaiming over, much to her Aunt Kitty's proud delight. *Hasn't he got the most beautiful blue eyes?* people would say. For some reason, they never saw the meanness that was waiting to come out later as a painful twisting pinch on Paula's arm or a foot stuck out to trip her when she was running or the slow, thorough dissection of a grasshopper while the tormented creature scrabbled its remaining limbs helplessly in the air. But she had seen it. Her mother had seen it, too, and wasn't happy about it. But Jeff was her only sister's boy, she'd told Paula, and they had to try to be nice to him. Maybe if he saw how people were supposed to behave, he'd try harder to be good and the meanness inside of him would shrink away to nothing. Paula had tried, but privately she felt that Jeffrey would always be a nasty little boy even after he'd grown up. And people would still be oohing and aahing over his beautiful blue eyes.

She hadn't wanted to come down to the pond with Jeffrey that day. But he was just there for the weekend with Aunt Kitty and Uncle Rob and there wasn't anyone else around to play with. Jeffrey had seemed a little nicer than usual but as soon as they'd gotten to the pond, he'd started making fun of her. She was a girl; girls were stupid and weak and scared of everything; he was going to catch a snake and scare her with it.

She wasn't scared of anything, she'd insisted, and there weren't any snakes anyway.

Are so, fraidy-cat. She could almost hear his voice, just as plain as anything, his childish, mocking treble, the way she had heard it twenty-five years before when they'd been eight years old. *Are so. There's snakes in the pond. If you're not scared of 'em, I dare you to swim in it.*

Steadfastly, she had shaken her head. He knew as well as she did that they weren't even supposed to go wading. Her father had warned them they could get sick from the water, which was murky and muddy. As well, the bottom was treacherous, parts of it suddenly dropping down ten feet or more without warning. But Jeff had kept after her. *I dare you. Double dare you.*

Darers go first, she'd said primly.

And then he had spotted her new watch that her father had bought her as a No Special Reason surprise. Jeff's parents never gave him No Special Reason surprises and he was very jealous. She'd taunted him a little about it; she couldn't help it. At last she had something she could lord over him. She should have known better, her mother had told her later. She should have realized she couldn't get the better of Jeffrey's meanness.

He had demanded that she hand the watch over. When she wouldn't, he chased her, tackled her, and tore the watch from her wrist. Paula still remembered her enraged frustration as, still sitting on her chest, he began to put it on his own wrist. Then he saw the picture of Cinderella on the dial.

A stupid girl's watch! Shoulda known it would be a stupid girl's watch! But he wouldn't give it back to her, no matter how much she demanded and pleaded. He got up off her and went down to the edge of the pond. *Let's see if it's water-proof.* Before she could stop him, he had lobbed it almost halfway across the pond. There was only a tiny splash when it hit the water and the ripples it made were soon gone.

Now you'll have to swim in the pond if you want to get your stupid watch back. Dare you to. Double dare you.

Paula had run home crying, knowing with bitter satisfaction as she sobbed and hiccupped out her story that Jeffrey was really going to get it for this one. He must have known it, too, she'd realized later, and it hadn't made the slightest difference to him. The pleasure of the act outweighed the consequences for him and that had frightened her. She could still see him as he had been, standing at the water's edge grinning nastily at her, enormously pleased with himself. The mental image chilled her. It was almost as if he was there still, standing in that exact spot and if she opened her eyes she would see him, still eight years old and every bit as nasty, daring her to jump in and get her watch.

The wind rustling the trees died down and a quiet settled over everything. Paula opened her eyes. A small figure *was* standing at the water's edge, leaning forward and peering curiously into the pond.

"Richie!" Paula jumped up. "Richie, get away from there!" She hurried over and jerked the girl back from the water.

"What? I didn't do anything!" Richie stared up at her with round, startled eyes.

Paula pressed her lips together, suddenly embarrassed. "I know, honey," she said after a moment, stroking the child's soft fair hair. "I just don't want you to go near the water. I've told you that before, remember?"

Richie nodded. "I just thought I saw something in there. Something shiny."

"You were wrong," Paula said firmly. "Come on now,

let's go back to the house.'' She didn't look over her shoulder at the pond as she and Richie walked up to the road.

"Did you and Richie have a nice walk?" Paula's mother asked as they sat in the kitchen drinking lemonade at the round wooden table.

"We ended up down at the pond. As usual," Paula said. "She likes that place so much."

Her mother pursed her lips. "It's a pretty spot."

"Yes. She seems quite drawn to it. She's made me take her down there every day." Paula half-rose from her chair to look out the window over the sink. Richie was in the back yard picking dandelions, presumably to try her luck at making a garland of them.

"You don't sound very happy about that."

"Why should I be?"

"Paula, that was such a very long time ago." Her mother's voice was gentle but Paula could detect a small hint of exasperation.

"I know, Ma, but I can't go there without thinking of that little bastard. That little sadist." Paula rested her head on her hand, digging her fingers into her dark, shaggy hair. "I know it's an awful thing to say. But I'm not sorry. I never was. There was something terribly wrong with Jeff. Aunt Kitty and Uncle Rob just refused to see it. Not Rob so much as Kitty, really. She thought the sun just rose and set on her darling Jeffrey."

Her mother sighed, folding her wrinkled hands around her glass. "Kitty had a lot of trouble delivering Jeffrey. It almost killed her and she never could have any more children. That was the saddest part, I thought." She sighed again and gave Paula a pained smile. "That was all Kitty had, being Jeffrey's mother. It wasn't like it is today for women. All Kitty ever really thought of doing was raising a family. When she could only have Jeff, she put a tremendous load on him. He had to be the best of every child she couldn't have. I think that may have helped make him the way he was."

"Maybe. *I* think he was born that way like some people are born deformed. Only his deformity was up here." Paula tapped the side of her head. "Things turned out for the best, Ma. I thought so then and I'll always think so."

Her mother raised her eyebrows, dipping her salt-and-pepper head slightly to the left. "I find it a bit disconcerting that after twenty-five years, you're still so bitter about the boy."

"It's the pond." Paula rubbed the back of her neck tiredly. "It's tainted now. Jeffrey polluted the place so that it'll never be the same. Whenever I go there, it seems like he's still around. I can almost feel him there. Hell, I *can* feel him there. His poison's seeped into everything, the water, the trees, the wind—" She made a face. "I sound crazy, don't I?"

"Obsessed. Perhaps you shouldn't go to the pond anymore."

"Perhaps I shouldn't." Paula sipped her lemonade. It had gone warm and the taste was sourly cloying. "But Richie would be so disappointed. And I certainly don't want her going down there alone. If something happened, I'd never forgive myself."

"Sometimes I don't think you *have* ever forgiven yourself."

Paula blinked. "Say again?"

"I don't think you're really glad about what happened. You're not that kind of person. At least I hope you're not. I think maybe the little girl inside you still takes Kitty's awful words to heart and keeps them there."

"Oh, for God's sake." Paula got up and dashed her lemonade into the kitchen sink with a flip of her wrist. She glanced out at Richie, who was squatting on the grass with her back to the house. "Ma, I *don't* blame myself for what happened. I never did. If you want to know the truth"—she turned away from the window—"I don't even feel guilty about not feeling guilty. It might have been me instead."

Her mother shook her head. "If you ask me, that's what's poisoning the pond for you. You were talking a little while ago about Jeffrey being abnormal, not quite right. What about the way you keep harping on this? You insist on working yourself up about it. If you could stop living in the past, you'd be a lot better off."

"I don't live in the past."

"When it comes to Jeffrey, you do. He hasn't been around to make you unhappy for a quarter of a century but you've managed to keep him closer to you than ever. You use him to make yourself miserable.'' Her mother pushed away from the table. ''If you continue this way, you'd better think about getting some help because it's going to turn you into a sad case.''

She left the room, her footsteps loud on the hardwood floor. Paula turned back to the window. Her mother had never known what it was like to be at Jeff's mercy. That was the sort of thing that could really leave a mark on a person. She fixed herself a glass of ice water to get the taste of the lemonade out of her mouth. If only she could rid herself of the taste of Jeffrey as easily. She leaned against the counter, sipping her water thoughtfully.

She had found the grown-ups sitting at the kitchen table playing whist when she had come home wailing from the pond. Through her tears she had seen each of their reactions, Kitty putting her hand to her mouth, Rob throwing his cards down, her mother looking to her father, who got up to wipe her tears away with his handkerchief. *That boy*, Rob had said angrily, *that boy is going to have to learn a few things*.

Now, Rob, don't hit him. Kitty, sounding syrupy about Jeff as usual. *Striking a child doesn't teach him anything*.

Her parents had kept quiet except to try to comfort her. Not long after, Jeff had come in and there'd been a scene, mostly Kitty shouting at her husband while shielding a smirking Jeff with her body. In the end he'd gotten a mild spanking, after which Kitty brought him to Paula so he could deliver an apology and promises to pay for the watch out of his allowance and never to do such an awful thing again, all of it dictated to him by Kitty and played back with occasional prompting.

Paula had stared at him through the whole thing until he got to the end. He smirked all the way through it. She knew all the adults were looking at her, waiting for her to be very grown-up and ladylike about everything and accept the artificial apology. But a devil had gotten into her and instead of pronouncing her forgiveness, she had reared back and exploded.

I'll never forgive you! she had screamed into his face, startling him so much that his smirk had actually disappeared for a few seconds. *I hate you and I wish you were dead*!

Kitty had clutched her son to her side in horror while Paula's father—a bit reluctantly, it seemed to her at the time—marched her upstairs to her room and told her to stay there until after supper. Paula had known her outburst would strain relations between the two families even further, but she hadn't cared. Or had tried not to. Later, her mother had had a quiet talk with her on the virtue of being civilized and not sinking to a certain other person's level. Her father had been more understanding; he tucked her in with a promise to teach her how to defend herself.

The next morning the situation had escalated into frenzy when Kitty discovered the front door open and Jeffrey missing. Sometime during the night or early morning, he'd gotten dressed and run away. Because of what Paula had screamed at him, Kitty said. He had run away because his feelings were hurt. Paula had doubted it.

Rob and her father had driven all over the county looking for him while Kitty sobbed and she hid in her room. It was just after lunchtime when the phone rang. Paula's mother had answered it.

She couldn't quite remember the exact sequence of events after that, or exactly when she had found out what had happened and from whom. Her father had stopped at the pond on the way back to the house and found Jeffrey's shoes and socks near the water. He and Rob had called the police from the grocery store down the road. The police had come out with a diver and several men to comb the woods, but the diver found him after all, lying at the bottom of a seven-foot drop-off.

Kitty had had to be sedated but Paula heard her screams through the whole house before the medication took effect. Paula had done it to Jeffrey. Paula had said she would never forgive him so Jeff had gone out to the pond to try to get her watch, just so they could be friends again. And it was Paula's curse that had done it. She had wished him dead and now he was.

Paula had found herself strangely numbed by the whole experience. She felt a little regret and a certain amount of horror for how the boy had died. But through it all she couldn't shake the thought that if Jeff had really been trying to retrieve her watch, it was only because he hadn't wanted to give up part of his allowance to pay for it.

But that hadn't been why he'd gone out to the pond.

Dare you. Double dare you, he'd said.

Darers go first, she'd replied.

And so he had. So that the next time they were away from the grown-ups, he could say he'd gone into the pond and then try to force her into the water. And when he'd gotten her there. . . .

Paula came slowly back to the present and shoved the memory aside. Her mother was right. She was rubbing salt in wounds that should have healed over at least two decades before. Even Kitty had apologized to her months after the funeral Paula hadn't attended, telling her she hadn't meant all the awful things she'd said. But the apology had had a curious flat sound to it, as though it had been fed to her the way she had fed Jeffrey's to him. But it didn't seem right, when Paula thought about it, that her feelings about Jeffrey should still be so strong. The image of the pond appeared in her mind and she felt herself tense. Jeffrey was the pond to her now and always would be. Well, she could help herself by refusing to dwell on it, starting right at that moment. She looked out the window again. Richie was still crouched down on the grass, studying something. Paula smiled. At least one good thing had come out of the experience. The memory of Jeff's death had persuaded her to take Richie for toddler swimming lessons at the Y before she was even three years old. She had decided there wasn't going to be another accidental drowning. The girl could swim like a little fish. Still smiling, she went out to see what her daughter was so involved in.

"What's up, buttercup?" she asked, ruffling Richie's hair.

Richie looked up at her guiltily. There was a pile of dandelions beside her and grass smears on her knees. Something small and brown wriggled between her fingers.

"Richie!" Horrified, Paula slapped the grasshopper out of her daughter's grasp and stamped on it. Then she yanked the girl to her feet and shook her. "What were you doing?"

Richie tried to shrink away. "Nothing, Mommy, I—"

"That's a terrible thing to do, a terrible, evil thing! How

would *you* like it if a giant tore *you* apart bit by bit! How could you? How *could* you?''

Richie flopped back and forth in her hands. "Mommy, you're hurting!"

"See? See what it's like?"

"I only caught him, I was only looking at him—"

Paula's grip tightened on the child's arm. "Don't ever let me see you doing anything like that again!"

Richie burst into tears. "I didn't do anything! I was just looking at him and you killed him! You killed him!"

Paula released her and the girl fled into the house, wailing for her grandmother. Uncertainly, Paula watched her go and then looked down at the crushed insect in the grass. With her shoe, she mashed the remains into unrecognizability and kicked the dying dandelions over them.

"You know," Paula's mother said, looking up from the magazine in her lap, "little kids don't really know that kind of thing is wrong. If, indeed, that's what she was doing. She may have been just looking at the grasshopper like she said."

Paula looked away from the television program she hadn't really been able to concentrate on and shifted her position in the overstuffed chair. "Maybe she was. But I recognized that position, the way she was holding her fingers. It was the way Jeffrey looked when he was pulling those poor things apart."

"Paula, really. Jeffrey again. And all over a *bug*."

"Really yourself, Ma. Suppose it were a puppy or a kitten?"

Her mother leaned against the arm of the couch and put her feet up on the cushions. "Richie would never do anything like *that*."

"Not anymore, that's for sure."

Her mother made a disgusted noise and set her magazine aside. It was this week's *Rolling Stone,* Paula noted with detached amusement. "You scared that poor kid almost into hysterics. And over nothing! *All* little children are fascinated by insects. Pulling them apart is just a way for them to try to figure out how they work. Like an experiment. It's curiosity, Paula, not sadism."

"It's sadistic, whether they realize it or not. I'm not going to stand for that. Richie is going to realize that other living things are entitled to exist unmolested."

"I suppose *you* never did anything of the sort," her mother said sarcastically.

"Did you ever catch me at it?"

"It's occurred to me that there was probably a good deal that I didn't catch you at."

"Well, I never did anything like that."

"Never? Not even once? Never picked the wings off a fly? Or a ladybug?"

"*No.*" Paula suppressed the memory of watching Jeffrey with horrified fascination when she had first seen him removing the hind legs of a grasshopper. What he had done after that had made her sick.

Her mother shrugged. "All right. You were good and kind and merciful, a sensitive little soul who never harmed a fly. If you insist." She picked up the magazine again and leafed through it to find her place. "But I still think your reaction was entirely inappropriate, no matter what Richie was doing or not doing."

"I am *not* going to have her turn out like Jeffrey."

"Jesus Christ!" Her mother slammed the magazine down on her knees. "Jeffrey, Jeffrey, Jeffrey! I had less of him when he was alive! Once and for all, Paula, lose this hang-up you've got about him. He's dead. Twenty-five years dead. Lay him to rest!"

Paula said nothing, turning her gaze back to the television set. The images on the screen made no sense at all to her.

"You only have a few more days of vacation left," her mother went on quietly. "Try to make them pleasant. For Richie's sake. And you ought to go up to her room right now and apologize to her." She looked at Paula sharply from under her eyebrows. "Believe me, it's far more important for grown-ups to apologize to children than vice versa. That is, if you really want a kid to grow up with the kind of integrity you want her to have."

"All right," Paula said resignedly. "I'll go up and talk to her."

Her mother was smiling as Paula walked out of the living room and into the front hall. At the foot of the stairs she paused, frowning at the open front door. The dying sunlight made a red-gold block on the floor. The screen door wasn't even latched. Paula shook her head. An authority on children and a subscriber to *Rolling Stone* and her mother still couldn't remember to lock the front door at night. Anyone could get in. . . .

She froze in the act of closing the heavy wooden door. Anyone could get in—*or out*.

"Richie!" she yelled, pounding up the staircase. "Richie!" She tore down the hallway on the second floor and burst into her daughter's room. "Richie!" She didn't have to turn on the light to see the empty bed, still neatly made. "*Richie!*"

She pounded back down the stairs, colliding with her mother at the bottom.

"What's wrong? What did she do?"

Paula pushed her mother's groping hands away from herself. "She ran away, she's not in her room!"

"Have you looked in the back y—"

"*You* look! I *know* where she is!" Paula ran out the front door, feeling her pocket for her car keys.

"Where are you going?" her mother called after her.

"The pond!" Paula jumped into the car and fumbled the key into the ignition, ignoring her mother's plea to wait.

It took her just a little over a minute to drive to the pond. She knew that was the only place Richie could have run to. To her favoritest spot, because she was angry and she knew she wasn't supposed to go there by herself. Paula forced herself to press lightly on the accelerator, in case the girl suddenly appeared walking in the middle of the road. "Richie," she moaned, her hands trembling on the steering wheel. "Richie, if I catch up to you—" Her heart thudded when she realized what she'd said.

When she reached the pond, she pulled onto the dirt shoulder and put on the emergency flashers. "Richie!" she yelled, running the fifty yards down to the spot where they'd been sitting earlier. "*Richie!*" Her voice echoed, shattering the quiet. A few feet from the water she stopped, listening for the sound of an answer. The trees rustled, patchy silhouettes against the darkening sky.

"Richie, please answer me! I'm not mad at you, I'm not going to hurt you, Richie—"

She spotted the shoes sitting side by side on the ground with the little white socks stuffed neatly inside them at the same time as she heard the splashing.

"*Mommy!*"

Far out in the pond, two little arms waved, scrabbling at the air before they dipped below the surface.

Then she felt it, like the terrible oppressiveness before the onset of a storm. She had been right after all. Jeffrey had poisoned the pond, but in a hideous, evil way she'd never dreamed of. He'd been there, waiting to get her for twenty-five years and when he knew he never would, he'd gone to work on Richie, drawing her to the pond, luring her into the water. If Jeffrey couldn't have Paula, he'd take Richie and, in a way, that was better for him. Jeffrey had always known exactly what would hurt her most.

All this passed through her mind in less than a second. Then she was tearing into the water, pushing with all her strength toward the little arms that had bobbed to the surface again and the choking voice that cried *Mommy!* with hopeless terror.

The filthy water splashed into her eyes and mouth as she struggled against it. It seemed as though she were moving with terrible slowness, as though the water were becoming as thick as hardening molasses. Every time she looked up, Richie seemed further away than ever, her voice becoming weaker. Paula strained against the water, feeling it resist her almost like a live thing. *You can't have her, Jeffrey!* her mind screamed. *You can't take her from me, I won't let you!*

The water suddenly churned around her, bubbling madly, sucking at her arms and legs, pulling her down. Panic exploded inside her like an electric shock. She fought to keep herself at the surface, to stay in sight of her daughter. The drag became more powerful, the water lifting when her arms lifted, swirling around her body like liquid ropes. She felt her head forced under and her hands lost the air; her legs kicked uselessly but she kept struggling, all the way to the muddy bottom.

•   •   •

The little girl sat at the water's edge, soaked, chilled, and panting. Several times she swallowed, making a face at the muddy taste in her mouth. The sun had set and there was only a little bit of a red glow left in the sky. She should start back before it was really dark. Mommy had always said it was dangerous to walk on a road after night had fallen, even if you were wearing light-colored clothing.

She stood up and looked out over the pond for a long moment. The surface was smooth again. "You got her," she said quietly. Then, a little louder: "You got her. OK? That means you don't need to get me, right? You said. You did."

She seemed to listen to something, but there was nothing to hear except the nighttime noise of crickets chirping. "You better not try to get me now, OK?" Her face puckered a little. "Well, you better not! You *said!*"

The pond lay impassive, not even a ripple disturbing it, promising nothing.

Richie turned and ran up to the road.

Coincidence rules much of our lives, no matter how hard we try to deny it. By denying it too hard and too often, however, we often overlook the fact that coincidence can also be terror in disguise—terror, when it defies its own definition and turns out to have rules of its own.

R. Bretnor's distinguished career continues without abating. Though his output has never been prodigious, it is always a delight to read and absorb what eventually leaves his typewriter. There is always more to a Bretnor story than meets the eye.

The Beasts That Perish

by R. Bretnor

SOME OF US on The Team don't even know that it exists. We're never told about it when we're hired; nor are we ever given the *real* reasons for our hiring. And those of us (like me) who do catch on seldom even discuss it with each other.

On paper, The Team doesn't exist at all. It permeates other agencies; we shuffle filing cards, or act as couriers, or translate documents, or diddle with computers, and each of us has been checked very, *very* carefully where security is concerned, not only by the hush-hush people but by Colonel Samuel Warhorse, who either is or isn't a displaced Army medic, and who once or twice a year goes back to Oklahoma to do his thing as a Medicine Chief of the Osage Nation, and who'd be captain of The Team *if* it existed, just as I'd be his second-in-command.

The best way to describe it is by using the example of water departments and their dowsers. Just about every major-city water department has one or more dowsers on its payroll—but never *as* dowsers, because water-witching still isn't quite respectable. They're hired as back-hoe operators, or truck drivers, or whatever, and there they are, ready to do their real job when necessary.

That's how it is with us. Somehow our real jobs filter in to us, always through Chief Sam, and we tackle them and do our best, and afterward everybody forgets all about them, just as people forget about water-department dowsers when they fill their bathtubs.

What sort of jobs? Problems that defy ordinary, logical solutions; puzzles that makes no sense; perils materializing for no reason out of nowhere; disasters that simply cannot be, but *are*.

For instance—

Chief Sam called me at 11:30. "We've got another one, Garry," he said. "Smells like a real collector's item. How's about lunch at noon?"

I didn't argue that I already had a date. I canceled it, and half an hour later, when he walked into the chophouse with three other characters, I was waiting for him.

I stood up and he introduced them. Two were State Police Captains, one out from Pennsylvania, the other a tall, rangy, local western type named Tod Welles; the third, with a French name and nice manners, was an R.C.M.P. Superintendent from up across the border.

"Douglas Garrioch," Sam told them. "He used to be a flyboy. Sometimes he turns out to be pretty useful." He grinned at me, his eyes black agate under his black Sequoia eyebrows and gray hair, and slapped me on the shoulder with a hand like a bear's paw. We ordered drinks, making small talk till the waiter brought them. Then there was silence. I looked at Sam.

"Our problem for the day," he said, "is simply stated. During the past week the *fatal* one-car accident rate has suddenly gone up—by four thousand eight hundred and some-odd percent."

"Where?" I asked.

"The entire United States and all of Canada. Garry, that means that almost fifty times as many people as usual have been smashing their cars into concrete abutments, plunging them into rivers, rolling them down cliffs—and at top speeds. And at night, *only* at night. Folks are getting spooked. Insurance companies are having fits. The press is getting too damn interested and making noises. So far nobody's released the true statistics, but there's no way to keep the local police and sheriffs quiet. It's lucky winter's almost on us, so there's weather to blame it on, but the whole story's sure to break wide-open before too long—and we just can't afford that kind of panic.''

"So?" I said, feeling those familiar small cold feet along my back.

"So you go back to work. You dig right in and find what's going on, and just who's killing whom—if there *is* a who. The boys here'll fill you in on everything they know. It's yours from there. Now let's have lunch."

They told me while we ate. They were experts in their field, specialists on highway accidents, and they had all the facts and figures at their fingertips, all the hows and wheres and whens—but nothing else, no *whys*. I asked the obvious questions, trying to find a pattern that would link everything together.

What about the drivers? What kind of people were they? That angle had been pretty thoroughly explored; they were just about every kind. The only thing they seemed to have in common was that most of them had done a lot of freeway driving—the percentage of big-rig truckers was astonishing—but there were too many exceptions to lay down a rule. Otherwise, they were of all ages, sexes, races, driving every kind of car or truck and a few motorcycles. Almost always they had been alone, or just about alone, on the road, with the next vehicle at least a quarter of a mile away; and always, *always* they had been going way over the limit—estimated speed 80, 85, 90, sometimes 100.

How about passengers? Well, there'd been a few—no busloads, no big groups, not even any foursomes.

"Any last words?" I asked. "Did any of 'em drop any kind of hint about why they did it? About what might've hit 'em?" And I was told that no, they hadn't, not really. There'd been a salesman in Ohio somewhere who was still alive when they pulled him out; they thought he screamed out something about hitting a coyote before he coughed up blood and died, but they weren't sure; and anyhow no coyotes had been anywhere around those parts since frontier days. Besides him, there was just a doctor in Saskatchewan, out on the motel circuit with his office nurse; she had lived long enough to whisper something that sounded like ". . . squirrel . . . squirrel . . ."

" 'The birds and the beasts were there,' " quoted Chief Sam. "An odd coincidence."

"Odd—but hardly pertinent." The R.C.M.P. man shrugged. "People say weird things when they're dying."

And that was that. They had no more to add. Chief Sam and I walked them to the door after he'd paid the check, and he said how I'd keep in touch with them, with Welles especially, and how they'd pass on all reports to me; and I guess somebody had briefed them—they asked no questions about how we'd operate. Then the Chief and I went back into the bar for one more drink and my instructions.

"Hit the road, Garry," he said. "Tonight and every night till you find out something. Stay on the freeways, particularly the Interstates. There've been a few bad ones on back-country roads, but its the freeways where everything's been really happening. Here are your credentials, State *and* Federal." He grinned. "They're sort of hoked up for the occasion, but they're genuine and guaranteed to impress everybody, even us Honest Injuns." He handed me two cards and an enamel-and-gold badge. "They make out you're sort of a cross between Ralph Nader, Oh-Oh-Seven, and the ghost of J. Edgar Hoover. Don't throw their weight around unless you have to."

"Thank you, Heroic Leader," I said, knocking off my drink. "You've put me in the ticket-fixing business. Now I can make my fortune and retire, and take Marina on a trip around the world."

"Any time," said Chief Sam. "*After* you stop those folks getting themselves killed off. Now don't forget to fill your tank—you're going to need it." His grin disappeared. "Take care, Garry, and give that lovely girl of yours my love."

I drove back to the office, and checked out early; and drove slowly up to the apartment, thinking about The Team, and Chief Sam and Marina and myself, and how the strangeness of our natures and our backgrounds and our lives had brought us together to do jobs that needed doing and otherwise would never have been done. Take me, for instance—three of my grandparents were of Scotch descent, by way of Nova Scotia;

the fourth was French and English mixed. And there was second sight on both sides of the family.

My great-grandfather Garrioch had seen visions, had known when death would come for friends and relatives there in the cold Western Isles. His son, my grandfather, had it also; but it was different in him, for almost never was it conscious. Usually it simply guided him in simple acts, things done or not done to keep one out of danger; he fought four years as an infantryman in World War I, in the Black Watch, and lived to emigrate—very nearly a survival record.

My father inherited it again, and it protected him after he moved down to New England to fish the harsh Atlantic, and in the Navy all through the Second War. In my case, it again had changed. I didn't know I had it until I took my first tour as a chopper pilot in Vietnam. Yes, it protected me—but it also told me, quite consciously and definitely, when death was going to strike—when Charlie was going to slam his rockets or mortar shells into the base, and who on any mission wouldn't make it back.

What do you do with that kind of talent? You don't report yourself to Headquarters. No, you worry about it, and maybe drop a hint to a close friend or two when you feel they ought to hit the sick list, and grieve when they won't take your advice and end up dead. Then, if like me you're very, *very* lucky, maybe you run into someone like Chief Sam Warhorse. He was doing his stuff there at the great base hospital in Saigon, and I was taking a routine physical; and next thing I knew somehow I'd told him everything, and his advice had been simply to accept it, to say nothing, and to keep in touch. We'd be seeing more of one another, he said.

So there I was, driving home to my golden girl, thinking that if it hadn't been for him probably I never would've met her. She had been born in Hawaii, on Maui, her father an Icelander, her mother Japanese, and she was golden-skinned and glowing, and so delicate that she looked almost breakable. She was as sensitive as a Gothic heroine, and as tough as whalebone.

She had to be. *Her* talent had just missed being her tragedy. She is an empath. Even as a child she could feel—in each degree, in every terrible detail—the agony of others. Not physical pain itself, but its tormenting tensions and terrors, the futile thrashings of trapped minds trying to cope with other kinds of pain. It is a talent unhappily too common, and children born with it often become autistic, withdrawing totally into themselves, for in societies that deny and fear the extrasensory, they have no way of learning how to distinguish between exterior agonies and those genuinely their own.

But Marina's parents were wise enough to listen, wise enough not to slap her down. They had no rules to follow, so—instead of calling in the headshrinkers—when she was seven they took her to her grandmother in Japan, who had retired to a convent for Zen Buddhist nuns. There she was cared for until she was 14, visited at least twice a year by one or another of her parents, and in constant touch with all her Japanese relations. And there she learned, not how or why her talent came to be, but how she herself, her being, could live with it and maintain tranquility.

When she returned to her father and mother in Hawaii, it had in no way been suppressed, but now she knew how to avoid the dangerous chains of emotional identification, how to say, "This agony's not mine, *it is not me*," how not to react to it. And yet a visit to a hospital was still, for her, an act of heroism, and she would ask me to detour for miles rather than pass a penitentiary, an insane asylum, or a slaughterhouse. For her talent differs from ordinary telepathy; distance is an important factor in it, and so are numbers. She can handle the impact of suffering individuals well enough, but groups still overwhelm her. She cannot heal; except very rarely, with people whom she loves, she is powerless even to ameliorate. She can only feel.

In the islands she went through high school and then on to college, taking a degree in librarianship—a wise choice, for libraries have more books than people, and books, whatever torments they contain, don't broadcast them. Then she got a job stateside, at a small college library in the state of Washington; and that was where Chief Sam ran into her—by accident, of course, the way he always seems to find his people. He was asking her a question at the reference desk when, without warning, she came out of gear, leaving the conversation dangling. She turned deathly pale; her pupils dilated; she gasped for breath. It took her several minutes to pull herself together, while he watched.

And *then* they heard the sirens. Some self-tortured kid, stoked up on speed and LSD and God knows what, had climbed the campanile tower and tried to fly. She had tuned him in that first dreadful second when he had found that he could not.

Chief Sam coaxed it all out of her and found her a new library job at a nice quiet computer center in Cinnabar, the little Colorado mining town where The Team works—still small enough so that you aren't psychically snowed under as you are in, say, Chicago or New York, but big enough to hold those government subagencies we need to keep us going plausibly. He introduced us. I saw her glowing skin, her strange, green golden eyes, her hair like the fine black lacquer of a household shrine in ancient Nara, and instantly I knew the joy and fire of her temperament, and the tempered strength under her gentleness and fragility. We drew together, feeling one another before we had so much as touched our hands; and it was wonderful that neither she nor I, nor Chief Sam even—neither then nor later—had to conceal why we were there, what we were all about.

That made it a whole lot easier, for we needed no barriers of security between us. I could tell her exactly what I was getting myself into, just as she could tell me. So as soon as I got home I phoned her on the job and asked her to take the rest of the afternoon off. I filled her in on the whole deal and told her there'd probably be nights I'd have to spend away from home. She shook her shining head and smiled ruefully. "I guess there's just no limit to the things some men won't do to get out of making love to their poor lonely wives," she said.

We went to dinner early and I told her everything again, somehow hoping that she might, intuitively, think of an angle we had missed. Those drivers, I repeated, driving at top speeds and late at night, must have seen *something,* something startling enough to make them swerve suicidally. The only alternative was to believe spooks were riding with them, or flying-saucer people were suddenly controlling them, or the Russkies or Red Chinese were playing with a new secret weapon. For a few moments she responded with that look people get when they are searching in themselves, but when she spoke it was only to say that she didn't like the freeways.

"I'm not happy on them," she said, looking a little puzzled. "There's—well, there's something *wrong* about them. But it's too vague. I can't get hold of it. It's only strong enough to make me feel uneasy." She took my hand in both of hers. "I know it's silly of me, Garry, with your—your talent. But you *will* be careful, won't you? Promise me?"

It was six days to Thanksgiving. The weather had been nasty for a week, but the night was clear. The highways had dried off, and though yesterday's snow blanketed trees, houses, and hillsides, when I reached I-25 it was all clear going and the traffic was moving ten miles an hour faster than the law allowed, with the big rigs and some other drivers pushing even beyond that.

I got my first signal around ten o'clock, near a side road leading to a little town called Penfield, so I followed my nose down the off-ramp and within three miles I came to it—a telescoped VW van, crushed against a cruelly jagged rockface. There was a wrecker there, and two State Police cars, and a sheriff's deputy, so I pulled off and showed the sergeant my credentials. He was properly impressed and treated me the way I wish people had when I was in the army.

"Another one of these damn one-car deals," he commented, "and not even on the freeway. The victim is on his way to Penfield in the meat wagon."

I spent twelve minutes with him, and though he kept repeating we wouldn't find a thing, he did help me search the area; and he was right, of course. There wasn't anything.

"I wish to God we could've found it!" he said. "Just once, to take the curse off this crazy business. If you're working on it, I sure wish you luck. Believe me, it's getting to us all!"

That was the first of five that night. The second was just about a duplicate, right off an interchange on 25, only the car looked as if it had been brand-new and probably a Cadillac. The third was a huge diesel truck lying on its crushed cab at the foot of a steep embankment; I got there almost right away, even before the ambulance, and it was a messy deal—

messy enough to shake me and the two policemen. The next was standard—a concrete overpass, ripped chunks of what had been a Porsche, a young man's body underneath a blanket. The fifth was something else again—a flaming, smoking heap of unidentifiable wreckage half a straight mile down the mountainside, with the cops and me and the trucker who'd reported it staring helplessly and talking about getting a crew down there come morning.

There were no clues at any of them.

I'd called Marina before midnight from a coffee stop, to tell her where I was and that I loved her; and by three A.M., more than a hundred miles from home, I holed up in a fleabag motel, ate a sandwich, drank half a pint of bourbon, and hit the sack.

I slept till noon—after all, my working hours were going to be from dark to dawn—then made my calls to Chief Sam and Tod Welles, and learned that there was nothing new except a scare story in a national tabloid, which wasn't making anybody happy. I spent the afternoon talking the situation over with State and local police, doing none of us much good, and had dinner with a superannuated sheriff who'd actually forbidden his wife and kids to use the highways after dark.

That night was like the first, only there were seven of them instead of five; it had rained and snowed a little, and we had bad slick spots here and there. I drove where instinct told me, and again learned nothing.

For the next three days the pattern scarcely varied. I followed 25 clear up into Wyoming and back down again. I followed I-70 for almost 300 miles west of Denver, coping with more bad weather, bedding down at night with my bit of bourbon to dream of Marina—with a nightmare or two about fatal crashes to keep me on my toes. I had nothing to report except somebody's testimony at third hand from the State Police, who'd had it from a sheriff's deputy, who'd had it from a sheepherder driving an old pickup: he'd been following one of them maybe a quarter mile away, and he thought maybe he'd seen some sort of shadow moving right in front of her before she hit.

Then, late on the fourth night, after two A.M., I pulled into a truck stop to get myself together. I'd just come from the nastiest wreck of all—a truck and trailer filled with something flammable. It had gone off at a sharp curve, hit some trees, and flamed instantly. I was there long before the police arrived—in time to hear the driver screaming—and there was absolutely nothing I could do but watch the flames. When it was over, I went into the truck-stop restaurant, ordered a T-bone and coffee to drink while it was cooking, drank half of the coffee, filled the cup up again from a pint I kept against emergencies, and found myself listening to four truckers in the booth behind me. They were fresh off the road and they knew the man whom I'd heard die.

They made the usual profane comments about the one-car crack-ups, only they said one-rig, and they indulged in the same foolish and futile attempts to explain them, or explain them away. Then, "Okay!" growled one of them. "That was a hell of a way to go, but—ah, hell, man, if it had to happen could you have picked any guy you'd rather have it happen to?"

"Don't talk like that, Slavich," barked another. "Grayber was scum, sure he was, but hell, he was human, wasn't he?"

"Human? Like hell he was human! Remember how that poor damn girl of his always looked like she'd been beat up on? Well, she had. And talk to anybody who's rode with him, or right behind him even. Twice I seen him try to nudge cars off the road when he figured nobody was looking. And he'd run over every critter crossed the road ahead of him—dog, cat, possum, you name it. The jerk would speed up to catch 'em. He'd swerve to cut 'em down. Hell, for my money he had it coming!"

They kept on arguing about the dead Grayber for a bit, with nobody getting really mad about it, and then the talk changed to women, and I quit listening. I ate my steak—a good one—but somehow it didn't really grab me. I kept remembering that driver in Ohio who'd screamed about hitting a coyote, and the nurse in Canada who'd died mumbling ". . . squirrel . . . squirrel . . ." My mind just wouldn't chase the thought away. When I drove off, I told myself to stop imagining a connection. Sure, there'd been people who'd killed themselves trying to keep from running down a dog, but chances were most had been inexperienced drivers.

There was only one more that night; and next day, when I phoned in, Chief Sam told me to come back for Thanksgiving. Marina and I could have the night together, and then next day, unless we had a date, would we have dinner with his family? I told him we were free as air, we'd love to; and then he told me that he and Tod Welles had been taking Emmie Bostwick to every crash site they could think of. She was part of The Team, a black girl from around Baton Rouge, with a genius for sensing felonious little plans being hatched or carried out anywhere near here—even a day or two afterward. She had a courier's job, a good cover for sudden traveling, and the Chief used her when terrorists or blackmailers were making threats. She was pretty close to being infallible; and she'd detected nothing, absolutely nothing. Chief Sam felt that if there was dirty work afoot it was a long-range deal, and it might even help me to take a two-day break.

So I called Marina and gave her the good news, and in her voice I could read not only pleasure but relief. "Oh, I'm glad, lover! At least I'll have you off those freeways for a while. Last night I had an awful dream—I guess it wasn't really *awful*, but in the dream it was. It scared me, and I've been worried for you ever since. Garry, don't laugh—I dreamed you ran over a poor raccoon."

I didn't laugh, partly because once I had; and coming home I drove more carefully than I usually do.

Thanksgiving Day I took time out in the afternoon to get together with Tod Welles and his R.C.M.P. friend and compare notes. We told each other what we could and ended up just where we'd started, on Line One. Then, at around 4:30, Marina and I drove out to the Warhorses'. Chief Sam has about 20 acres a dozen miles out of Cinnabar, near a weird little place called Dudgeon, where there's nothing but a service station, a general store, a bar, a hashhouse, and a combination City Hall and volunteer Fire Department—but only half a mile off the good main road, where you can snake around the mountains without losing too much speed and with about half of it freeway so nobody can really hold you up. It didn't take us long to get there; there wasn't even a whisper of bad weather.

We were greeted by Chief Sam, his wife Connie, three kids, a pretty Warhorse cousin from some university out West, two big brown Labs, a Siamese, and a striped tabby cat. The Warhorses told us it was heap good for stupid palefaces to come in out of the cold and drink firewater with the friendly natives; and we all sat there before the huge fireplace, surrounded by dogs and cats and kids, talking, laughing, and forgetting that along the miles of road that hold our world together people were suddenly smashing to their deaths.

Our conversation flowed from one culture into another; tales were told born in traditions continents apart. Nobody spoiled things by trying to hog the floor; when disagreements showed themselves they became friendly fencing matches instead of duels. Then we went in to dinner, and let the turkey dictate to us.

We left just after midnight, still glowing, and at the door we were kissed good night; and when I shook Chief Sam's hand I knew that he, even as I myself, at once regretted that tomorrow it would be back to work—and yet looked forward to it.

The night was frosty; the air was crystal-clear; never had there been so many stars across the sky. Quickly we left Dudgeon sound asleep behind us and in moments we were at the freeway entrance. I turned into it and speeded up. And as I did, I felt again, suddenly, that something was all set to happen—and the feeling, as it always is, was laced with fear.

"Damn!" I said, only half aloud. "Not tonight!"

Marina heard me. "Garry," she whispered, "are you sure?"

The feeling, oddly, was a little different. I couldn't tell exactly how, but that didn't change it. "Yes, I'm sure," I told her. "I wish to God I wasn't, but I am."

"Can't you—can't we ignore it?"

I shook my head. In the rearview mirror I could see the single light of a motorcycle coming—coming fast.

That's him, I thought, as he swept by, doing 80 or 85—and yet, somehow, I wasn't sure it *was* him. Still, whatever it might be, I knew he was part of it.

"This one may be special," I told her, stepping on the gas. "There's something strange about it. We'll have to see."

She didn't say a word. Her hand moved over and rested lightly on my knee.

For three miles we followed him, taking the mad curves, never letting him get more than a quarter mile away. Then we came to a long, straight, downhill stretch. We passed a sign saying JEFFERS PASS, TURNOFF 2 MI. There ahead of us was the interchange, a concrete bastion pierced by two sally-ports. Our motorcyclist was heading straight toward it. I could feel apprehension building in me. I could feel the tightening of Marina's hand against my thigh.

The concrete rushed toward the motorcyclist. It rushed at us. It seemed to grow. There was the second sign. There, very suddenly, was the turnoff.

And, so abruptly that for an instant I thought he'd lose control, the motorcyclist hit his brakes and, tires shrieking, swerved sharply to the right, taking the turnoff, barely making it. I forced my eyes back to the road in front of me. I heard Marina scream—

In my headlights, right in the middle of my lane, less than a hundred feet ahead of me, there was a wildcat, white fangs bared, ears back, eyes burning bright—

And he was 25 feet high.

How many impressions can you crowd into a quarter of a second? How many decisions can you make in half of that time? I recall Marina screaming; my hands doing their damned-est to twist the wheel; my brain, in shock, still forcing my foot to floor the throttle instead of trying for the brakes. I remember my mind telling me that cars are not as hard as concrete. I don't recall whether or not I closed my eyes.

We hit.

There was no impact, none.

There was a timeless instant in which I felt surrounded by flesh and fur, by the idea of fur and flesh, by an animal odor, musky and far away.

Then we were through, and under the overpass, and nothing lay ahead of us but open road. I looked up in the mirror, and there was nothing there.

Then the reaction hit me. Fearing that in a moment I would be trembling uncontrollably, I let my foot leave the throttle. I let compression slow us down. Finally I pulled off onto the shoulder and stopped the car with a jerk.

Beside me, Marina's scream had dropped to a small wailing moan, ululating hysterically. I switched the engine off. Trying to control my almost spastic hands and arms, I reached for her. "Darling, *darling!*" I cried out, shaking her by the shoulders. "It's all right! We're safe! Everything's all right!"

She stared at me out of enormous eyes. Her moaning stopped. "Let me *go!*" she cried out, pulling violently away. Then she covered up her face and wept, her head thrown back, her whole body shaken with her weeping.

"Sweetheart! Marina! It's all *right!*" I kept repeating foolishly. "It was a hologram—some kind of projection. That's *all* it was. I tell you, we're *safe*. There's no need to be afraid!"

She dropped her hands. Still weeping, she threw herself at me. "Afraid! *Afraid!* Of course I'm not afraid! What was there for me to be afraid of?" Her small fists hammered at my shoulder, at my chest. "My G-G-God, are you a log? A stone? *C-can't you feel anything at all?*"

I simply stared at her, helpless before her terrifying intensity. "My God, *my G-G-God!*" she sobbed, covering her face again. "Those animals! Those poor, *poor* animals! When I think of the c-callousness, the utter emptiness, the—the abandonment, the *uselessness!* Oh, damn you, *damn you!* You'll never *understand!*"

Once more her weeping shook her; and I, shaken by her words, made no attempt to touch her. An endless minute passed, lacerated by her sobbing, a minute and another and a third—then suddenly it was over. She dropped her hands again; she sighed, a sound so sad and so forlorn that any hurt I might have felt was swept away. Gently she reached out to me.

"I never should have said that," she whispered. "Garry, not to *you*. I'm sorry. It's just—just that you're a westerner. In Asia we see things differently. Besides, though you can see perils in the future, I—I share agonies right now. *Have you ever thought what we've been doing to the animals?* On every highway, Garry? We run them down, but it's not death that counts—" Her hands clutched at mine. "We all die, men and beasts. In the wilds an animal will die, and it'll be eaten, by other beasts and birds of prey and scavenging insects. At least its substance goes to sustain more life.''

"How about men killed in war?" I said. "By earthquakes, tidal waves, tornadoes?''

"We're on a different level. Most of us. Animals *have* to feel their deaths aren't purposeless.'' Her voice rose. "Garry, did you know that sometimes one caribou will actually *allow* a pack of wolves to eat it? That antelopes in Africa have done the same for hunting lions? They *know*. They know it in the group-souls they share, life after life, until they individualize as men. I know you don't believe that, but it's what Buddhists teach—''

She stroked my face; she let me hold her close. "What have we done to them, for years and years, as our highway speeds went up and our concern went down? Have you ever seen a dead animal even thrown off a freeway, Garry—except deer, because they're big enough to cause accidents? No, no! We leave them there, to be crushed, flattened thin, rubbed into the fabric of our concrete—even their hair, their hides— until they vanish. No other animals can get to them to profit by their deaths, not even buzzards—no, not even ants! And that is what they do not understand, their useless dying, the contemptuous coldness of our disregard; and in their chilly emptiness *they hate us for it*. More and more and more of them. They—they've reached critical mass. It was no hologram that tried to kill us! *They're striking back!*''

I thought about Jung's theory of a mass-subconscious, of group-souls. I remembered the stories of Lord Buddha, feeding his own body to hungry tigers.

"Garry, you've seen Kuniyoshi's prints of monster cats! You've heard the legends, from every continent, of monster dogs and jaguars and wolves! They aren't just legends. They're *real*—but never, never, *never* on this scale. Lover, you *must* believe me! I felt it all when—when we went through that beast.''

I did remember the legends I had read. Even the one about the monstrous cat that's said to haunt the lower corridors of the Capitol in Washington—still terrifying patrolling guards at night. I remembered, and in spite of logic, and my own training—and also just because I knew my girl so well—I did believe.

"Marina," I said then, "what can we do?"

"In Japan," she told me, "the people who grow cultured pearls have *segaki* services performed for the spirits of all those oysters who die in making them. Samisen makers have them said for the dogs and cats whose skins are stretched over their instruments. It is an explanation, an apology. This is all they ask."

"Who could we get to do it here? Christianity tells us animals have no souls. You know, 'the beasts that perish.' "

"Not all Christians believe that," she answered, "nor all ministers, and there are many others who would help."

"And how are we supposed to sell Chief Sam on the idea?"

She kissed me, there next to the haunted highway. "We'll have no trouble there," she declared. "*His* people never did deny that animals have souls."

It took Chief Sam a little while to get things organized, quietly, and without stirring up a mess of controversy. But he managed it, and we were surprised at how many people from how many different faiths came to our assistance. (The media hardly touched it, and when they did they treated it as nut stuff, as a joke.) In ten days the one-car fatal accident rate plummeted; in three weeks it returned to normal. In a month almost everyone had forgotten it completely, and I was trying to.

Then, in February, the Chief and I had to take Emmie Bostwick up to Denver to check out an anonymous assassination warning, which turned out to be baseless. We had an early dinner and headed back, praying that the roads would all be dry and open. We did have bad weather for the first two hours; then it cleared and before we knew it the traffic was all passing us, trying to make up time.

Our first hint of trouble came around ten o'clock when the feeling came to me. I thought, "Not *again!*"—still seeing that enormous wildcat in my mind's eye. Then, to my relief, Emmie started breathing hoarsely, as she always does when one of her impressions starts coming through. "I get a great big car, or maybe it's a bus," she told us. "It's full of men, just men. They—oh, they scare me! Something's gonna happen! One of 'em's up front where he oughtn't to be, up past the—I guess it's wire—and—*oh, no, no! Don't you do it!* Oh, Chief Sam, he's goin' to do something to the driver—with a knife! And—" She shuddered and was silent. "Man! I'm sure glad *that's* gone," she muttered finally.

Chief Sam soothed her and we drove on. It was a full hour before we saw the traffic block, the blue lights, ambulances, wreckers, all clustered around an overpass. I swung our own light down against the windshield, and on the shoulder we passed the long halted line. We stopped behind a knot of police cars. Sam and I got out. The freeway for a hundred yards was strewn with shattered metal, torn metal, twisted metal, metal charred out of all recognition, shattered glass, and—well, other things. Above it all there was a great gap in the railing of the overpass.

We found Tod Welles there, in charge. He filled us in. "At least, Colonel," he told Sam, "it's not a one-car deal, so you don't have to worry, but it's really going to be a hell of a mess to clean up. The bus—"

The bus had been State-owned, on its way from Andriess Hospital, maximum security for the criminally insane, loaded with more than 30 of their hopeless cases—all killers who had killed again inside, or tried to. They were being moved to a special new even-more-maximum facility, and one of them—though nobody could figure how—had got to the driver and cut his throat—

Sam and I looked at one another, thinking of Emmie.

—and the bus had plunged straight down into the path of a truck and trailer loaded with steel pipe, trying to make 90 miles an hour. It was like being hit by an express train.

Welles gestured at the road. "Two survivors," he told us. "One guard, one prisoner. About a dozen of the bodies are sort of in one piece. The rest have all been through the shredder. And now it's fixing up to snow." He gestured at a few flakes that had started falling. "We'll be lucky to get the road opened before a storm hits."

The wrecker crews were hauling and pushing metal off the

highway; the ambulance men, some carrying stretchers, some with baskets, were going about their grimmer business.

Welles kept looking at his watch. "At least," he said, "it's not like we were dealing with real people, except the driver and the guards. Those men were subhuman, every damn one of 'em. No loss." He shrugged. "Hell, what we can't find of them the big riggs'll take care of."

Chief Sam and I looked at each other once again, and I knew that he and I were thinking the same thing, and I could feel gooseflesh all along my arms.

Then he took Tod Welles aside and spoke to him quietly and very seriously; and we left him there after we'd said good night.

"What's he going to do?" I asked, as we walked back.

"He's going to stay till every piece is found—each ear, each finger bone, each scrap of flesh. He doesn't understand, but he'll do what I asked him to." He drew a deep breath. "Garry," he said, "there are some things we mustn't take a chance on. Not *ever*."

Another one of those people we see, and we ingore. They're characters, all right, but it seldom occurs to us to pay them any heed. They're crazy. They have to be, of course, or they'd be just like us.

Julie Stevens is just beginning her career, lives in Oregon, and has an uncanny grasp of knowing when to end a story that has, in fact, more than one ending—at the bottom of the page, and in the corners of your closet, the one you thought you'd just cleaned out.

Cassie, Waiting

by Julie Stevens

CRAZY CASSIE. Cassie, the bag lady. Cassie, who staked out her territory on Eighty-third and Lexington one sunny afternoon five years ago and told an unheeding world that the next president would be a Hollywood actor. She stands there today, shouting unheard prophecy into the flow of traffic.

Crazy Cassie keeps business hours. She's there, in command of her street corner, five days a week from ten to three. Then she disappears into the hordes of nameless New Yorkers. Those who pause to wonder where she goes when she is not verbally accosting them, do so only in the hope that she will not return.

People pass the bag lady with wary glances, and though the sidewalks are crowded, a circle of bare concrete surrounds her. People show much interest in Crazy Cassie but pay no real attention. They might note the dirty green plaid coat and the frenzied shouting, and maybe they see the fevered eyes peering through bangs of matted gray hair. But they never look at her face. Crazy Cassie could pass them on the street, and if she were clean and if she were not shouting, she would go unrecognized.

Not that recognition was important. People still would not listen to her. Nor would they believe her. Would anyone ever believe that the charming and gracious Dorothea Lindsay, wife to Dr. Charles F. Lindsay, fond parent of Shaun and Barbara Lindsay, the doer of good deeds approved by the Junior League and Charlie's mother, was, in fact, Crazy Cassie?

Naturally, not.

Or, rather, unnaturally so.

Cassie amused Dorothea. The babbling woman on the streets was as accurate a persona as Dr. Lindsay's devoted wife, and no doubt, a more sincere one.

Cassie was born of an affair. One lousy affair. The one and only affair Dr. Lindsay's monumentally bored spouse had attempted. Maybe there was something in the way Dorothea asked. Crying into her embroidered pillowcase late at night, she had asked the darkness to provide. But provide what? Surely not this.

She had waited later than any of her friends. She had put up with Charlie's infidelities longer than his first wife ever did.

Bring me happiness, she whispered into the dark. It was a request made safe by its impossibility. She asked for happiness every night as she cried herself to sleep.

Tell me what you want, a voice inside herself responded one night. It never occurred to Dorothea to be frightened. Her reaction was amazement that anyone had even listened to her plea. She found herself answering that she wanted a perfect lover. And, so, the two of them, she and the voice from the dark, created Matthew. Not for Dorothea Lindsay the suntanned tennis instructors or German-speaking ski bums favored by her friends. Matthew was nineteen, beautiful, and the son of Charlie's favorite mistress. Matthew, the philosophy major, whose need to understand the meaning of life had been so intense that he bypassed day-to-day living. Matthew understood theories of the universe but not life with Dorothea. He was hers to teach, hers to make perfect. Though she knew that Matthew truly existed, so, too, did she realize that this boy was a gift from the formless voice in her midnight thoughts. It was the fact that he had a real name and a real place in the universe that made him all the more mysterious to her.

Their days together took on the unreality of a slow-motion

movie sequence. Dorothea drifted in the warm, happy haze of being loved.

"I'll stay with you forever," Matthew said.

But the day came when it was not enough to have a perfect lover. She had to know if he would stay, if it would always be this wonderful.

Tell me, she demanded of that inner voice.

It doesn't matter, the voice answered.

Tell me, she pleaded.

Enjoy what has been given, was the response.

Tell me.

If you really want to know. For the first time, Dorothea knew the voice in her head was male, and that it spoke sadly.

He told her. He told her about Matthew and herself and all of her friends, and people she had never met. He would keep telling her for the rest of her life.

Matthew laughed at her. "I'll stay with you always," he said. But he had already met the girl with dark eyes and darker hair, who smoked too much and studied medieval literature and would have him married within a year and a father within two years and a widower within ten.

People always laughed at Crazy Cassie, some to hide their nervousness, some in disgust that society had found no suitable means for removing the Cassies from the street.

People laughed at Dorothea Lindsay, too. They smiled covertly behind manicured hands and monogrammed napkins. Dr. Lindsay's sweet, demented wife—nothing to require hospitalization, you understand, and such a charming hostess; but Charlie's spouse said such funny things, had so many strange opinions, and was always wrong.

Cassie. A good name for a crazy prophet, Dorothea thought when she selected the name. Perhaps she should name her midnight voice as well. But what? Apollo? Or Lucifer? It was hard to decide. Her Episcopal girlhood had not prepared her to identify sad demon voices.

"Gilford's a shoo-in for mayor," the portly businessman was saying to Charlie as Dorothea handed both men their drinks. "Don't you think so, Dot?"

"I doubt it," she answered softly, but Charlie responded in

the affirmative and the two men's conversation swirled on past Dorothea.

She thought of the wig upstairs in her room, sitting on its stand at the very back of the closet. And there was the green plaid coat hidden in the Bloomingdale's box underneath the rack of blouses.

"We've got to do something about the neighborhood," Dr. Philbin's wife said, punctuating every other word with a forward thrust of her gin and tonic. "The Mental Health Department will have to step in, won't they?"

Why was she never believed, Dorothea wondered. Why, after events turned out exactly as she said they would, did no one remember that she had said it first?

Apollo/Lucifer/Crazy Cassie? Who was Dorothea Lindsay?

"Dottie, for heaven's sake. What do you think?" Dr. Philbin's wife pressed. "Do you know she was yelling about germ warfare yesterday? That old woman will be locked up before winter, won't she?"

"I doubt it," Dorothea answered.

But no one listened.

Leanne Frahm has had her first stories showcased in Terry Carr's Universe *series, as Australian, and here presents us with an old-fashioned (though not so old-fashioned as all that) story of the sort sadly lacking these days. It is very reminiscent of the 1950s' British disaster novels that took over the field for a time. It is also as compelling, and in its implications just as terrifying.*

High Tide

by Leanne Frahm

"HEY, MR. CLEAVER, he's fallen asleep again."

Peter Cleaver took his eyes off the rutted road for a second and glanced across the seat of the truck at his son. Michael's head hung down on his chest, rocking gently with each bump. His fair hair flopped across his closed eyes. Cleaver smiled briefly at Drip, on Michael's other side, and received a blank stare in reply. He looked back at the road, feeling slightly foolish. Drip had that adolescent ability down to perfection. Cleaver wondered, not for the first time, whether it had been wise to include Drip in the trip.

"Hey," he said, nudging Michael with his elbow. "Wake up. Greet the dawn. Look like you're interested."

A ragged banner of screeching lorikeets swooped by, across the paling sky, adding their own noisy encouragement.

Michael jerked awake and gazed sleepily through the dust-smeared windscreen. "Are we there yet?" he yawned.

"Nearly," said Cleaver.

"We just passed the Seaforth store while you were asleep," Drip volunteered, his tone supercilious.

Lord, thought Cleaver irritably. Can't he talk any other way? Not everyone found it easy to get up at four A.M. He stifled a yawn himself. Including me, he added. Obviously

Drip would have no trouble—vampires and werewolves and kids like Drip were at their best through the night.

Michael didn't seem to notice the sarcasm, and was peering at the lightening scenery as they rattled through the bush. Cleaver wondered how long it would be before even he noticed Drip's antagonism. He winced inwardly at the prospect of three days with him. Still, it had been impossible to refuse Ralph Buckley's appeal when he'd mentioned the fishing trip he'd planned for Michael and himself.

"It'd mean a lot to him, Pete," Ralph had confided over a dripping stubbie of Four-X. "I just can't get away again this weekend, and he needs to get out and mix with men. Better than lying around the house all day, annoying his mother. He'll be real thrilled with the idea."

Drip now looked anything but thrilled, feet up on the dashboard, glowering at the sunrise as at a personal affront. At sixteen he wasn't a very bright or likeable boy, and at seventeen he'd be mean. Cleaver sighed resignedly. He resolved to make a determined effort to have a good time with Mike despite Drip.

The truck lurched over the furrows, sending up a mist of fine red dust, bleached to pink by the sallow light of the rising tropical sun. The small aluminum boat, a thirteen-foot Kestrel, jounced behind them on its trailer, rocking the truck even more. Michael was fully awake now.

"Look—there's the causeway. How many cars?" he said anxiously.

In the distance they could see the area of flattened guinea grass where an assortment of cars and trucks, with their attendant trailers, were parked near the top of the boat ramp.

"Seven," said Cleaver, rapidly casting an eye over them. "No, eight. There's a little Subaru over to the side."

"That's a lot already," said Michael. "Do you think any of them will be going to Mud Island?"

Cleaver shook his head. "I don't think so. Most will be just fishing for the day, or going to the bigger islands with water where the camping's better."

"Yeah," muttered Drip.

Cleaver continued over him. "Besides, not many people know the way through the mangroves to Mud Island."

They bumped across the causeway and finally drew up at the top of the boat ramp above the tidal creek. Cleaver turned off the ignition and pulled on the handbrake. It was a relief to be stationary.

"O.K.," he said. "Let's load up."

Michael scrambled out of the cab of the Homer Datsun and up into the tray, while Drip followed slowly. Cleaver walked back to the boat and loosened the straps that held it to the trailer. He checked the safety gear again, and then began lifting the equipment into the boat as Michael and Drip passed it to him.

Tent, containers of water, Esky full of ice and cold food, a carton of tinned food and bread, eating utensils, air mattresses, gas stove and light, petrol can, fishing gear, oars, spare clothes and toilet paper. He mentally checked again. Everything seemed to be there. What they didn't have they could go without.

"Christ, your mother doesn't mean us to starve," he grunted, lifting the carton. He nodded at a large bottle of vinegar among the tins. "I know I like vinegar with fish, but this is ridiculous." Michael laughed, and tried to say "Yeah" in his father's tone, man-to-man. Cleaver grinned at it.

The boat loaded, they stood for a moment while Cleaver lit a cigarette. The light was brightening rapidly, casting long shadows of gum and fig trees around them. A figbird uttered its rich musical call, and a spangled drongo scolded noisily back at it. Insects began to hum the morning's cantata. Below them, the waters of the creek surged sluggishly, the tide almost full. In a few hours, its mirrorlike skin, now disturbed only by the concentric rings of surface-questing fish, would be as chopped and furrowed as the road, as the waters dashed back out to sea. Far out near the mouth, they could hear the remote whine of a powerboat.

"Come on, Dad," said Michael, breaking the spell. "They're beating us."

"Right, better get a move on," said Cleaver. "We can only reach Mud Island at high tide, so let's hop to it." He swung himself into the cab, and turning on the motor, began to swing the truck round in a semicircle. Michael ran alongside the boat, yelling directions as Cleaver began to reverse the trailer down the boat ramp.

"Left hand down a bit," called Michael, giggling.

"You're nearly in the water," yelled Drip. "You'd better stop."

Cleaver ignored them both and stopped when he judged the wheels of the trailer were half-submerged. He leaned out of the window and said, "O.K. Take the boat off."

Running to the front of the trailer, Michael released the ratchet lock on the winch and began paying out the wire rope that held the boat to the trailer. Drip waded distastefully to the back and started tugging it off the sloping trailer. The flat stern hit the water with a muted smack, and the boat glided down to float in the shallow water.

"We've got it," called Michael, holding to the prow. He laughed as Drip wiped at the spray that had hit his face. Cleaver nodded in the rear-vision mirror and drove up the ramp, towards the makeshift carpack. He checked again that nothing had been left in the back of the truck and locked the cabin carefully. He was never very happy about leaving the truck parked at a boat ramp. Too many vehicles had been broken into. Some fishermen had returned from a trip once to find their cars up on blocks and the wheels gone. He shrugged. You pays your money and you takes your chances.

He frowned as he walked toward the creek and caught sight of the boat. Drip had left Michael to hold the prow alone, but luckily the pull of the tide was slight now. Drip was busy tossing stones at the small shoals of baitfish that hung over the ramp, feeding on the algae that encrusted the submerged concrete. Michael wasn't objecting, though. He was laughing as the wavelets splashed up their thighs, and his laughter and Drip's irate voice echoed from the other side of the creek, where the mangroves grew thickly, forming a dark impenetrable barrier.

Cleaver halted for a moment's indulgence in the sight of his son's enjoyment. Twelve. Next thing he'd be a teenager, next a man. It was a strange thought, both depressing and exhilarating. Could you ever pinpoint the times of transition, say yes, now this boy is a man? Cleaver couldn't remember from his own childhood. He wondered if he'd notice Michael's.

He shook off the mood of introspection that the quiet dawn engendered and found himself laughing at Michael's comic expression as he floundered on the slippery moss, at the fresh, bright morning, at the prospect of a fine bag of fish. Drip would be no trouble at all. It was going to be a great weekend. He ran down the boat ramp.

"Hold tight now," he said to Michael. Sliding into the boat he swung the outboard down over the stern. He connected the fuel lines and pumped the bulb a few times. The motor purred at the first pull.

"Right. Push off and hop in," he said, grimacing as Drip hopped and Michael pushed. Soon they had both clambered aboard, shaking the water from their jeans and sprawling over the gear. Michael's eyes were sparkling as he took the center seat opposite Cleaver.

"Up to the sun, Dad," he whispered, shy of Drip's overhearing him. Cleaver laughed again. It was always "up to the sun" when they had taken the boat out, right from when Michael was a toddler. He'd believed they could follow the golden path the sun made on the water right up to it, and the words had become a sort of incantation to them. Cleaver winked solemnly, and reached out to tousle Michael's hair, but he ducked under the hand, scowling backwards at Drip, who snickered.

Cleaver stayed at half-throttle, following the winding creek carefully. As with most tidal creeks, long sandbars lurked beneath the waters, shifting from time to time. He knew this creek well, but still remained alert. It paid to be careful.

The creek widened imperceptibly, sand dunes to their left, mangroves to the left. Gradually the smooth surface turned to swells, then waves, as they met the sea proper. They were in the huge Seaforth Bay. Ahead of them lay Rabbit Island, Newry Island, The Mausoleum, the remnants of rolling hills before the sea rose up around them eons ago. But these were resort islands, popular for Sunday boat trips, with the fishing so competitive that you could almost walk from boat to boat—not the sites for a real camping and fishing trip.

Cleaver turned north, cutting across the bay to where a slash of deep green signaled the far shore. The green was a wide strip of mangroves, and within it, in a maze of small creeks that meandered through the black ooze of the swamps, was Mud Island.

Cleaver felt his pulse quicken.

The water darkened visibly as they drew near the mangroves. Till then, it had been the clearest of aquamarine, sparkling under the sun's rays, with only a gentle swell. It had been transparent enough for them to make out a shoal of bright blue jellyfish floating on a current far beneath them. Michael had seen a turtle surface, its broad wet shell gleaming. It had stared blankly at them for a second, then it had dived hastily. Michael had laughed at it. Drip had ignored it.

He'd been remarkably quiet so far. Only once had he roused himself out of his studied lethargy. "What's that?" he'd asked, pointing at some well-defined patches of water far off that glistened more palely than the surrounding sea.

"I don't know," Cleaver said. "Perhaps . . ."

"Figures," Drip grunted. Michael had looked at his father in surprise, and Cleaver shrugged.

Now the mangroves loomed up before them, forbidding in their silence and dark opacity. Cleaver cut back to idle and scanned the wall.

"Where do we go?" said Drip.

"Through—ah—there?" said Michael uncertainly, his finger wavering through a ninety degree arc. He turned to his father. "I've forgotten," he said.

"It's O.K.," said Cleaver. "I've got it now."

He headed towards a narrow break in the barrier, where only the tips of budding mangroves thrust through the surface of the water. He moved the boat gingerly across it, zigzagging around the larger bushes. A tunnel formed as the mangroves closed in again, shrouded by the overhanging branches.

"You see, the tide's at about fifteen feet right now," Cleaver explained to Drip. "At low, this is a mud flat between the mangroves; you can't get in or out. That's why we always come at full tide. Then you have to wait about twelve hours for the next high, or at least make sure you're coming out on a making tide. We'll have all today, tonight, and tomorrow before leaving on tomorrow evening's high tide."

"Uh-huh," Drip responded.

They followed the winding stream, the water murky and sinuous beneath them. Trails of brown seaweed floated past, or decorated the branches around them. Small crabs crawled among the bushes, waving huge red claws defiantly at them as they passed.

"What's that stuff?" asked Drip, pointing into the water beneath the mangroves.

Cleaver peered through the dim light. He could make out patches of a clear glutinous substance floating among the twisted trunks. He shrugged.

"Some kind of jelly. I don't know what it is, maybe oyster-spawn, or something. You get a lot of peculiar stuff in the mangroves."

The bushes on their right gave way abruptly to a long sandy spit. "There you are, that's Mud Island," said Cleaver, as they rounded the spit.

"Where's the mud?" asked Drip in surprise.

Cleaver laughed. "The back of the island's mud and mangrove all right, but this side has sand." He pointed to a small beach about a hundred yards long. It rose to a ridge where scratchy wisps of salt-grass grew. Behind it the mangroves manifested themselves again. "I wouldn't think much of camping on mud, would you?" he asked.

Drip scowled self-consciously.

"Anyway," Cleaver continued, "there's plenty of mud around us. You can see how the creek widens into a small bay facing the beach. The sand shelves out about another six feet, *then* it's mud. You'll see it as the tide goes down—even walk right through it, which is not very pleasant."

He moved the boat into the shore, shut off and lifted the outboard. Michael crawled past Drip and leapt ashore, pulling the prow into the sand. It made a squeaky, grating noise, loud in the silence that hung about them with the cessation of the motor.

"Get the anchor out," Cleaver said to Drip, "and take it up on the beach. Then we'll start unpacking and set up camp."

Drip dropped off the edge of the boat onto the damp sand with the light reef anchor. Cleaver was gratified to notice that he didn't complain about getting wet again. Maybe Drip would enjoy the trip after all, now that it had really started.

"Hey, stop tracking sand into the tent," said Michael indignantly. He pushed the last tent-peg into the soft sand and sat back on his haunches, glaring up at Drip who was trying to maneuver an inflatable mattress through the entrance.

They had erected the tiny tent on the beachward slope of the ridge. There was barely enough room for the three air-beds inside, but Cleaver knew they would spend little time sleeping. Night-fishing was even more enjoyable—and profitable—then fishing by day.

He was fixing a light tarpaulin over some long bleached bones of driftwood a little way from the tent for a windbreak.

"Mike," he called. "Get the eating gear. We'll set the primus up here out of the wind."

There was no wind at present. The spikes of salt-grass barely moved, and the glossy mangrove leaves lay unstirring. But later, after sunset, he knew the shorewind would rise and gust over the mangroves to be lost at sea.

He heard a sudden call from Michael. "Dad, look at this!"

Michael had wandered along the beach a little, down to the water's edge. He was pointing to something white at his feet. Cleaver shrugged aside the question of the food and sauntered over, with Drip following. The object resolved itself into a small skeleton. Michael was bending down, delicately touching the bird's skull. The wings and body were completely free of feathers or flesh—even the tough skin of the webbed feet was eroded.

Michael glanced up at his father. "Can I keep it, Dad? Look, it's all there."

"What do you want that for?" said Drip disdainfully. "Probably stinks."

Cleaver sniffed. There was no odor of putrefaction. "Well," he began, "I suppose so. . ."

Michael started to gather the skeleton up, but immediately the myriad small bones fell apart into an unrecognizable heap. "Aw . . ." His voice was disappointed.

Cleaver smiled gently. "Looks like all the sinews and ligaments are gone, too. Why not just keep the skull?"

"Oh, O.K.," said Michael. He stood up, pocketing it.

Cleaver glanced at the sun, hanging high and white above the palisade of trees. Barely eight o'clock, and the camp set. Everything ready.

"Listen, boys," he said. "The tide's on the way out now. First we'll net for bait, then we'll fish from the island till nightfall. The tide'll be on the way in then, so we'll take the boat out into the deeper area—and fish till we get tired."

"We won't," Michael protested.

"When'll we eat?" Drip said sarcastically, scuffing at the sand.

Cleaver ignored him and grinned at Michael. "Even fishermen get tired," he pointed out.

Michael shook his head vigorously. "O.K.," he said. "We'll see. Now, get the net out—we need bait before we can start."

It was Drip's turn to hold the end of the net on the beach. Cleaver frowned at him. "Higher," he said, more sharply than he had meant to. He was wading deep in the mire that met the sand of the island, water up to his waist, black glutinous mud up to his knees. He moved a slow step at a time, parallel to the beach, his legs aching from the repeated effort of pulling each sandshoe loose from the muck. His back hurt with the strain of keeping the net upright as it unfolded behind him. The water darkened around him, stained with puffs of mud that wafted to the surface around his legs.

He ducked his face under the murky water to rinse the sweat and mud away, and shook his head fiercely.

"O.K., I'm coming in," he called. "And keep that leading edge *up,* or the bloody fish'll swim over the top!"

He floundered ashore onto the firm sand and they hurriedly hauled the net in from both ends, running it up the beach as it cleared the water.

Michael joined them as they began to pick over it for some bait-fish, swinging his bucket. A couple of prawns had flung themselves clear and were making single-minded efforts to leap back into the sea. Drip grabbed them and tossed them into the bucket.

Michael was diligently untangling small mullet that flopped in the mesh. Several miniature Johnny Dories, flashing silver in the sun, lay supine, caught by their raised spines, gulping air, and a tiny flathead wriggled like a snake. Michael looked up at his father questioningly.

"Keep the mullet," said Cleaver, "but those others are worthless, and the flathead will be more use if it grows to eating size. Throw them back." He ran his fingers through his mud-streaked hair in exasperation and turned to Drip. "How many's that?" he asked.

Drip tilted the bucket slightly so Cleaver could see the level of fish and prawns inside.

"I don't know," said Cleaver. "There should be shoals of bait-fish around here right now. If we're going to do any real fishing, we'll have to use the prawns too. To hell with eating them." He sighed, squinting up at the noonday sun. "We'll give it one more try."

Disconcerted by Cleaver's annoyance, the boys silently began to concertina the net, ready for the next drag. Cleaver stretched, steeling his muscles for one more back-breaking effort, and wiped the encrusted salt from his eyebrows. He looked out over the water. The only signs of life were a few patches of the odd-looking jelly floating calmly on the surface and some seagulls spiralling listlessly overhead.

"Right," he said, and picking up the end of the net, trudged into the water until his feet fell into the irresistible pull of the mud.

He suddenly heard a rasping burble and turning, saw a boat glide round the spit at the end of the island. He stared at it. The boys had heard the cough of the ancient outboard and were watching it too. It was a small wooden dinghy, paint-flaked. A mound of wire-netting crab-pots balanced precariously from prow to stern, and as it chugged closer, Cleaver could see a grizzled face shaded by a nondescript felt hat squinting at him between the wires.

"G'day," said the face in a cracked voice. The motor cut to idle, and the boat swung slightly. "Fishing, are you?"

"Yes," said Cleaver, feeling slightly ridiculous, standing

waist-deep in water, peering up over the gunwhale. He tugged alternatively at his feet to stop them slipping even farther into the mud.

The old man shook his head lugubriously and spat over the side. "Won't do much good," he said positively. "Fish're off now. Haven't caught a decent size one in days now."

His certainty annoyed Cleaver. "Well, it won't do any harm to try," he said, growing more and more conscious of the weight of the net over his shoulder. He gestured to the crab-pots. "How's the crabbing?" he asked.

The old man spat again, more venomously. "No better than the fishing," he replied. "The dillies been empty for a week now, if you don't count a few undersizers." He winked, and Cleaver knew that taking the "undersizers" hadn't worried the old man a bit. "Still, gives you something to do," he went on, turning the boat's prow towards a narrow opening in the mangroves opposite the beach.

"Indeed it does," muttered Cleaver. He watched the dinghy disappear, leaving only the remote droning of the outboard trailing in the air.

He turned to Michael and Drip. They were giggling, obviously at the old man and his crab-pots. Funny how youth thinks old age so amusing, he thought. Until you suddenly get to forty and see mortality more clearly. He shook himself.

"Settle down," he called, "and get on with it." He served inshore slightly to miss one of the floating masses of jelly, and began trailing the net after him again.

Blackness wrapped the boat as it rocked gently on the high tide. The inky reaches of the moonless night were mirrored in the warm dark waters beneath them, and the darker ebony of the mangroves encircled them. Above, the cold and lightless points of stars enhanced the plush velvet of their cocoon. A gentle breeze ruffled the waters, flickering an occasionally brighter star's reflection.

The boat swung lazily as the current tried to pry it loose from the anchor, and Cleaver glanced over his shoulder at the one sphere of light that relieved the darkness. The gas lamp shone steadily at the camp on Mud Island, a beacon for their return, a reassurance.

The boys were as silent as he was, enjoying, he hoped, the loveliness of the night. Maybe the fishing's just an excuse, he mused. An excuse for a grown man to wrap himself in the warm blackness and gentle rocking. He shrugged off the Freudian explanation, grinning. Why let it spoil the sensation?

But the fishing. He sighed. That was the only disappointment of the night.

"Any bites?" he whispered.

"Not yet," said Michael hopefully.

"Nope," said Drip in a loud and bored voice. Cleaver fingered his own line once more. It was rigid, a faint tremor vibrating along the nylon as the current pulled at it. But there had not been one jerk on it since they'd begun hand-fishing from the boat two hours ago. The afternoon's fishing from the island had proved equally fruitless.

Cleaver felt a wave of irritation. For those that knew of it, Mud Island was famous for its fishing. He couldn't understand it. There had been no storms, no runoff of fresh water, the tides weren't exceptionally high or low—but still, no fish. Thank God for the tinned food, he thought wryly.

A strangled squawk from Drip broke the silence.

"I've got one!" he yelled at the top of his voice. "It's a bloody big one," he gulped. The boat rocked in confirmation.

"Can you manage it?" said Cleaver sharply.

"Course I can," Drip gasped.

"Get your line in," Cleaver said to Michael, swiftly reeling his in. "We don't want it tangling in our lines when it gets near the boat."

He could hear Michael fumbling in the dark to obey. His own tackle cleared the water with a popping sound and putting his reel in the bottom of the boat, he reached for the torch. He switched it on, and saw Drip shirtless in the prow seat, his shoulder muscles straining as he pulled on the line. Michael, in the center, was still reeling in.

"You're right," he said. "It is a big one. Just keep pulling, nice and steady."

"Shut up. I can do it," grunted Drip. Cleaver was taken aback. He saw Michael staring at him, eyes wide. O.K., he thought, do it, and sat back.

Drip was staring into the water as his taut line circled back and forth. Michael had forgotten the exchange in his excitement, and was leaning over to look. Cleaver played the torchlight along the line, into the greenish water. "Michael," he said quietly, "pick up the gaff and be ready to stick it under the gill as it surfaces."

Michael's shadowy head nodded.

The sinker and trace-line emerged as Drip pulled hand over hand.

"Ready," said Cleaver to Michael.

The head and the upper part of a body broke free as Drip stood up, and Michael automatically swung the gaff hook into the straining gill slits.

Both Drip and Michael paused. "What *is* it?" asked Michael, staring into the flat, elongated snout. Eyes gazed back at him from either end of it, and the mouth opened to show rows of small sharp teeth.

"Why, that's a hammerhead!" said Cleaver.

"A bloody shark?" said Drip angrily, looking at him. "I caught a bloody little *shark?*"

Cleaver tried to stifle a burst of laughter. "Well, you've got to admit it was a good fight," he said.

Drip glared at him. "All this time for a shark. Big deal," he said scornfully.

"Now just a minute," began Cleaver.

"Hey, Dad," Michael interrupted. He had been looking at the shark, still tethered by the hook, feebly thrashing the water with its tail. "What's this?"

He pointed to its back, and edged the gaff round slightly to show them. Cleaver shone the torch full on it. The pearl grey of the wide back was discolored, reddish. He peered closer. It seemed to be a wound.

They clustered round the edge of the boat to examine it. A long sore was embedded in the skin, the flesh and muscles showing grey, white broken veins wept blood into it. The white of cartilage showed through in places, and the whole was covered by a film of mucus.

"Has something bitten it?" Michael asked.

Cleaver shook his head slowly. "I don't think so. It looks more like some sort of disease." He eased the hook from the hinge of its jaw, carefully keeping his fingers away from the ulcer. "That might explain why there are so few fish, an epidemic, perhaps. We'd better keep it, and get the disease identified. The Fisheries Inspector will want to know about this. . . ."

The shark heaved in one last desperate effort and threw itself off the gaff. It hit the water with a splash and disappeared into the murky tube of torchlight.

"That's that, then," said Drip maliciously.

Cleaver ignored the bait. "Well, we might as well get back to fishing and see if there *are* any fish left."

"I've had enough," said Drip.

Cleaver kept his temper. "Then you can sit quietly till Michael and I are finished," he said.

Drip shrugged, but said nothing more. Cleaver turned off the torch.

Silence. As the minutes crept on unremarked in the deep blackness, Cleaver noticed the silence. One of the others would shift on his seat, material brushing on metal, or a floating piece of driftwood would touch the boat on its interminable journey through the currents with a scrape. Small waves would slap idly on the hull as the boat rocked. But apart from those small sounds, the stillness was absolute.

That's not right, Cleaver thought. There should have been sounds. The sharp crackle of something—you never knew what—crawling over the lower branches of the invisible mangroves; the soft bubble of a big fish sounding, the panicky ripples of small fish scared across the surface; the sticky plop of mudcrabs in their burrows beneath the black mud. The noises made a continuous muffled chorus in the ubiquitous life of the nighttime swamps.

But tonight there was silence.

Cleaver's thoughts went back to the hammerhead, and its disfigurement. How widespread could an epidemic be, he wondered. The mangroves swarmed with animalculae, a burgeoning cauldron where the sea's plenty was born. An epidemic spreading from here could impoverish the oceans for generations. He shifted uneasily, finding the hard seat suddenly uncomfortable.

He sensed movement. "What are you doing, Michael?" he said softly.

"Just reeling in, Dad. I want to check my bait."

Cleaver grunted, and tugged lightly on his own line. Wishful thinking, he thought. Nothing was disturbing the bait tonight.

He turned idly to watch. Michael was a blurred silhouette as he swung the sinker and hook into the boat.

"Do you want the torch?" Cleaver asked.

"No," said Michael. "I can see it's there." The small white baitfish gleamed palely, picking up the almost imperceptible starlight. "I'll just make sure it's on tight. . . . Hey!" He yelped in pain and astonishment.

"What is it?" Cleaver said quickly, reaching for the torch.

"I don't know . . . it *bit* me!" Michael's voice was scared.

Cleaver thumbed the button and directed the light onto him. He was crouched in the center seat, his line dropped, clutching his hand. Behind him in the prow Drip's face was a pale skull, his eyes wide with interest. Cleaver felt the skin on his cheeks tighten.

He swept the light into the bottom of the boat and stared hard at Michael's hook, then he burst into laughter, a part of his mind surprised to find himself so relieved. Michael looked up at him reproachfully, nursing his right hand, and then down to where a fat white spiny slug writhed on his hook.

"It's a bristleworm!" Cleaver exclaimed.

"What's *that?*" asked Drip.

"Look." Drip moved forward to peer over Michael's shoulder. "It's a segmented worm, but it's covered with hairs, or rather chaetae—almost like tiny glass splinters. Give me your hand, Mike. There. See the spines?" Michael's thumb and forefinger bristled with tiny white hairs. Already the skin around them was turning red.

"It must have been feeding on the bait. It's pretty painful, I know." He grasped Michael's shoulder as he nodded. "There must be some kind of poison in them." Drip's eyes opened wider and Michael recoiled under his hand. Cleaver went on hastily. "It's not fatal, just uncomfortable. But we'd better get back and get them out—put some cream on the swelling. I'll just get rid of our unwelcome visitor and we'll head back to camp.'' Suddenly he was very glad to be leaving the silent dark waters and returning to the sanctuary of the bright gaslight.

He picked up the filleting knife and edged the blade under the bristleworm, which wriggled frenziedly. In one swift motion he tossed it overboard. ''Right,'' he said, switching off the torch. ''Drip, you get the anchor in when I start the motor. Can you manage that?''

Drip's sneer drifted audibly back to him, and Cleaver mentally bit his tongue. He'd said the wrong thing again. He pulled hard at the cord. What with Drip, and no fish, and now Michael's injury, the fishing trip was rapidly sinking to disaster level.

The motor caught, and above its idle he could hear the water swish as Drip pulled in the anchor rope.

''Shit,'' said Drip, stopping suddenly. Cleaver could see his outline in the prow, a deeper black against the invisible mangroves.

''What's the matter?'' he called.

''The rope—it's all covered with that jelly stuff.''

Cleaver could hear the disgust in his voice. ''Well, go on, it won't hurt you,'' he said.

''But it's splashed all over me,'' Drip whined. Cleaver sighed in exasperation. ''Look,'' he said sharply. ''Michael can't pull it in, not with his hand. I've got the motor. *You* pull in the anchor.'' He nearly added that he had told him to wear a shirt, but swallowed the words. That would be too juvenile, even for Drip.

''Shit,'' mumbled Drip again, and began pulling slowly. Cleaver heard the clatter as the rope gave way to the chain, and winced as he visualized the paint scraping off the side. Hold it *out* from the boat, you vicious little bastard, he muttered inaudibly. The throttle throbbed regularly under his hand as he waited.

''Hey!'' Drip's voice came again.

''Now what?'' said Cleaver.

''It's hurting,'' said Drip hesitantly.

''Oh Christ. What is?'' Cleaver said angrily.

"I don't know." Drip's voice sounded confused. "It must be that jelly stuff. It . . . it's *burning!*" His voice rose.

"Dad . . ." said Michael uncertainly.

"O.K., O.K., just hold on." Cleaver fumbled for the torch, his palms suddenly sweaty. He missed the button.

There was a splash and a slithering sound. Cleaver jerked up. Drip had dropped the anchor back into the water.

"Mr. Cleaver!" screamed Drip. "It's *burning* me!" His outline blurred as his hands brushed at his body. The boat began to rock as he moved violently in the prow.

"Drip!" Cleaver yelled. "Keep still! You'll have us all . . . Michael—you stay still!"

He cursed at the torch, suddenly upside down in his hands. Drip was screaming incoherently now, jerking and squirming. He slapped at his torso, at his face and arms. Cleaver could hear a sucking sound as flesh met flesh, and his stomach contracted.

He found the button, and a swathe of light leapt out. For a moment Drip was caught in it, frozen. Cleaver had only a glimpse of him, but it was a glimpse that brought bile searing up his throat. The healthy brown skin was gone, replaced by a glistening mucus, streaked pink and yellow.

Before Cleaver could react the boat topped violently and the torch fell from his hand to land with a solid jolt that extinguished the light.

"Dad!" Michael cried again, barely audible above Drip's hoarse screams. "Stay there!" shouted Cleaver. "I'll . . ."

The boat rocked again, and there was a loud splash. Drip's screams were cut off abruptly, and there was the sound of a frenzied wallowing.

Unthinking, Cleaver hurled himself over the side and into the water. He surfaced and flung the water from his hair. Dimly he heard Michael crying in the boat, a monotonous "Dad, Dad, Dad," but he ignored it, listening for Drip's splashings. The surging water was suddenly incredibly quiet. He trod water for a moment.

"Drip?" he called loudly over the purr of the motor. "Drip!"

He dogpaddled helplessly in small circles, wondering why he was doing this odd thing. It's a joke, he thought. Drip's sort of sick joke. But he kept paddling and calling. If he gave up and climbed back into the boat, then he was admitting that Drip was gone, that he had lost him. The water seemed suddenly cold, and he closed his eyes, shivering.

"Please, Dad, come back." Michael's voice broke through to him. The untended motor had stopped and the silence had crept closer through the blackness. Oh Jesus, he's alone in that boat—thank God the anchor was out.

"It's O.K., Mike. I'm coming back."

He swam tiredly towards the slap of small waves against the aluminum and heaved himself over the edge. He slumped for a moment in the stern seat, streaming water.

"Are you all right?" he asked finally.

"Yes, Dad," Michael whispered. "What was it?"

What was what, Cleaver thought fuzzily. Oh, yes, Drip. Trust a kid to get straight to the heart of things. What *was* it? Cleaver realized he didn't have an answer, didn't even want to think about an answer.

"I don't know," he said. He straightened. "Come on, we'd better get you back to camp. I'll get the anchor. . . ." He stopped, his heart lurching. The anchor rope. What was on it? What was in the water? He saw Drip again, jerking spasmodically, flayed, and himself, plunging into that water. His hands shook.

"Listen, the torch is busted, Mike. I'm going to climb past you and cut the anchor rope. Then I'll start the motor and get us back to the island. We can do without the anchor."

"All right, Dad." Michael's voice was small and distant. How much had he actually seen, Cleaver wondered. He felt a lump in his chest that hurt physically. Mike was too young for this.

He climbed to the prow and, standing on the seat, leaned over to the hitch where the rope was knotted. The knife grated for a few minutes on the tough nylon before it finally parted and slithered into the water. He was careful not to touch the hull.

He went swiftly back to the stern as the boat began to move with the current. The outboard started at once, and he turned them towards the steady beacon of the gaslight.

They traveled in silence. Michael was a small hunched

figure in front of him. Terribly small, Cleaver thought. He cleared his throat and spoke to break the silence that was waiting for them. "Mike, I'm going to ram the boat hard up on the beach and swing it sideways. *Don't* climb over the front, jump out sideways, over the water. O.K.? And don't let yourself touch the water."

"Yes, Dad." There was no further comment.

Cleaver wondered if Michael realized what he meant, whether he had worked it out, that there was something in the water. . . . Or on it, he realized suddenly, remembering the pools of jelly floating by the island and caught in the mangrove roots. Christ, he shuddered. It was all around us all the time. And I ignored it.

The camp was directly in front of them now, and close. The tiny waves made phosphorescent ripples on the sand. Jelly was often phosphorescent, he thought abstractedly, and refused to follow the thought further.

He throttled the boat hard at the beach, then killed the motor and lifted the outboard clear of the sand at the last moment. Even so it caught for a second, making a high-pitched screaming sound as the skeg knifed through the sand. It sounded like Drip, so much so that he spun round foolishly, peering over the turgid waters behind them.

Stupid, he thought. Stupid, stupid. He grabbed savagely at an oar and pushed the boat sideways, levering it as hard as he could onto the beach. "O.K.," he said to Michael. "Jump clear."

He couldn't see if Michael's legs were shaking as he stood up on the seat, but he could feel his own. Michael jumped awkwardly, falling onto his hands, but well clear of the water's edge. Cleaver pulled the oar out of the water and threw it up onto the beach. "Don't go near that," he called. But Michael just stood, holding his right hand with his left, gazing up the slope to the campsite.

Cleaver leapt out himself and, grasping the stern, pulled the boat more firmly onto the sand. It should hold, he thought. With the tide on the way out, it would be left stranded for the rest of the night. They'd be up well before the morning's high, when they could get out of here.

He trudged up the beach and put his arm around Michael. "Come on," he said. "Let's look at that hand."

Under the glare of the gaslight, Cleaver removed the last shiny sliver from Michael's fingers with the tweezers. Gently he rubbed Xylocaine gel over the swollen red areas and sat back.

"There. How's that?" he said, glancing anxiously at Michael's set face. There was no response. He felt at a loss.

He knew he should talk to Michael, should make Michael talk to him. But he felt an unutterable weariness. How could he speak about Drip now—dead Drip, his neighbor's son? All he could say would be, "I didn't know." Fathers always knew, didn't they? They were always right. But not him. He didn't know. No wonder his son would not look at him. He forced himself to cover his helplessness with words and action.

"We can't leave the gaslight on all night," he said, getting up and dusting the sand from his jeans. "What say we collect driftwood and make a fire?" He refused to wonder why he felt this sudden passion for light and warmth, but he was sure Mike would be feeling it too.

Michael rose automatically and began casting around for wood, keeping within the circle of light. There was plenty, and soon Cleaver had a decent-sized fire in a depression scooped out of the sand. It was far enough from the tent to be safe, but close enough to be secure.

"We'll rest now," he said. "Try to sleep. We'll get back first thing in the morning on the full tide." Michael said nothing. Shock, thought Cleaver. Partly shock, anyway.

They lay down on the inflatable mattresses, close together in the confines of the tiny tent. Drip's unoccupied bed lay hauntingly to one side.

Cleaver found he couldn't sleep—he'd known he wouldn't. Lying down was simply an excuse to get Michael to sleep, to wear away some of the horror of the evening. But he lay still, trying not to move. The distended rubber of the mattresses twanged with every motion. He listened to the dark silence outside. The only sounds were the liquid ripples of the waves receding on the beach, the tinkle of shells and pebbles washing over the sand. At any other time this would have a lulling effect, but now Cleaver found himself tensing with every wave, visualizing its serenely floating burden.

He decided to let himself think objectively about the jelly, to strip away its horror, and regard it analytically.

First question. What was it? How had it originated? God knew, not Cleaver, he thought. Analyst's score—zero.

Somehow something had been added to the evolutionary soup of the mangrove mud, and the jelly had resulted. But its potency was unbelievable.

He thought back over the numerous swarms they had seen, the lack of fish—of crabs, too. The old man had mentioned it. And the hammerhead. It must have just been infected—attacked—but its primitive brain hadn't recognized that message from its rudimentary nerves, and it had stolidly followed its instincts to take the bait. He suppressed a shudder. Thank God they hadn't touched it.

They. Thoughts circled inevitably to Drip. He had to face it. Drip was being *eaten* by that stuff. It must multiply at an enormous rate when feeding. It had attacked his skin and was down into the flesh and fat and muscle when Drip plunged overboard, dying. It would have been with him when he sank into the water, still burning, still silently screaming, eating remorselessly into organs and sinews, until his white skeleton joined the white driftwood, current-driven and grinning, surging with the tides, like the skeleton of the bird. . . . Stop it, he thought savagely. Analyst's score—minus ten.

But there was one consequence still to be considered. He and Michael were on an island surrounded by suspect water. They had to travel several miles across said water by boat to reach safety, and whatever else he surmised, he knew that that jelly should not touch them.

I will be careful, Cleaver thought. As long as I can avoid the patches of jelly, as long as I can prevent waves washing into the boat, as long as I keep spray to a minimum, we'll be fine. And until we start off, we're safe on the island. . . . These thoughts were more comforting. He dozed off.

Cleaver woke with a start as a dim grey radiance filtered through the thin walls. He woke knowing Drip was absent. There had been no forgetting in sleep. Michael still slept, his face puffy and pasty, unhealthy-looking. Cleaver shook him gently, stiffening as the first sleepy look of inquiry in Michael's eyes deepened into a blank fearfulness.

"Come on," he said abruptly. "We'll get the boat and go—forget about all this stuff, it isn't important. We'll have something to eat when we get home." And after I've seen Ralph Buckley and explained to the police and convinced the fisheries. The enormity of the day ahead enveloped him like a pall.

They emerged from the tent, the salt-tainted air strong and vigorous under the dawn. Cleaver fumbled in his pocket for a cigarette. Michael glanced down the beach.

"Where's the boat?" he asked, his voice curiously detached.

Cleaver dropped the packet, blood hammering through his veins like cold oil. He stared at the shoreline, where the tiny waves continued their monotonous dance. The oar still lay above the highwater mark where he had flung it, but the boat was gone.

He raced down to the water's edge. The water was still washing over the depression the boat had ground into the sand, but the boat was gone. He jerked his head up. There was no sign of it floating on the oily water. But his fisherman's mind reasonably pointed out that the current would have taken it round the end of the island, and it would be beached on the mainland, probably several miles away. . . .

"Oh, Jesus," he whispered. The water looked oily, he realized, because huge patches of jelly covered it. It stretched across the open water like a continent, with only narrow alleys of blue water intersecting it. It was growing. He looked down. Where the waves met the sand, small banks of jelly glistened in the early light, pushed by the waves, like spume-froth. He backed away. "No boat," he whispered.

"The boat's gone," Michael said conversationally at his elbow. "How, Dad?"

Cleaver turned to him. Michael's pale face smiled up at him, but his eyes were deep and mocking. He looked suddenly like Drip.

"Because," Cleaver snarled, "you smart-arse kid, because your dumb father didn't pull it high enough on the beach! Satisfied?"

Michael took a step back, but gazed intently into his father's face.

"How do we get back then?"

Rage suffused Cleaver. He raised his hand and slapped at the smiling face. "I don't know!" he yelled. "I don't know!"

The blow knocked Michael to the ground. Cleaver fell at once to his knees beside him.

"Oh God, Mike, Michael, I'm sorry." Michael began to cry.

"Don't cry, please don't cry," said Cleaver, hugging him hard.

Michael's teeth were chattering. "Dad, I'm frightened," he sobbed. "It killed Drip, didn't it? What is it, Dad?"

"It's O.K., Mike, don't worry," Cleaver whispered. "We're all right, we'll get back. I'll think of something."

The hooded look in Michael's eyes was gone. He was a child again, trusting. Cleaver felt an enormous relief, an absolution of past mistakes—his ignorance of the jelly, Drip's death, the loss of the boat. There was only now, and this he would concentrate on.

Michael's shaking eased. Cleaver sat back and regarded him. It was time to talk honestly.

"Here's how we stand, Mike. I don't know what that jelly stuff is, but it's deadly if it gets on you. So we avoid the water. We're safe on land." Michael looked around apprehensively at the small hump of the island. Cleaver managed to laugh. "That's all right. We're a couple of feet above the high tide mark. Now we've got food and drink to last for several days if we're careful. People know where we are, so when we don't get back tonight, the Air and Sea Rescue will start searching for us, and we're not all that hard to find. We might even start a smoky fire to help them."

Michael began to look interested. Perhaps there was something glamorous about their situation after all. Rescue from a desert island, maybe by helicopter . . . His eyes lit up. "I'll collect as much driftwood as I can, Dad," he said.

"Good," Cleaver agreed. "We can use mangrove branches to make it smoke. And don't forget there's the chance of someone else coming along, like that old crabber." He thought for a moment. "Pity about the flares. They're in the boat.

Otherwise they would have seen them from Newry or Seaforth. Well, can't be helped. The fire will do instead."

Michael started to get up. "Wait a minute," Cleaver said. "Let's have breakfast first. Thank God your mother packed enough food for two weeks—hey, that was a joke! We won't be here more than a day or two, I promise." He grinned at Michael's solemn face.

"But," he added, "when you go for that wood, keep away from the water."

Being a castaway, thought Cleaver, is bloody boring. He sat under the tarpaulin out of the heat of the sun, squinting abstractedly over the water. It was low tide, the mud flats exposed, but the white glare of the narrow beach hurt his eyes. The jelly-laden water had receded, and he felt that somehow the danger had receded with it.

There was nothing to do. Michael, floppy hat on head and zinc-cream on nose, was still out collecting driftwood to add to the huge pile he had placed on top of the sandy ridge. There was no point even fishing, especially considering the fact that the bait was in the vanished boat, Cleaver thought wryly, let alone the scarcity of fish.

He kept his thoughts firmly off Drip. Already his death seemed a long time past. When they were rescued, then would be the time to release those ugly memories. . . .

"Dad! *Dad*!" Michael's scream jerked Cleaver to his feet. He stared up the beach for a second, orienting himself to Michael's call. At the opposite end of the island to the spit, where a few hardy seagulls still nested in season. He remembered the birds' irate calling as Michael had invaded their territory only a little while ago. Even now he could hear angry screeching.

He ran along the beach, oblivious of the searing sand beneath his bare feet and around the corner. He grunted with relief as he saw Michael standing on a level area of sand above the hightide mark. Michael turned to him.

"Dad, look!" He was pointing to the sand in front of him. His finger shook and the zinc-cream was an incongruous rosy stripe across his pallid face.

Cleaver looked. A seagull sat on her nest in front of them.

Her feathers were ruffled, and her long wicked beak was open to attack. Even as he watched, she emitted a series of sharp caws. But she was facing away from them, towards the water.

Cleaver looked further. His scalp tingled as he realized what she was threatening. The sand shelved away sharply here, and the water at low tide was much closer than around on the beach. And a lump of jelly, as big as a football, was oozing towards her over the sand.

But that's crazy, thought Cleaver. It can't live out of water—no jellyfish can.

Bemusedly he bent towards it. It was different, he realized. Instead of the familiar clear homogeneous colloid, small round spheres interspersed the lump throughout its interior, like lather. And it trailed a long cord of substance that ran back to a bank of the stuff at the water's edge.

The seagull raised her wings as the mass drew nearer, and lowered her head.

Cleaver straightened, trying to understand what the change meant. Suddenly he knew with a chill that the spheres were bubbles of water, not air. The jelly had learned to take its water with it.

He and Michael stood unmoving, fascinated. The seagull reluctantly climbed to her feet, revealing two large speckled eggs. She moved nervously from foot to foot as the jelly progressed inexorably over the smooth sand. Finally her courage broke, and she took to the air as the jelly gained the rampart of her nest, and enveloped the eggs. She swooped overhead in a circle, then flapped slowly away, uttering desolate cries.

Cleaver heard them as in a nightmare, unable to take his gaze from the nest. The eggs were visible through the gelatinous surface. Slowly they changed color, whitened. Suddenly the shells were gone and the yolks showed briefly before they were dispersed in yellow streaks that grew fainter as they were absorbed.

Cleaver felt disoriented, as if all his certainties were being slowly stripped away, leaving an abyss of ignorance. His eyes refused to focus. He could vaguely feel Michael trembling beside him. Then there was a tug on his sleeve.

"Dad!" said Michael sharply. Cleaver blinked and shook himself.

A finger of jelly trembled out of the nest, wavering in their direction. Behind it the mass humped up, as if preparing to embark on further exploration.

"Get back to the camp," Cleaver whispered hoarsely. He spun Michael round and they raced along the ridge to the campsite. They flung themselves, panting, under the tarpaulin, out of the stinging sun. Cleaver's mind was in a turmoil, a part refusing to believe what he had seen, a part frantic with unvoiced implications.

Michael's shaking voice shocked him into reason. "How did it do that, Dad?"

How? Cleaver tried again to analyze it, to banish a growing terror.

"I don't know exactly, Michael," he began feebly. "But a lot of jellyfish carry poisons. This one seems—well—less differentiated, more diffuse, than others. I don't know where this one came from—maybe some kind of mutation—but instead of poisons, it must carry a sort of acid that breaks down living matter to feed it. . . ."

"I don't mean that," said Michael impatiently. "I mean how did it know to go to the eggs? It can't see or hear."

Cleaver stared at him, astounded once again at the perspicacity of youth. Michael knew what was important, while his father covered his fear with bumptious chatter.

He cleared his throat. "Vibrations, perhaps," he said, suddenly conscious of a trickle of sand that showered into a cavity as he moved his elbow. "Vibrations carry well in water. Maybe it can feel vibrations in the sand as well."

"That means we can't move." It was a statement, not a question.

Cleaver searched the edge of the water. Masses of jelly floated quietly on the wavelets as they beached. For the first time he recognized what might be exploratory pseudopods reaching for the sand.

"Well, when the tide's out, like it is now, I don't think it could—feel—us. But later . . . if we're careful, and move slowly, perhaps." Doubt reflected in his voice. "No running, or dropping anything heavy." The resigned terror in Michael's eyes frightened him. "Don't worry, Mike," he said, trying to sound casual. "We'll be all right until the rescue team gets to us."

"Over that?" said Michael, pointing to the water where incrustations of jelly rocked, virtually covering the surface.

Cleaver wondered how far the jelly had spread. He considered the files of parked cars and trucks at the boatramp. How many others had been on the water this weekend? Had there been other casualties? How many? Did the authorities already know of the danger? If so, would they consider rescue was feasible, or would they simply put him and Michael—and Drip—into the category of "disappeared without trace" along with the others? He shook his head. He refused to believe that.

"They'll come," he said firmly. "Remember the helicopter." But a picture of the invaded nest flashed through his mind again, and he wondered to himself if they would come in time.

They sat quietly for some time, watching the jelly-covered water. Cleaver tried to get his thoughts in order, to cover the unknown possibilities of the situation. They would have to spend the night on the island. Nightfall would bring high tide, and the jelly that much closer. Asleep, they might move, violently perhaps, in nightmare, he thought anxiously, glancing at Michael. The tent zipped up—by vinyl would be little protection, considering the ease with which the egg shells were penetrated.

What else? He could stay awake all night, quieting Michael if necessary, in the comforting circle of the gaslight's radiance, but the risk of falling asleep in the silence was too great. Already he felt lethargic. A wave of panic threatened to confuse his thinking, but he fought it down grimly.

The wood . . . Michael had collected an enormous quantity of it. What if they placed it in a ring and set fire to it, with themselves in the middle? It would burn down eventually, but the embers would stay hot for hours—the sand would act as a natural furnace.

He felt suddenly elated, as at a small victory. Besides, it

would give them something positive to do. He looked at the small figure beside him. Less time for dwelling on fear.

Michael seemed to cheer up slightly as he told him of the plan. They spent the long afternoon carefully and quietly making a circular hollow in the sand and arranging the collected driftwood in it. The sand squeaked continuously, and insisted on sliding underfoot as they moved back and forth over their own footprints, making the work awkward. We must look funny, Cleaver thought. Like someone caught in a slow motion film, or one of those nightmares where you can't run.

He paused continually, glancing anxiously at the water's edge after a stumble, or when a piece of driftwood dropped clumsily into place. The water was rising, slowly covering the mudflats, carrying the glutinous mass closer. Several times they froze, as a questing lump formed on the water line, but each time it dissolved back into itself.

Finally Cleaver was satisfied. The sun was setting redly beyond the swamps, drawing answering crimson streaks from the jelly that lined the shore. If I were superstitious, Cleaver thought, I wouldn't like that omen. But I'm not, he added angrily.

"I'll get some food," he said aloud to Michael, who was sitting near the tent. "Then we'll light the fire."

He brought back tinned meat and a packet of dry biscuits, and a cup of water each.

They ate by the last light of the sun, quietly. The familiar silence and darkness formed in the mangroves, and seemed to grope menacingly towards them. Overhead the first cold stars glinted. The waves made no sound at all on the beach, muffled by the jelly.

Cleaver got up, determined to break the spell. They had stuffed whisps of dry salt-grass under the smaller pieces of wood. He set to work lighting them round the circle, and was gratified to see the speed at which the fire took.

"We'll sit here for an hour or so," he whispered, "until the fire dies down. Then we'll move into the middle of the circle and sleep." Michael nodded, his face bright in the firelight, his eyes already looking tired.

"It's lucky it's summer," Cleaver went on. "We won't be

cold, especially with the fire around us.'' Michael's head dropped onto his shoulder. A few minutes passed, and Cleaver realized he was asleep. How vulnerable he is, thought Cleaver. Able to sleep, now. A fierce surge of protective love washed over him, shaking him. It'll be O.K., he promised silently.

Time passed. The heat and vigor of the fire lessened to an occasional flicker of flame. Cleaver judged it would be safe for them to cross, and not too hot within the circle. He gathered Michael in his arms. Michael showed no signs of stirring, and Cleaver mentally groaned under his weight.

Carefully, a step at a time, he moved into the circle. The sand was only pleasantly warm underfoot. He put Michael down and stretched out himself. The warmth of the sand permeated his body, relaxing muscles tense with exhaustion. He slept.

A loud snap woke Cleaver abruptly. He wondered groggily for a moment what had happened, then as his head cleared, he realized that a burnt branch must have broken off a bigger log. He sat up and looked around. There it was. It had rolled a little way down the slope towards the water. Nothing to worry about. He started to lie down again when he sensed a movement beyond it. He rose slowly to his knees and stared into the darkness.

The embers still cast a wavering illumination from the remnants of the fire. A dimly discernible humped stream of jelly was undulating from the shadows that marked the water-line, towards them.

Ice coursed through his veins as he sat perfectly still. It'll go away, he murmured voicelessly. The falling of the branch had attracted it, but it'll go away if there's no more movement. He kept repeating the words with the intensity of a rosary.

The mass seemed to slow, as if it were hesitant of its next move. It reminded Cleaver of a dog, sniffing the air for a scent, its bulk shifting slightly. He stopped breathing. Behind him, Michael rolled over in his sleep and muttered. Cleaver felt the heavy movement. Not now, he screamed silently. Not now.

Michael kicked at the sand.

The lump moved forward again. Cleaver reached blindly behind him to still Michael's legs, his eyes locked on the jelly which seemed to be growing massively every second. It had the purposeful intractability of a tank as it moved over the sand as if on treads, breasting the ridges, the water bubbles flashing in the firelight as they moved constantly beneath the surface.

At least we can run, he thought wildly. Run up and down the island for hours, never sleeping, while it crowds in at every step . . . No, mustn't run.

Michael heaved again and Cleaver flung himself across his body, whispering "shush, shush," but Michael didn't wake, and Cleaver was too terrified of his reaction to rouse him.

The jelly reached the edge of the hollow. A fragment searched the air before it, then dipped down towards the glowing embers. Cleaver's chest was tight.

The finger drew back abruptly. Cleaver could see that the end was ragged. A few drops of liquid dripped from it, sizzling as they fell on the coals. Unperturbed, the mass moved slowly to the right and tried again. Cleaver found himself relaxing, his breathing shallow.

The jelly receded. Gradually the strand linking it to the water thickened, as it drew itself back. Michael seemed quieter now, and Clever sat up, wiping at his suddenly greasy face. Granules of sand stuck to his cheeks, irritating among the stubble, but he ignored them. He sat unsleeping for several hours, his thoughts jangled, but always returning to one inescapable fact. The wood was used. There would be no protection the following night.

They must get off the island tomorrow.

The rising sun had struggled through a dull overcast and had retired, defeated. They had breakfasted on bread and vegemite. Michael had asked no questions, either of the night before, or of the coming one, and Cleaver found his silence harder to bear than expressions of fear. He seemed totally dispirited, and Cleaver had given up attempts at conversation that brought no response.

The pale circle that was the cloud-masked sun had traveled

overhead and was now dipping towards the west. They sat on top of the ridge, near the tent. They had risked attracting the jelly when the tide was at its lowest to change into jeans and sweaters from the duffle bag, but despite the low clouds, there was no sign of rain and the air was mild.

Cleaver stared out over the water, completely covered now with jelly. It had built up thick layers at the water's edge, and he could see grotesque formations of it shifting among the mangroves where the stilted roots rose above the water. As the day had worn on, the sight had lost some of its repugnance, and his mind seemed to become curiously torpid whenever he tried to think of a solution to their predicament. He realized vaguely that this should have alarmed him, but he felt more indifferent than frightened.

"DAD!" Michael's urgent voice roused him from a blank reverie. He jerked up and searched the shoreline for signs of an incursion by the jelly, but it lay placid. Michael grabbed his shoulder. "Look, Dad, look!"

Cleaver saw it then. The mangrove swamps opposite the island were closest at a point to their left, near the spit of sand round which they had come to reach the beach. From a narrow opening in the greenery drifted a small wooden boat, it painted sides peeling, wire-netting crab-pots still piled helter-skelter inside it. There was no sign of the old man.

Cleaver's first thought was an immense dismay that the old man was gone. Then the image of the boat seared through his brain and he forgot everything else. He stood immobile for a moment, calculating the drift, then "Come on!" he cried to Michael. "It's going to pass the spit. We've got to get it!" His mind worked overtime. Swimming was out of the question. They had to bring it ashore somehow. He looked frantically over their possessions.

"The rod!" he exclaimed triumphantly. "I can cast from the end of the spit. The current's not running too fast—I should be able to drag it in."

"But Dad," said Michael. "The jelly . . ."

Cleaver looked at the spit again. It suddenly seemed very narrow, foolishly narrow, with the banks of jelly on either side. Waiting. He tried to think.

"The vinegar," he breathed. "Michael, remember the vinegar we brought?'' Michael nodded, staring at his father with puzzled eyes. "They use vinegar to treat jellyfish stings, the acid dries the tentacles! This is a type of sea-jelly, the vinegar should work on it too—at least it won't like it!" He thought for a moment. "Michael, you'll have to come too. With the vinegar. If the jelly starts getting closer, you'll have to sprinkle it on it. Just sprinkle it, it won't go far. . . ." He bit his lip, looking into his son's set face. "This may be our last chance. Can you do it?" he said gently.

Michael nodded again.

Cleaver grabbed the barra rod from where it rested against the tent. The line was twenty-two pounds, he remembered. Pretty strong. Have to do. Michael picked through the box of food for the bottle of vinegar. They set off, lightly loping down the beach. Cleaver imagined he could hear an interested ripple from the seaward side, but refused to look back.

The spit was low. At high tide it was covered, but now, with the tide only half-in, it jutted thirty feet into the water. It was about eight feet wide before it rounded off. Cleaver hesitated as they reached it. Jelly mounds glistened dully on either side. He set his jaw and walked forward. Michael followed behind him.

He halted at a spot where the spit began to narrow. The boat was drifting sluggishly on, perhaps not as close as he had first thought. He clamped down on a preliminary thrill of fear. There would be no failure, he thought firmly, and blanked his mind to everything but the mechanical motions of his hands and arms.

The rod was rigged for the king salmon he had hoped for that long time past, with a 40 khale hook and a medium ball sinker. Good for a long cast. It balanced in his hands fine, just fine.

Rod backed, he measured the distance. He cast. The line spun out in a graceful arc, line whirring through the bailer arm. His heart jumped as the hook snicked the gunwhale with a faint whisper of sound, then rolled into the water. "Shit," he muttered. But he could do it. He could make the distance. He reeled the line rapidly in.

"It's coming," whispered Michael, standing close to his back.

Cleaver paused and looked down. Pseudopods of jelly were protruding from the clumps on all sides. Their space had perceptibly narrowed. Sweat beaded his lip.

"O.K.," he said, "start sprinkling it with the vinegar. All around us." Michael stood unmoving, staring glazedly at the advancing jelly.

"Mike," said Cleaver sharply. "*Do* it!"

Michael jumped and clumsily unscrewed the top. Hesitantly he sprinkled some of the liquid over the nearest finger that was rapidly forming itself into a clump. As the brown drops showered onto it, it twitched. The colloid writhed and drew back to the water's edge.

Cleaver bared his teeth exultantly. "Go on, Mike. It's working." Michael moved to the other side and Cleaver began reeling in once more, hurriedly. The boat would not stay in range much longer. Small gobbets of jelly fell from the line as it wound through the ferrule, but Cleaver ignored them. If they landed on him, the vinegar would handle them.

He paused, ready to cast again. He kept his eye fixed on the boat and put every muscle into an accurate throw. The line sang from the reel again. The tackle glided smoothly through the air and seemed to hover over the boat for an instant. Then it was down, with an audible clunk, inside the boat. Cleaver delicately tautened the line and watched the prow of the boat swing slowly round. The tackle was holding. He released the breath he had been unconsciously holding.

"Dad," said Michael anxiously. "A lot's gone already."

Cleaver looked down. Some clumps were retreating, but larger masses were creeping forward. He ground his teeth. "Keep going, Mike. I've got the boat." He twisted the ratchet, and held the rod steady. There was the chance that the line would break, but it was a chance they had to take. There would be no others.

The veins stood out on his forehead as he struggled to rotate the handle of the reel, and the muscles of his hand began to ache. The boat wallowed for a moment, as the pull of the line began to counteract the influence of the current, then gradually he found he was reeling in more quickly. He wound the lever gently, letting momentum build up to aid him. The boat crept towards them.

"How's it going?" Cleaver said between clenched teeth. "O.K," Michael whispered, but Cleaver could hear his struggle to keep the terror out of his voice. He glanced down. There was little vinegar left, and the sand-borne masses of jelly seemed bigger. Fear prickled down his spine, but he kept winding evenly.

Suddenly he could bring the boat no farther in.

It swung a mere yard from the spit, and those three feet were plastered with jelly. He realized sickly that the current was stronger near the shore, and the line had reached its limit. Any further strain would snap it. He stood trembling with muscular fatigue, sweat dribbling down his cheeks. Tears of frustration sprang to his eyes.

Angrily he shook them away. They could still make it.

"Mike," he panted. "There's a stronger current running close in. I can't bring the boat any farther in or the line'll break. Run up the beach and bring that oar back—the one I threw onto the beach the other night. Remember?" He didn't wait for a reply. "I might be able to lever the boat in with that. Sprinkle the last bit of vinegar all round and then run."

He looked down to where Michael was crouched on the sand, bottle ready. Michael stared along the narrowing spit, and back at their own small area. He stood up and looked at his father, his face expressionless. "Do you think there's time?"

Cleaver was taken aback. Michael's gaze was no longer wide-eyed and fearful, but a level and calculating stare that disconcerted him. Even his voice sounded different, lower. Cleaver hesitated.

"Do you?" he said finally.

Michael considered for a moment. "Yes," he said.

Cleaver returned his attention to maintaining the boat's position, feeling strangely jubilant. A question he had asked himself eons ago had been answered, the transition was pinpointed. They would talk about this moment, later. . . .

He heard the vestiges of vinegar gurgle from the bottle, heard the dull thunk as it fell to the sand, heard Michael's footsteps pounding as he turned and ran. He took one look back. Michael was running confidently along the center of the spit, his stride long and steady.

But the jelly's advance was also steady. He refused to look down, refused to count the seconds. He stared at the boat, so close, swinging resentfully at the end of the taut line, and concentrated on tensing now painful muscles.

It seemed an age before he could hear Michael's footsteps again. He disengaged his right hand, feeling the surge of weight pull remorselessly at his left biceps. In a second the oar was thrust into his hand and Michael stood on his left, taking a careful hold of the rod to ease the strain.

"Hurry, Dad," Michael breathed.

Cleaver glanced down involuntarily. Sweat stung his eyes despite the cooling sea breeze. The jelly was close on both sides, surging and building its leading edge, as if it knew that it had something larger than a seagull's egg to tackle.

He spat bile at it as he reached forward with the oar. His hand trembled, but he managed to wedge the blade under a wooden seat, and, straining every muscle of his back, began to drag the boat towards them.

The pull on the rod slackened. "Take it," he hissed.

Michael seized the rod, and Cleaver put both hands to the oar. The boat moved obliquely, jelly swirling before it as it came reluctantly.

"We'll have to jump as soon as it's close enough," he panted. "I can't drag it over the sand."

Michael said nothing. A reply was unnecessary.

Time seemed suspended, its progress marked only by the imperceptible movement of the boat as he struggled at the oar. Surprised, he felt the pain of tears starting in his eyes again, and thought incredulously that that was very foolish. He blinked at them, preoccupied, and abruptly the keel was grinding on the sand, crushing into the jelly.

"Now!" he shouted.

Michael threw down the rod and leapt for the prow, scrabbling across it. Cleaver felt the boat rock violently, almost tearing the oar from his grasp as it swayed back from the spit. He wrenched hard at it and as it rasped on the sand again, threw himself forward over the gunwhale.

He landed across a seat and a crab-pot, head down and legs

kicking in the air. He felt the boat detach from the spit and slide sluggishly into the current. Righting himself, he crawled onto the seat, sides heaving. He looked back in time to see a wave of jelly surge over his footprints in the sand. He tried to laugh, but the laughter sounded like crying, so he turned it into a fit of coughing instead.

"Are you all right?" Michael asked anxiously.

"Fine," said Cleaver, clearing his throat. "Terrific."

He looked round the cramped interior of the small dinghy. It seemed dry and watertight. A bit late for that, he thought wryly.

"First, we'll get rid of these," he said briskly, laying a hand on one of the crab-pots. They tossed them overboard one by one, and watched them sink through the jelly with hardly a splash. Cleaver estimated that it would be six inches deep in places. Plankton, he thought. With the fish gone, it's moved on to the plankton. And after that, he wondered?

With the last of the crab-pots gone, he climbed to the stern to check the petrol tin. "We're in luck," he grinned, shaking it. "There's plenty left, more than enough to get us home."

"We're going to make it, aren't we, Dad?"

He smiled easily. "Certain to," he replied, but the thought of the trip across the bay with its heavy swell and spray nagged at him. If the jelly's range now extended into the bay, then one wrongly-judged wave and they'd both be drenched with it. He began to understand the concept of fatalism. It wasn't bravery to keep forging ahead despite the danger. In the absence of any other course, it was simply resignation, and a dull determination to make the best of it.

He busied himself with the outboard. It had been stalled in gear. (And the old fisherman? Cleaver pictured him stepping out onto a mud bank, perhaps, or grasping at a root for balance. Maybe his eyesight was failing, maybe the jelly had seemed unimportant. . . . Another thought to ignore for now, along with Drip, and maybe others. . . .) But it wasn't flooded, and he pulled it into life on the second tug.

Michael grinned at him, and he grinned back. He called over the rattle of the motor, "Tide's not full for a couple of hours, but I think we can make it through the passage and over the mudflat. We'd better do the trip in daylight. I don't want to spend a night drifting on the water.''

Michael shook his head violently, and Cleaver grinned again.

While they had been busy clearing the boat, it had drifted along Mud Island, close to the point where the seagulls nested. Cleaver swung the tiller and brought it round to traverse the beachfront again. The ancient motor made a peculiar burbling noise as he increased the throttle, and he realized that the jelly was having a dampening effect on the water turbulence. He wondered if it would affect the swell in the bay, cutting down on spray. Don't get too hopeful yet, he cautioned himself. Wait and see.

He scanned the beach as they cruised past, hardly noticing the cheerful red tent that stood out amid the muted greys of the overcast afternoon, or any of the equipment lying forlornly about it. The jelly had crept even higher on the rising tide. He imagined a second night there, and shuddered.

They cleared the shallow water round the spit and an abrupt turn brought them face to face with the corridor between the mangroves through which they had entered the swamps. Cleaver cut to idle, and they gazed at it silently.

He was dismayed at the forest of mangrove seedlings that confronted them. At high tide the bulk of them was covered: he had never realized how thickly they grew. Even more dismaying was the advance of the jelly here. It trailed up the saplings, festooned the branches of the bigger bushes, seemingly in constant, oozing motion. Beneath the layer of jelly the water was brown and thick. It was impossible to tell its depth.

Several hours to high tide, he thought. Night would fall, they had no light. Unthinkable to grope through the dark, uncertain of what they might blunder into. Their best chance was now. . . . But still he hesitated.

Michael glanced at him over his shoulder. ''We're going to lose the light, Dad,'' he said. ''We'd best go on.''

Cleaver nodded to him gratefully.

He revved the engine and they crawled forward into the twilight of the passage. He steered for a middle course, deviating only to miss the spirelike seedlings and their viscous coating by as wide a margin as possible.

Once the propeller burred sharply as it struck something, perhaps an old log hidden by the murky water, and they both jumped. Twice they had to duck under jutting jelly-smeared branches, holding their breaths.

The tortuous journey began to take on the essence of a nightmare, so much so that Cleaver was amazed to find the light paling, and a slow swell raising the boat. They were out of the swamps.

He breathed deeply. Another one down, he thought triumphantly. One to go.

"Mike," he yelled above the din of the motor. "We'll be taking it slowly, so we don't ship water. O.K.?"

Michael turned and nodded. Cleaver could see his own relief mirrored on the boy's face, and a fleeting expression of hope. It sobered suddenly as he pointed ahead. Cleaver nodded. It was as he'd expected.

Before them stretched the bay. To their right the mangroves were a green-and-black wall that marched into the distance. Far ahead, a speck of mustard yellow showed the dunes where the mouth of the creek merged into the sea. The islands reared to their left, protecting the bay from the onslaught of heavy waves, but creating complex currents to be navigated.

And over the wide expanse of water, as far as they could see, the gelatinous glaze floated, gleaming faintly under the diffused light of the feeble sun.

Cleaver took a deeper breath, set his mind to neutral, and headed the boat out into the bay, steering as directly as he could for the patch of yellow.

The waves rose under them. He tried to get them behind him, to coast along on the crests. But their slow speed made the boat wallow in the troughs, and there was a constant risk that an oncoming wave would splash over them. Each wave became an obstacle to be overcome until it had petered out, when another one would take its place.

Cleaver's forearm ached from the strain of holding the tiller steady, and he could feel his hand cramping on the throttle. He tried to ease it slightly by flexing it, using his left hand for a second. They seemed so low in the water, he thought. Dangerously low. The jelly swirled and eddied only inches away. . . .

A white object off to his left caught his eye. He half-rose to see it better. It was the hull of a capsized powerboat, a large one. The propellers of the twin outboards stuck up in the air, like children's windmills. He sank back to his seat. Another one.

Michael twisted to watch it out of sight, his face expressionless. Then he turned back to his vigil at the prow.

Gradually the dunes crept closer. Cleaver was squinting now to see them. The light was failing, evening hurried by the lowering clouds, but he was certain they would make it. Already the pounding of waves on the shore came faintly to him.

Suddenly the land seemed to rush at them, and he steered exultantly for the mouth. One moment they were riding a crest as it surged to meet the creek, and the next they were chugging steadily up the mirrorlike waters towards the boatramp. On a sandbar to one side lay a beached yacht, its sail fully rigged and drooping into the jelly-infested water. There was no one in sight. He noticed Michael look away.

He sighed and sat back, releasing the throttle and rubbing his hands. The right one felt numb. He glanced at it. The rough pattern of the rubber handgrip was etched deeply into his palm. He shrugged and took the throttle again.

The mottled grey of the concrete ramp materialized against the deeper grey of the mud banks and the startlingly gay colors of the vehicles in the carpark, almost luminescent in the dusk. Cleaver realized the carpark was crowded, much more so than when they'd arrived. Does that make us the first ones back, he wondered? Surely not the only ones . . .

As the boat drew closer to the ramp, he was startled to see a flashing blue light at the top. Of course. A police car. The alarm had been raised already. He felt an enormous thankfulness for that. Blue-clad figures were moving through the parked cars and trucks, checking licence plates. Cleaver saw their heads jerk up at the whine of the outboard.

One detached himself from the others, and ran down the

ramp as they circled in, waving its arms vigorously. It stopped well short of the wash of jelly that plastered the water's edge.

"Hey!" the policeman yelled. "You'll have to jump ashore. Whatever you do, don't touch this stuff here—this jelly-stuff. It's dangerous!"

Cleaver started laughing, he couldn't help it. Michael turned to him and began giggling. Their howls of laughter rang out over the water as they faced each other, echoing from the brooding mangroves. Eventually Cleaver regained control. He looked at the shadowed and perplexed face of the policeman and wiped his eyes.

"Ready for one last jump?" he said.

The young man opposite him smiled and nodded.